KEEPING KAMA

EMI HILTON

5 PRINCE PUBLISHING
5PRINCEBOOKS.COM

Published by 5 PRINCE PUBLISHING & BOOKS, LLC

PO Box 865, Arvada, CO 80001

www.5PrinceBooks.com

ISBN digital: 978-1-63112-386-3

ISBN print: 978-1-63112-387-0

Cover Credit: Marianne Nowicki

F103024

To my family, and the many beautiful memories we share together in Hawaii.

ACKNOWLEDGMENTS

As always, thank you to my readers. Thank you for your support, encouragement, and for sharing my novels with your friends and families. Thanks for leaving five-star reviews, commenting on my posts, and following along with me on this writing journey. You are the reason I am inspired to write.

Thank you to my fantastic editor, Cate Byers. Once again, it was a complete pleasure to work with you on this manuscript. I am beyond grateful for you helping me to grow and develop as a writer. Thank you for pointing out my many mistakes with grace and wisdom. A million thanks.

To my publisher, 5 Prince Books. Thank you once again for believing in me and my story. Thank you for staying with me as I improve and develop in my craft. I appreciate you beyond words, and I am forever grateful my stories have found a home at your publishing house.

A huge thanks to Ali Ward for helping me better understand and represent the Hawaiian culture in my novel. I appreciate you taking the time to guide me as I tried my best to write a story that embraced the beautiful aloha spirit of Hawaii.

To my husband, Tyler. Everything is better when we are together. You have been my constant friend and companion, and I have lived and breathed in your love. My life is only whole because you are in it. Thank you for your never-ending support and for staying by my side these last seventeen years.

To my family and friends who are near and dear to heart. Thank you for believing in me from the very beginning as I started this writing journey. You have lifted me up when I questioned my abilities. You have offered words of encouragement when I needed them the most, and it means the world to me. Thank you.

Last, I thank my faithful Father in Heaven. God, I know all things are possible with thee. I know despite my many shortcomings and flaws; I can always land safely in your warm embrace. I thank thee for granting me the gift and desire to grow and develop in my craft. I pray through my written words that others might embrace thy goodness. In all things, may the glory and honor be thine forever.

ALSO BY EMI HILTON

KEEPING KAMA

CHAPTER 1

From behind, a fast car dipped over a bump, making their headlights cast a brief glow on Leia. "Geez," Leia muttered under her breath.

Taking a quick glance over her shoulder, Leia reverted her gaze to the road in front of her. As the headlights approached, Leia tried to maintain her running pace. Only a few months remained until the Honolulu marathon, Leia planned on getting her personal best.

Her shoes crunched into the gravel. The headlights grew closer, Leia peered over her shoulder a second time and said to herself, "I hope they plan on slowing down." The words were carried away with the ocean breeze.

Readjusting her headlamp, Leia counted on it, along with the lights on her shoes, to be enough for the driver to make out her silhouette in the darkness of early morning. Leia moved as far as possible to the side of the road. The car violently came closer and closer. An annoying low beat from the car made her body vibrate. Did the driver have their windows rolled down, belting out loud music? At this hour?

Twisting halfway, Leia caught a better view of the small

Honda. Yep, the windows were down, making the blaring music louder with each passing second. And it wasn't good music, it was annoying music. Like maybe Tom Petty?

Concentrating, Leia recognized the tune, 'I Won't Back Down', confirming whoever was driving recklessly also had bad taste in music. Two knocks against them. Leia never understood the singer's appeal, an opinion she knew enough not to voice out loud to others, though. People became awfully touchy when it came to Mr. Tom Petty.

Besides her dislike for the driver's music choice, why did they feel the need to broadcast it at a deafening volume at five-thirty in the morning? Especially on the North Shore? Ugh. Leia purposely started her long runs early in the morning to avoid cars, commuters, and tourists.

As the car loomed behind her, Leia abruptly stopped and twisted to face it. Lifting her hand to block out the blinding light of the car's headlights, it took Leia's vision a moment to adjust. It was barreling toward her and getting dangerously close to hitting her. Leia jumped into the grassy plain next to the shoulder. A near hit, the car passed, taking its annoying music with it.

Once it was out of sight, Leia moved back onto the road, brushing off her arms, and continued running. Forcing herself to forget the encounter, Leia dug out a gel from her side pocket. Ripping off the top with her teeth, she gulped it down in seconds, sliding the empty packet back into her pocket when she was finished. Five miles down, five more to go.

Glancing to her right, Leia took in the beautiful sight of the ocean. Sunlight skimmed an inch above the water enough to make the black sky turn to a milky dark blue. Slowly, the warmth of the sunrise hit her skin.

When she was only a mile from home, Leia ran by Shark's Cove. A popular destination for both locals and tourists alike, Shark's Cove had the best snorkeling around. Though getting into the cove, past the break of rock, tended to be a bit dangerous this time of year for an inexperienced swimmer. It was equally important once in the safety of the cove that one did not swim past where the waves broke or venture out on their own.

Usually, people don't swim in the cove this early in the morning. Rarely did Leia spot anyone in the water on her early morning runs. But today, a lonely Honda was parked on the road, next to the path leading down to Shark's Cove. Leia wasn't positive, but she believed it was the same car as earlier.

Out of breath, Leia stopped, walking over to the lookout point. Down below, in Shark's Cove, she spotted someone way past the basin of the cove, snorkeling. The water past the basin was choppy, deep, and dangerous. Leia hoped the person out there *alone* was a strong swimmer.

For a few moments, Leia watched the swimmer, wondering if they were aware of how far they were from the calmer waters in the cove. Then a huge wave came, pulling the person further out past the cove and into the treacherous open ocean. Leia scurried down the rocky path to the shoreline.

Hitting the sand, Leia cupped her mouth with one hand while she waved frantically with the other. "You are out too far. Come back!" She knew it was fruitless. Her voice couldn't carry that great a distance. But to no avail, she yelled again, "It's not safe. You're out too far!" With a frenzy, Leia waved both arms, trying to catch the swimmer's attention.

Another wave came, hitting the shore. Leia took a step back to keep from getting wet. When she glanced back to spot the swimmer, the person was gone. Leia ripped off her shoes and shirt, dumping the contents of her pockets onto the sand. Then she waded past the choppy break of the shore, once beyond the rocky portion, Leia dove into the water, swimming with her entire might toward where she last spotted the swimmer. Her lungs burned. Salt water stung her eyes. Every so often she came up for air, peering around to try and locate the person. When she didn't see anyone, she dipped her head back in, using her strong lean legs to catapult herself forward.

Finally, several yards ahead, Leia clocked a man's head bobbing in and out of the water.

"I'm coming, hold on!" shouted Leia. With another several strong, fast strokes, Leia neared the man in distress. "Calm down. I'm almost to you!" His body floated up and down like a buoy. "I'm here to help!"

With only a few feet left between them, Leia reached out, wrapping her arm under his armpits in a move she learned in her lifeguard training course.

Teeth chattering, the man attempted a reply, "I'm— I'm—" the man replied. Then his eyes rolled back.

Leia secured him in a football hold, swimming and dragging his body with her free arm, depending on the strength of her legs to catapult them forward. A rip tide attempted to drag them in the opposite direction. Each stroke was a fight against the strength of the tide. Why had she done this? This rash decision might cost her life. Adrenaline pumped through her veins, giving her a bit of herculean strength. Leia forced herself to not think about how far she still needed to swim, or how she might not make it back to the safety of the shore. No, Leia swam and swam, fighting for each inch, dragging the man behind her.

"AHHH ..." Leia screamed as the man's weight made every part of her body throbbed from exertion. Her shoulder popped, and Leia wondered if she had dislocated it. "What were you thinking?" she tried to yell, but salt water filled her mouth. She spit it out, gritting her teeth against the stinging grime coating her tongue.

Another wave rolled over them, but Leia didn't let go. She couldn't let go. Then another wave broke on them, but Leia held on, refusing to let herself or this guy die. After spending every summer from eighteen to twenty-two as a lifeguard at Waikiki

Beach, Leia's training took over. Pure muscle memory allowed her to swim and drag the man back to safety.

Eventually, they reached the calmer water of the cove. Her toes hit the rough bottom of the ocean floor, making them sting as the rocky coral cut through her socks and into her skin. After a few steps, the rock gave way to sand, making the end almost near. The water eventually danced around her waist then her knees. Leia jumped out of the water, pulling the man by the arms onto the sand.

Every part of her hurt, but Leia didn't stop. Ready to begin CPR, Leia kneeled next to the man. He rolled to his side unassisted, coughing and sputtering out water. His hand flew to his chest, as he continued to cough up water.

Leia pounded on his back with a closed fist. "Good. Get it all out," instructed Leia.

Eventually, he stopped coughing and Leia helped him sit up. Still kneeling beside him, she scanned him, looking for any injuries. "Are you okay?" Leia practically shouted.

"I—think—so," his words came out in short spurts. He coughed some more but appeared to be regaining his normal breathing. Swiping his hair out of his eyes, he said, "Just a bit shaken up." His voice evened out while his chest slowed its heaving.

Relieved, Leia dropped onto her backside. Sand stuck to her shorts and legs. Leia paused, waiting for the commotion in her chest to subside enough for her mind to clear. Salt stung her eyes as water ran down her face in long continuous streams. Leia reached for her tank top on the sand next to her, using it to wipe her face dry. She tossed it back onto her pile of stuff.

Running her hand over her hair, Leia waited for her own racing pulse to return to normal. The adrenaline from before left her body, leaving her completely limp and exhausted. She cradled her knees to her chest, to keep her body from shaking uncontrollably. The tremor in her hands sent shock waves through her.

They almost died.

She almost died.

And this guy was to blame.

Turning her face toward him, Leia found his gaze. Shaking her head, Leia hissed, "What were you thinking? You could've died." Her jaw tightened. She turned away from the man, closing her eyes for a moment to find her equilibrium. "The sun is barely coming out," Leia forced herself to calm down. Opening her eyes, Leia found his gaze again. Sparkly blue eyes matching the color of the sky looked back at her. Placing her cheek against her cradled knees, Leia exhaled, "Did you get in the water when it was still dark?"

Shrugging, he leaned back on his hands. "Maybe." He shook out his dripping hair, casting his glance out to the cove.

After staring at him for a few moments, Leia forced herself to look out at Shark's Cove too. "Unbelievable," muttered Leia. Clearing her throat, Leia desperately wanted a drink of water to rid her mouth of the frothy saltwater tickling her tongue. "Who do you think you are? Unless you're some Olympian swimmer I don't know about …" She shifted, letting her gaze settle on him. "You can't swim in the ocean when it's dark. You just can't— especially not on the North Shore. The tide is incredibly strong." Her voice faded off.

His eyes locked on hers. For a moment, Leia stared him down. Then he laughed, a deep bottom of his belly, laugh. Gripping his middle, the man almost keeled over. And Leia hated him a little bit more. The guy almost killed them, and he was laughing? Swiping at his eyes, he eventually stopped, meeting her stone-cold stare.

"You're right, it wasn't my smartest move." He held up his hand in defeat. "I agree, a minor lapse in judgement on my part, but you saved my life. So, thank you." Casually, he leaned back again, stretching his legs out in front of him, he crossed his ankles. "How did you do that? I can't believe you swam all the way out to me, and then dragged my body back to shore. You're ..." His gaze glided over her, making her acutely aware she looked like a wet soggy dog. "You're like half my size." He peered at her like she was some sort of mesmerizing Greek goddess.

With no attempt to hide her disdain, Leia jutted up her chin. "I was a lifeguard for years, and I'm stronger than I look." She glanced away out toward the water.

The sun rose higher in the sky, making the blue turquoise water glisten beneath its rays. If she wasn't so exhausted, Leia imagined she would have appreciated the beauty of the quiet cove. It was a place she loved passing by on her many morning runs. The peaceful serenity would be short lived, in another few minutes, the place would be swarming with people, tourists and locals wanting to snorkel or wade in the tide pools.

Squinting up toward the sky, the man remarked, "Obviously ... you are strong. I mean that was amazing. I didn't realize how powerful the current was, because one minute I was in the safety of the cove then ... bam." He slapped his hands together, making Leia flinch. "Next thing I knew, I was being pulled further and further out by the current. I believe I might've been in a rip tide."

Pursing her lips together, Leia didn't even know where to begin. Leia remarked, "You were in a rip tide, which clearly means you aren't from here."

Leia allowed herself to peer over at him. He reminded her of the many washed up California surfers that came to Hawaii to reclaim their youth. Usually, Leia wasn't attracted to that type, but there was something about his blond hair and blue eyes that made her stomach twist against her consent. If she was betting, she'd peg him to be in his mid to late thirties. No doubt, he had a way with women and was used to getting whoever he wanted. Leia had plenty of experience with men like him, and she stayed far away. Even if his five o'clock shadow helped accentuate his chiseled jaw line, Leia didn't care.

Bringing his stretched legs up to his chest, he cradled them with his hands. "What makes you say that?"

Catching herself checking him out, Leia stood, walking a few steps over to where she'd dumped her stuff. "If you were from here ..." Leia plucked up her tank top from the sand. She pulled her tank top over her sports bra, covering her bare abdomen. She continued, "You would know this time of year the current is extra powerful. Plus, you would never have ventured out there alone."

With a soaking wet body, the tank immediately stuck to her skin. Water continued to cascade down her legs. Leia ripped the band from her hair, placing it in between her teeth. Bending her head forward, she gathered up the messy strands of her long dark hair, readjusting it into a knot on top of her head.

From his place on the sand, Derek peered up at her and said, "Guilty. I'm not from here. I'm from Los Angeles." He stumbled to his feet, wiping his sandy hands on the front of his wetsuit. "I'm here on business. I was trying to squeeze in a little bit of fun before I head to a meeting this morning."

Clearing her throat, Leia said, "Whatever dude ... I don't care. Just don't ever do that again. I won't be there to save you next time." Bent down, Leia swiped her running shoes and pushed her soaking, sand covered, socked feet into them. Her final mile home was going to be a doozy in these socks. She hoped it didn't give her blisters. After shoving her phone and keys into her side pocket, Leia put a hand on her hip. "How are you feeling? Any lightheadedness? Trouble breathing?"

In one swift movement, Derek captured his zipper on his back and tugged at his wetsuit. Then he shimmied his arms out of the top, pulling it down to his waist. It revealed a chiseled abdomen. Warmth pooled in her gut. Heat splashed her cheeks. Leia forced herself to look away and out toward Shark's Cove.

"I think I'm okay," replied the man. Leaning against a rock, he yanked off the remaining part of his wetsuit, leaving him only in his swim trunks. *Dang, he looked good.*

A hand plunged through his sandy blond hair, and he added, "Just a little shaken up."

Sand coated the bottom of her shoes. Leia tried to kick some of it off but it was fruitless. She paused and peered over her shoulder at the path back up to his car. It was steep and uneven. The true test would be if he could make it without assistance.

After she contemplated the dilemma, she shifted back to face him, and Leia finally replied, "That makes two of us." Her gaze skidded across his body, forcing herself to only double check for any injuries she might have missed and not the delectably perfect shape of his broad shoulders. Leia raised an eyebrow and asked, "Do you think you can make it up the path to your car?"

"Of course," he waved her off, "I've never been better."

"Mm." Leia narrowed her eyes, crossing her arms. She gnawed on her cheek until she tasted blood. There was zero chance she could leave this guy down here on his own. Her conscience wouldn't allow it. "I'll wait for you. I don't want you climbing that alone. After we get to the top, I can decide if I need to call you an ambulance."

"I'm fine. I'm perfectly okay to make it home on my own." He walked a few feet, snatching his towel. Water cascaded in mesmerizing streams down his entire body. First, he patted his face dry then moved onto his dripping temples. As almost an afterthought, he held the towel out to Leia. "Would you like to use this to dry off, too?"

Leia glanced down at her drenched body. There wasn't a point. Nothing was going to dry her off enough to be comfortable on the rest of her run home. Her toes were no doubt shriveled inside her soggy sand covered socks. "Nah, I'm good." Ready to leave, Leia took a step toward his pile of stuff. After she nabbed his beach bag, she continued, "But I need to get going. We need to walk up to your car. I can't leave you down here alone." Leia didn't ask for instructions, but instead she shoved whatever she saw into his bag.

"Go," he said. Toweling himself off further, he didn't appear to be in any hurry. "I'll be fine."

With his beach bag in her hands, Leia leered at him. "No way," replied Leia. "I can't leave you. I'm sorry, what's your name?" She straightened herself.

His towel now firmly around his waist, he walked two steps closer to her. The distance between them was cut in half. She shifted uncomfortably, because Leia had suddenly become much too aware of his rugged handsomeness. "I'm Derek." Derek placed a hand over his chest, while he held his free hand out to her. "And what's your name—woman who saved my life?"

Leia had no choice but to take a step closer. She quickly shook his hand. "Leia," she said a bit brashly. All business, she took a step back and surveyed his remaining stuff. "So, now that we have the introductions out of the way, Derek, are you ready to go? The path back up to your car is rocky. I don't need you slipping and becoming unconscious." Leia closed his stuffed beach bag, throwing it over her shoulder.

His wet towel unwrapped from around his waist, Derek snatched it before it hit the ground and flung it over his shoulder. He clutched his wetsuit then said, "Aye, Aye, Captain, you lead the way." He smiled, revealing blinding white teeth.

Leia wondered if he was one of those vain guys who whitened their teeth or if he simply hit the genetic lottery. Either way, it made her uneasy. The sooner she left Shark's Cove and him, the better.

With an eye roll, Leia turned toward the path and muttered under her breath, "I've got it. You're Mister funny guy. Perfect." With a huff, she walked to the bottom of the rocky path. He moved at a slower pace, and Leia was forced to wait for Derek to catch up with her. Once he arrived, Leia held out a hand to help him up and onto the first rock step. "I'll follow you. You go first."

Without protest, Derek slipped his hand into hers, passing by her onto the rock ahead of them. "Thanks, Leia." Derek paused, dropping her hand. An odd tension bubbled up between them. His crystal blue eyes bore into hers. She might have swooned a tad. Then with a voice full of sincerity, Derek said, "Thanks for saving my life."

The icy block in her heart thawed. "Anytime, Derek." With a tremor in her hand, Leia motioned toward the road. "Just drive slower on this road up here. You almost hit me while I was running, too."

Derek cringed. "I did?" Slowly, his cheeks reddened. "I'm sorry," he said, with a voice full of remorse. "I didn't realize how fast I was driving. The rental car I have, the speedometer is broken." He held up his hand. "I know, no excuse, but I apologize."

"It might help too if you don't drive with your windows down and blasting your music at an excruciating volume at five-thirty in the morning." Leia shrugged. "I'd start there. I'd think it would help, especially if you were driving around with zero ability to know your speed."

Derek took another step up the rocks. "The air conditioning in my rental car is broken too. I rolled down the windows to keep myself from melting. I'll never trust a buddy to hook me up with a good *deal* ever again. It's been more like I was scammed big time."

"I'm sorry to hear it." Leia stepped onto the rock next to him. The path was wider and could fit them side by side. "But come on," Leia tsked, "*Tom Petty?*" She cocked an eyebrow.

"Noo." Derek groaned and placed a hand over his heart like he had been stabbed. "Tom Petty is a legend. I don't even know how to unwrap that. I'll pretend you didn't just insult a total musical icon. I mean 'Free Falling' alone is enough to debunk your opinion."

"But you're in Hawaii for crying out loud." Leia scoffed. Her patience wore thin, and she made zero attempt to disguise it. "Listen to Hawaiian music. Nobody will care if you have that blasting out of your car, but Tom Petty …" She climbed up onto the next rock, holding out a hand to him.

Derek took her hand and moved onto the rock next to her. "Message received. I'll save Tom Petty for when I'm back in California." Climbing onto the next rock on his own, Leia followed behind him. "My late dad was a huge Tom Petty fan. I listen to it when I want to remember him. Last time I came to Hawaii was with him and my mom." He shrugged. "I guess I wanted to feel him close to me."

"When did your dad pass?" asked Leia.

They took the few remaining steps up to where the ground evened out, Derek stopped at the top until Leia joined him. Then he replied, "My dad has been gone so long, sometimes I forget he was ever even here." His voice faded away. "My mom is gone too. A few years now."

Leia's throat grew tight. "I'm sorry," she offered. "I'm sure it's nice to have some wonderful memories of them here in Hawaii."

They walked the flat path to the car, stopping in front of the side door. "Yeah …" Derek ran his free hand over his blond hair. "But I'm in Hawaii now, and I promise the next time I want to blast music; I'll make sure it's Hawaiian."

Tilting her head to the side, Leia observed Derek's movements. "Much appreciated on behalf of us Hawaiians." A beat of silence followed. Leia took that as her cue their exchange of pleasantries was over. She held his beach bag out to him, and Derek took it from her. "You do seem okay. How are you feeling? Any lightheadedness? Confusion?"

Derek dug into the bottom of his beach bag, pulling out his keys. "Nope, I'm fit as a fiddle."

Leia forced a laugh. "Are you sure? Do you want me to call an ambulance for you?"

Off came the towel slung over his shoulder and Derek replied, "No, I'm fine." He walked to the back of his trunk and opened it, hurling his wetsuit and towel into the back.

Leia bit her bottom lip and studied him for a few more seconds. "If you say you're feeling normal, then I'll have to trust you. If anything feels off later today, you should take yourself to the ER to get checked out." Taking a few steps away from him, Leia continued, "I need to go." She waved a hand between them. "This whole thing has put me behind schedule, but I hope you enjoy the rest of your stay in Oahu."

After the beach bag landed in the trunk with a swift toss, Derek shut it. The keys jangled in his hands as he fidgeted with them. Derek said, "Hey, let me give you a ride."

A backpedal, Leia shook her head. "Sorry, no way." She held up a single finger. "The first rule of being a woman is you don't take rides from strangers. Ever."

"But you saved my life," Derek emphasized. "So, we're not strangers, not anymore."

"It doesn't matter. I get you're trying to be a nice guy, but I'm not getting into your car." Leia took another step away from him. "I would say I'll see you around, but I won't, so, Derek from Los Angeles, I'm glad you didn't die."

Immediately, Derek busted up laughing again. *Maybe Derek did hit his head?* Tears streamed down his cheeks. He swiped at them with the back of his palms. Leia lingered. Her gaze roamed over him, reassessing if he did indeed need an ambulance.

Finally, he regained his composure and appeared completely normal. Derek leaned up against his car, crossing his arms. "Okay, Leia from—" shaking his head, "sorry, I didn't get where you were from."

"Oahu," said Leia.

His annoyingly perfect blue eyes twinkled back at her.

Derek straightened himself. "Leia from Oahu," he smiled, revealing those perfect bright whites again, "thanks again for saving my life."

Leia stumbled a few feet back. She needed to get away from Derek, and his earthshattering smile. "Anytime. See you, bye," Leia managed.

With a wave over her shoulder, Leia sprinted away toward home, refusing to look back.

Her soggy socks squished with each step. Resolved her feet would be covered in blisters; Leia tried her best to ignore the rubbing of her feet. Still soaking wet, water cascaded down her arms and legs, leaving a trail of water drops behind her. But Leia didn't slow down. Running twice as fast, her legs and lungs screamed.

When her childhood home finally came into view, Leia slowed her run to an easy pace, trying her best to gather her breath. With each step, her breathing evened out and soon she arrived at the walkway leading to the front lanai of her parents' home. Leia lived in a small one-bedroom apartment attached to the back of her parents' garage. Sitting out on the front lanai was her mom, Teresa. Leia smiled and waved as she turned up the gravel walkway.

"Good morning, Leia!" Teresa's gaze skidded over Leia's soaked body as she climbed the front steps to the lanai. Once Leia stopped in front of Teresa, Teresa asked, "What happened to you? I know you sweat while you run, but you look like the cat dragged you in."

"Umm. Thanks?" Leia lowered herself into the wingback chair next to Teresa and sat. Her hand roamed over the top of her damp hair, and Leia continued, "I had to save some idiot from drowning in Shark's Cove."

Teresa jolted forward. "Say what?" Her eyes widened.

Gingerly, Leia slipped off her hairband and put it between her teeth while she gathered her hair together. Through her teeth,

Leia said, "Some guy, who almost hit me with his car while I was running, decided it was a good idea to take a morning swim by himself in Shark's Cove." Leia took the band and retied her long dark hair.

In an attempt to relax, Leia leaned back in her chair. But to no avail; nervous energy pumped through her veins. She tapped the armrests of her chair with closed fists. Her jaw twitched as she remembered Derek's tauntingly perfect body. Ugh.

"And …" inquired Teresa.

"And, I couldn't let him die, so I dove in after him. He was carried out past the safety of the cove." Her eyes narrowed as Leia reviewed the encounter in her mind. "I swear when some of these tourists visit Hawaii all of their rational thought goes out the window."

"I can't believe you jumped in to save him. Why didn't you simply call 911?" screeched Teresa.

Leia stared out at the beautiful view of the Pacific Ocean from her parents' lanai. Her parents and she lived on the North Shore. In fact, her family had lived there for generations and generations. And Leia understood why. It was the most beautiful place on the planet.

Shifting to meet Teresa's gaze, Leia said, "He wouldn't have made it. I didn't think, which is probably for the best, I just went in after him so he wouldn't drown."

"Ahh, Leia." Teresa reached over and patted the top of Leia's hand with her own. "It brings back my memories of the times I worried about you when you worked as a beach lifeguard out at Waikiki Beach."

"I was a really good lifeguard, and it helped me earn enough money to pay for college," stated Leia.

With a smirk, Teresa replied, "And you were the only woman, so that certainly didn't hurt. You loved hanging out with all those male lifeguards every summer."

Leia smiled, remembering those summers so long ago. It

seemed like yesterday and today wrapped up into one. "You didn't hear me complaining," stated Leia.

"Yes, but it didn't stop me from worrying about you. But what were you thinking going after a grown man? You could've been killed." Teresa turned her gaze away from Leia, folding her arms, she stared out at the view of the ocean. "Leia, you're not young like you used to be. If you're not more careful, you might injury yourself, or worse, die."

"Hey, I'm only thirty-six," replied Leia. "And I run marathons. I think I'm in decent shape."

"Yes, but you haven't been a lifeguard in like a decade and a half," countered Teresa.

Holding up a hand in defeat, Leia said, "OK, it wasn't my smartest move, but at least Derek isn't dead."

"I'm glad you and *Derek* survived." Teresa's stiff posture slowly loosened as they both stared out at the view, admiring the idyllic setting of the crystal blue waters and sunny blue sky. There wasn't a cloud to be seen which was exactly how Leia liked it. Interrupting the silence, Teresa asked, "Was the guy, Derek, at least cute?" Shifting in her seat, Teresa faced Leia.

"*Mom*," Leia tugged at her wet shorts, avoiding eye contact. "I wasn't checking him out." *Lie. A complete lie.*

Leia wished she hadn't found Derek attractive, not that she would ever see him again.

Teresa shrugged. "I know, but it sure doesn't hurt if you happened to save a good-looking guy." Then she chuckled, touching Leia on her forearm. "Remember how Dad and I met when he saved me when I was learning to surf?"

Her parents loved to retell the story of their meet cute. "Oh, I remember ..." Leia smirked.

Teresa, a native Washington girl, went to the University of Hawaii for college to escape the cloudy depressing skies of her childhood. Noa, her dad who was a local, went surfing like he did every morning. That morning, Teresa was attempting to surf with some friends. Supposedly, after Noa helped Teresa get up on her surfboard for the first time, he knew Teresa was the one for him. After the encounter, they began dating and fell in love. Since then, they'd never wanted to spend a day apart from one another. Teresa stayed in Hawaii after college, marrying Noa. Leaving the overcast skies of her childhood for constant sunny weather, Teresa swears meeting Noa on the water that day was destiny.

Leia enjoyed hearing her parents' love story and was grateful they still loved each other. Life certainly had thrown them numerous challenges over the years, but they'd stayed in love with each other through it all. As for Leia, she was still waiting for her knight in shining armor to show up. For a while there, she thought her college boyfriend Bane might have been the one, but he dumped her after college graduation. Bane high-tailed it to Idaho to live out his cowboy dreams. Last she knew, Bane was still in Idaho. Apparently, his cowboy dreams became a reality.

Since college, Leia rarely dated. After a long string of bad first and second dates, Leia stepped away from the dating scene. Sometimes family and friends tried to set her up, but it never materialized into anything. Unfortunately, now most guys around her age were divorcees with issues or eternal bachelors, making her pickings slim. Leia needed a freaking unicorn. Maybe one with blond hair and blue eyes?

"See," Teresa smiled. Her voice softened. "All I'm saying is people have met their person in the most unusual of circumstances. This could be one of those examples."

"*Mom*," said Leia pointedly. "I highly doubt that. Let's not get carried away with your romantic notions."

Teresa held up a hand in defeat. "Fine." Teresa picked a random piece of lint off the front of her dress. "But, Leia—Tick. Tock. How else are you going to meet someone? When you aren't teaching, you spend all your time here on the farm. The people who work here are your relatives so that isn't going to work."

"I'm well aware of my singlehood," mumbled Leia. This

seemed like a suitable time for her to make an exit. Leia scooted forward, about to stand. "By the way, what time is the meeting with that potential investor?"

"Ten," replied Teresa.

Shaking her head, Leia said, "I don't like this one bit. I still don't see why we're meeting with this person. I told you I'd take out a loan to try and cover the remaining balance that's owed."

"Leia," Teresa said pointedly. "You're a teacher. Come on, you need to be realistic. No bank is giving you a loan." Staring down at her hands, Teresa continued, "And, we owe more on the farm then we've told you."

Leia's heart sank. She loved Kama Farm, the small fruit farm her family owned. It wasn't huge, but her dad Noa's family, had lived on the land for generations. Their roadside shop sold the produce they grew. Mainly, they sold fresh pineapple, guava, mango, and coconut drinks. Her older brother, Kai, had recently taken over running the store and Kama Farm. His wife, Alana, and their two kids lived in a small house on the property too. Leia, being a teacher, helped balance the receipts of the fruit stand.

She knew the expenses to run Kama Farm had increased significantly when both Teresa and Noa could no longer work the farm. Their troubles hit big time in the past year or so when Noa suffered a brain aneurysm. Noa had lived and breathed the farm. Teresa had overseen workers in the store. But Noa's brain aneurysm which caused a stroke, left him with paralysis on one side of his body. In addition, Noa now had slurred speech and memory loss. Teresa spent her days caring for Noa, leaving both Leia's parents unable perform their usual duties on the farm.

Kai had done his best to pick up the slack of losing two integral people, but it was impossible to do everything on his own. Alana, Kai's wife, had taken over working the store, but she had two small children who needed her attention as well. Leia had contemplated leaving her teaching job to help full-time on the farm, but Leia's family knew how much she enjoyed teaching and wouldn't entertain any of her suggestions regarding her quitting.

Fidgeting with the end of her wet shirt, Leia asked, "Will it only be you and Kai and me at the meeting?"

"He'll be there. I won't. I'm taking Noa to his physical therapy appointment," said Teresa. She paused then added, "Plus, I don't have the heart to be there. I know we don't have a choice, but I'd rather stay out of it." Her eyes misted. "I've lived here my entire adult life, and your dad was born here. I hope this investor is the answer for us to save the farm. The whole thing breaks my heart. I really don't know what we will do if it doesn't work out."

With a desire to ease Teresa's worries, Leia gave Teresa's forearm a squeeze. "Then I'll hope this is the answer." Leia stood, stretching for a second. "I guess I'd better go. I need to shower before this meeting." She walked toward the front steps. "I'll talk to you and Dad tonight."

Teresa replied, "Sounds good. Please behave." She raised an eyebrow and gave her a pointed look.

Leia stopped in her tracks, glancing back at Teresa. Innocently, Leia asked, "Don't I always?"

Wagging a finger at Leia, Teresa replied, "You've been getting into trouble since you were a child. Kai will be fine. You on the other hand …" With an eye roll, her voice trailed off.

Taking the steps down, Leia said over her shoulder, "It's not my fault if people need to be shown how to do things right."

Teresa laughed. Speaking to her back, Teresa asked, "Is that what it is?"

Waving off their exchange, Leia said, "I'll see you later."

CHAPTER 2

Holding up a mango, Derek asked, "How much are the mangos?" He peered over at the shop worker.

The woman rearranged some papaya, making sure the ripest fruit was on top of the fruit stack. Without glancing up, she replied, "Two for a dollar." A papaya started to roll, and the woman grasped it before it fell to the ground. She slowly moved it to a free spot, securing it in place.

Setting the mango back down, Derek dug into his pocket, pulling out his money clip. "I'll take four." He peeled off two dollars, handing it to the woman.

Moving closer to him, the woman took the money from his outstretched hand. Her face brightened. "Wonderful." After putting the money into the front pocket of her apron, she plucked four mangos from the pile. After she placed them into a paper bag, she held them out to him. "Mahalo. Enjoy," she said cheerfully.

Shoving his money clip back into his pocket, Derek took the bag from her. "I will. Thank you." He glanced around the small store one more time. "Do you happen to know Kai? I have a meeting scheduled with him."

With a hand over her chest, she said, "Kai, is my husband. I'm Alana." Alana motioned a thumb over her shoulder. "You can make an exit through the back door. Follow the path to the right, following it around until you see a trailer. It doubles as the office. You can't miss it. Leia will be there too. Leia is Kai's sister. She takes care of balancing the books for our store."

Leia? Derek wondered if it was a popular Hawaiian name. The woman who saved him on the beach this morning was also named Leia. *Leia. Leia. Leia.* He couldn't get her out of his mind. But then again, if a gorgeous and incredibly strong woman, single-handedly saved your life, you'd remember her too.

"Great. I'll do precisely that," said Derek. He shook the bag of fruit. "I look forward to eating these later."

Alana nodded, stepping away from him toward another customer. "It was nice meeting you." Alana left him, joining the customer over by the pineapples.

Derek heard Alana ask the customer if they were looking for anything specific before he exited through the back door.

Following Alana's directions, Derek walked down the dirt path. On one side of the path, it led to a large house with a detached garage. Then several yards behind it were a few bungalows. The other side of the path was covered with wildflowers, plants, and what Derek guessed were banana trees.

After walking for a few minutes, the trailer came into view. Behind the trailer were signs of the beginning of the fruit farm. Acres and acres of rows with what he figured were different varieties of fruit plants and trees. Derek admired the impressive landscape of the farm. From the information he received, Derek didn't envision the farm to be on this grand a scale. He mostly imagined a mom-and-pop operation, but this farm was awe-inspiring.

With only a few minutes on the property, Derek sensed the pride of ownership and careful design of the farm which appeared to utilize every available square inch. Nothing was overgrown or needed to be trimmed. No wonder the farm had thrived for so many generations. From his understanding, it was only recently, the last year or two where the farm had fallen on challenging times with increased operational costs.

As he approached the trailer, Derek straightened his blue-checkered collared shirt. Though he recently showered, the cotton fabric already stuck to his skin. Los Angeles was hot, but the humidity here was stifling. Glancing down at his blue dress pants, Derek wondered if he had overdressed for a visit to a fruit farm. He opted for the short-sleeve shirt instead of one of his usual long-sleeve dress shirts, but even it suddenly felt too formal.

Before he had a chance to knock on the door, it swung open, revealing a middle-aged Hawaiian man in a t-shirt and flip flops. Derek at once regretted his attire of choice. The man looked comfortable and at ease, while Derek was hot and itchy.

With warmth in his voice, the man greeted him, "Aloha. Derek?" He held the trailer door open partway with his hand.

Derek tugged at the collar of his dress shirt. "I'm Derek." He studied the man for a moment. "Are you Kai?"

With a wide smile, he replied, "I'm Kai. Welcome to Kama Farm." Kai pushed the door open wider, motioning with his other arm. "Come on in. I'm glad you found us way back here. My wife texted me and told me to send out a search party if you didn't show up in the next five minutes." He paused, and Kai scrutinized Derek's attire. Kai cleared his throat and continued, "I'm afraid your clothes might get dirty from the tour. I wouldn't want you to ruin those nice shoes of yours." Kai's eyes stared down at Derek's brown leather loafers.

"Oh, yeah." Derek ran his free hand through his blond hair, while his other tightened its grip on his bag of mangos. "I can see I overdressed for our meeting." Shuffling his feet, he peered down at himself. "My apologies." His neck stiffened, and Derek wondered if he was already off to a bad start with Kai.

"No worries. You are in Hawaii now. It's much too hot to dress so formally, especially on a farm. You'll know better for next time." Kai gave him an encouraging smile, easing the tension between his shoulder blades. "Come on in. The trailer at least has a window AC unit."

Derek passed through the open door. A blast of cool air hit his skin. "Thanks. I appreciate it." The door slammed shut behind them.

"You!" said a woman's voice.

Jolted, he snapped his head in the direction of the voice, Derek's gaze landed on Leia from this morning, seated behind one of the two desks. Leia shook her head. His jaw dropped.

Swimming in Shark's Cove early in the morning wasn't something he was proud of, but Derek blamed it on a temporary lapse in his usually sound judgement. The night before, his girlfriend, Heather, dumped him via text message. Heather hadn't even dignified him with a phone call. Boy had Derek been off with where their relationship had stood.

Derek tossed and turned most of the night, and since his entire world was crumbling and sleep wasn't happening, he figured he'd get a jump start on his day. Several people had recommended snorkeling in Shark's Cove on the North Shore of Oahu while he was here. Without thought or even checking the time, Derek had stumbled out of bed, thrown on his swimsuit and headed out before the sun had even come up.

Forcing a smile, Derek replied, "Leia. What are the odds?" He scratched his chin.

Kai walked to the other desk next to Leia, taking a seat. "Wait, you two know each other?" Kai's gaze darted between them.

Sighing, Leia rolled her eyes. "Technically, we don't really know each other." She waved her hand flippantly toward him. "I pulled this guy out of Shark's Cove this morning, after he nearly hit me with his car."

Kai held his hands up. "Whoa, back up." He then leaned

forward, his forearms resting on his desk. "You went swimming in Shark's Cove? *Alone?* Early in the morning?"

Derek tried not to shrink into himself. "It wasn't my most brilliant move." Then he motioned toward Leia. "But thanks to your sister and her remarkable strength, I didn't die." He set his fruit down on the ground. Shoving his hands into his pockets, Derek lowered himself into the available chair facing the two desks.

Defensively, Leia crossed her arms. "I thought I wasn't ever going to see you again." She pushed her chin up. "But here you are, trying to buy Kama Farm."

"That's not true." His hands shook as he removed them from his pockets. Derek pulled back his shoulders and regained a tad of his confidence. "I'm not buying Kama Farm outright. It'll still very much be your family's farm. I'm an investor."

With a heavy sigh, Leia flipped her hair over her shoulder and scooted closer to her desk. "But you'll own some of it." She shot him a pointed gaze.

"I wouldn't think of it that way." Derek rested one ankle on his opposite knee. "Think of me as an investment partner who's here to help improve the functionality and profits of the business. I've been doing this for years. My goal is always for the businesses that I invest in, for the owner to maintain their control and vision for their business. The goal is for me to eventually disappear, not take over."

Kai slapped his hand across his desk, glancing toward Leia. "See. I like the sound of that."

Leia blinked at Kai, then she turned her stone-cold stare to Derek. "I don't like the sound of that." Narrowed eyes met his gaze. Leia added, "There's always a catch, so what is it?"

With a tug at his restrictive collar, Derek tried to calm himself. Finally, he forced himself to pull his hands away and fold them on his lap. "Yes, I'm an investor. I can't change that. This is what I do for a living, but I want for the farm to be profitable again." Derek cleared his throat, meeting Leia's gaze head on. "Your success will be my success."

Rolling her eyes, Leia peered at Kai. "I'm not buying it." Leia shifted toward Kai and pointed at Derek. "Kai, you can't let him do this. Why can't we take out a simple loan from the bank?"

Without hesitation, Kai said, "Because a bank won't give us a loan. Trust me, I tried." Kai pinched the bridge of his nose. "I know this isn't ideal, but with Dad's current state we have to do something." Removing his hand, Kai continued, "Leia, we could lose everything and not only the forty percent Derek's investment company wants to buy."

Leia jolted forward, nearly toppling out of her seat. Clutching onto the desk, Leia shrieked, "Forty percent!"

Derek flinched but forced his expression to remain neutral.

Nodding, Kai steepled his hands together. "Forty percent," repeated Kai calmly.

Glancing between Leia and Kai, Derek said, "Your family will remain the majority shareholder of Kama Farm. This means your family remains in control of the vision you want for this place."

With an edge, Leia commented, "How very generous of you." She opened a desk drawer and pulled out a tube of Chapstick, yanking off the cap. After applying it to her lips, Leia threw it back inside and slammed the drawer shut.

His back stiffened. Derek tried his best to keep his emotions from giving away any sort of reaction. Through his years of investing in different companies, Derek knew the initial meeting tended to be the hardest. People approached his investment firm when things weren't going well for their business. Leia's family was in a comparable situation, but Derek had an excellent history of turning companies around. As an outsider, without any of the emotional attachment to the business, Derek could pinpoint what needed to change for the businesses he invested in to thrive.

Kai leaned back in his chair, cupping the back of his head with his hands. Speaking directly to Leia, Kai said, "I know he's here to buy a portion of the farm, but Leia you must know this is our last-ditch effort to keep Kama in the family. We have no other options. The farm has been running in a deficit for the last year or two. None of us predicted how severely Dad's absence from the farm would affect our bottom-line. But Leia ..." shifting toward her, Kai continued, "if we don't turn things around, we will lose everything."

Leia's shoulders slumped.

Silence followed.

Derek knew his presence wasn't wanted, but if he didn't think the business could thrive with his investment, he wouldn't have come to Hawaii. After looking at Kama Farm's financial records, Derek had already found numerous areas to improve the business; ways to save money, be more efficient, and keep the integrity and heart of the family in the farm. All these things were doable, but the family needed money to do them.

Cradling his propped knee, Derek said, "I know you aren't happy with me being here." He motioned toward Leia, "I completely understand. But if you don't mind, I'd like to explain to you the process I take before we even begin to negotiate me purchasing part of the farm."

Kai peered over at Leia. With a raised eyebrow, Kai said, "Leia we asked Derek to come all the way here to Hawaii. The least we can do is hear him out."

Raising both her hands in defeat, Leia replied, "Fine." Then Leia met Derek's gaze, crossing her arms against herself. She prodded, "Go on. I'm listening."

Clearing his throat, Derek dove into his spiel. "So, usually I stay for a week or two. I'll shadow both of you so I can learn how Kama Farm functions, make notes of ways to become more efficient, point out trouble areas and make suggestions to improve on them. Then at the end of that time, if I find this is a business I want to invest in, I'll give you an offer. Think of the next few weeks as a trial period." Gesturing at himself, Derek continued, "You'll get to know me, and I'll get to know you. If we gel, and we're comfortable with one another, we'll proceed with the negotiations of the investment. Does that sound reasonable to both of you?"

Leia exchanged a look with Kai. "I'm a teacher." She peered back at Derek and continued, "I'm only here on the weekends and do most of the bookkeeping from my apartment. There won't be much for you to shadow when it comes to me."

Slowly, Derek nodded. "You're correct." He glanced at Kai. "I'll mainly be shadowing you, Kai."

Leia smugly asked, "So, will this be the last time we have to talk for a while?"

Derek scratched his chin. Even though the window AC unit buzzed on the wall, sweat poured down his back. Somehow, he kept his voice even as he replied, "Sure if that's how you would like it." He shrugged, though his middle churned. A trickle of sweat ran down his temple, and using a single finger, he swiped at it. "I believe most of our interactions can be done over email. And if you want, you can email my business partner Tyson instead of me."

Holding up both his hands, Kai interjected, "Leia, if we're bringing Derek in to invest, I need you to feel comfortable with him too. His business partner isn't here. This guy is, so..."he shook his head. With a voice colder than before, Kai continued, "I don't know what happened this morning, but you need to get over it." Kai shot Leia a pointed look, "Leia ..."

Defiantly, Leia crossed her arms and replied, "Okay, *Kai.*"

Kai tilted his head toward Derek, staring at him directly. "How about you? Are you embarrassed my sister had to save you this morning?"

Derek shifted, lowering his propped leg back to the ground. "I don't have a problem with Leia. She saved my life." Derek met Leia's gaze and spoke directly toward her, "And I think she's amazing."

Leia's cheeks tinged pink. She flipped her gorgeous long silky black hair over her shoulder.

Clapping his hands together, Kai said, "Perfect. Then we're in agreement." He pushed his chair out, standing. Kai continued, "Let's give Derek a tour of the farm."

As Leia stumbled to her feet, she said, "Okay then."

Derek rose to his feet too.

Kai's gaze ran over Derek's body. "We need to get you something else to wear. You're going to ruin your clothes. We just put down new fertilizer."

Tugging at his shirt collar, Derek's cheeks warmed as he peered down at himself. "I'm sure I'll manage." He shuffled his feet.

"No way." Kai strode across the trailer toward the door. Over his shoulder, he said, "Let me run and find you a shirt and some flip flops. I'll be right back." Kai exited.

The door banged shut behind him, leaving Leia and Derek alone for the first time since the meeting began. Derek rubbed his hands together, before shoving them into his pants pockets. Palpable silence followed, making his skin crawl. Leia reached out and straightened a few piles of papers on her desk. Without glancing at him, Leia moved to tossing a few things from her drawers into the trash.

Derek said the first thing that came to his mind, "I'm really sorry I almost hit you with my car."

A long pause followed, and Leia shifted toward him. "You need to be more careful when you're driving early in the morning. I can't tell you how many close calls I've had with reckless drivers like you." Shaking her head, Leia picked up a pack of post-it notes from the top of her desk and moved them to a drawer. Leia didn't appear to want to continue the conversation.

"Do you always run so early in the morning?" asked Derek.

Leia glanced quickly toward the door, no doubt wanting Kai

to return. Derek tracked her gaze. With Kai nowhere in sight, Leia said, "Yes." She brushed her hair once more over her shoulder. The long, dark strands glistened from the sunlight peeking through the window next to her. Then to his surprise, Leia added, "I'm a teacher. I've gotten used to getting up early to run. Even in the summer, when I don't have to rush off to work, I still get up early to run. It's nice to be up before everyone else."

"I wish I could say I was an early riser," replied Derek.

"It's not for everyone." Picking up another stack of papers, Leia leafed through them.

"Are you training for anything?" Derek stepped closer to her desk. "Or do you run for the joy of it?"

Setting the rearranged papers back down on her desk, Leia said, "I'm training for the Honolulu marathon in December." Walking around her desk, Leia sat down on the corner of it. She placed her palms flat on both sides of her.

Derek took two steps to Kai's desk, sitting on the edge of it. Their knees nearly grazed one another's. "A marathon— wow." Derek nodded. "I'm impressed."

Leia kept her gaze on the trailer door, but without prompting, she revealed, "I hope to run every major world marathon someday. The ones they have in London, Tokyo, and Berlin, but on a teacher's salary …" Leia scoffed, "I don't know when I'll manage it. So, when the sign-up rolls around for the Honolulu marathon, I sign up again out of convenience." Lifting her hand, Leia examined her fingernails.

Derek crossed his ankles in front of himself. "How many marathons have you run?"

Leia's shoulders relaxed as she crossed her ankles too. "I lost count at twenty," said Leia with a half-smile.

Nearly choking on his own saliva, Derek exclaimed, "Twenty!" His eyes dilated. "That's unbelievable."

Leia shrugged though she appeared pleased with herself. "It's not a big deal."

"Umm," Derek placed a hand over his chest and continued, "It is to me. I only tried to run a marathon once. I did all the training, but the night before I ate some bad seafood. I couldn't get out of bed to make it to the race. I never tried again." He sighed. "I still regret it. It's on my bucket list. But I can't kick my booty into gear to try and train again."

A slight shift and Leia finally looked at him. "You need to do it." Her gaze captivated him. "Life's too short to live with regrets. You never know what will happen." Railroad tracks formed on her forehead. With a heavy sigh, she added, "Just look what happened to my dad, Noa."

After Derek contemplated for a moment, he asked, "What happened to Noa? If you don't mind me asking."

Leia bit her bottom lip. "He had ..." Then she waved a hand. "The point is, don't wait, Derek. If it's something you've always wanted to do. Then do it. You could run a marathon. You look like you're already in decent shape. Just start training and stop waiting."

Derek started to ask, "Would you ever want to go running—" but was interrupted by the creaking door.

Kai entered, closing the door behind him. Quickly, Derek stood, overly aware of his casual demeanor with Leia.

Proudly, Kai presented a t-shirt and pair of flip flops and said, "I didn't know your size, but I pegged you for a medium." He strode the five steps to Derek.

Graciously, Derek took the t-shirt and flip flops from Kai, Derek replied, "Medium works. Where should I change?"

Kai pointed to the only other door in the trailer. "There's a bathroom in there."

"Okay, give me a second." Derek moved toward the bathroom. "I'll be quick."

"Take your time." He smiled brightly, putting Derek at ease. "You're in Hawaii, you know, island time."

Without a further word, Derek entered the small bathroom.

Taking off his button-down shirt, Derek pulled the tight shirt over his head. Leia remarked earlier that he was a guy who looked like he worked out, a comment he thoroughly wanted to unpack later. But Derek wondered if he had gained weight. This shirt was super snug. Was this really a medium? Derek attempted to reach for the tag behind him to double check the size, but he failed to see what it said. Instead, Derek tugged the ends of his shirt down a few more times, but the cotton material felt like Teflon.

As he stared at his appearance in the tiny mirror over the sink, Derek couldn't help but laugh. He looked absurd. The shirt looked like it belonged to a toddler and made him look like he was a gym rat trying too hard to show off his physique. But Derek didn't have another shirt and didn't want to ask for a different one. Next, he removed his oxford loafers and socks, replacing them with flip flops a good two sizes too big. Dang ... he laughed again as he peered down at himself. This certainly was going to raise an eyebrow or two.

With nothing else to do, Derek gathered his items in his arms and exited the bathroom. Without meeting Leia's gaze, Derek set his shoes and clothing on a chair next to his bag of mangos.

Kai chuckled. "You look ... ridiculous."

Derek shrugged. "It is a bit tight." He tugged on the bottom of the cotton tee. His glance flickered to Leia, and he caught her smirk. "Are you sure you this is a medium? Unless— I mean, I haven't worked out for a while, so I might be wearing a large t-shirt these days."

Leia's eyes roamed over Derek's body, making his senses heightened. "I think it looks good on you." Tilting her head toward Kai, she asked, "Are you sure you gave him a medium? I mean he could pass for a body builder."

Derek's ears perked up.

Kai regained his composure and stopped laughing. "It's a

medium," replied Kai. "I promise." Then he made a motion of an X over his heart.

Taking a step closer to Leia, Derek asked, "Do you really think I look like a body builder?"

Holding up a hand, Leia shook her head. "Simmer down. It was a joke. You look …" Her voice trailed off. Wiping the back of her forehead with the heel of her hand, Leia remarked, "You look *buff*."

For a moment, the air crackled. Both stared at one another. Derek gulped. His insides did a somersault. Was Leia flirting with him? One could certainly dream. For a second, Derek forgot Kai was even in the room, because in this moment the world was only orbiting around him and Leia.

Kai cleared his throat, snapping Derek back to reality. "Are you ready for your tour?" asked Kai.

Throwing his hands down at his side, Derek said, "I guess I am."

They filed out of the trailer, turning toward the dirt path winding behind the trailer then leading out toward the rows of fruit plants. A few feet onto the path, Kai's phone rang. They continued walking while Kai answered. Derek tried to listen to one side of the conversation, but he was too distracted by Leia directly in front of him. Her hair swung back and forth, whipping across her shoulder blades. Derek reminded himself mixing business with pleasure never worked. Time to check himself and place his attraction toward Leia into a locked box.

The path became narrower, and Derek remained directly behind Leia. Slowly, Kai trailed a few yards back, talking on his phone. Leia pointed out a few plants, native to Hawaii, while explaining that the narrow path circled the entire farm.

Suddenly, Leia halted. Derek nearly tripped on her heels. Kai came up from behind deep in conversation.

Pointing, Leia said, "If you look past this curve, to the right where it veers off. Do you see where I'm pointing?" She shifted her weight, peering over her shoulder at him.

Quickly, Derek tried to focus on what Leia was asking him. He traced the length of her arm toward the direction she pointed. "Yes, I see it," said Derek.

"At the end of that path, is the original bungalow where my second great grandparents lived when they started the Kama Farm. Kama Farm was the brainchild of Alelo Kama, my second great grandpa. He needed a way to provide for his large growing family. He and his wife had ten children together." Leia started walking again. Derek leaned in a bit closer to hear her. Leia continued, "I mean generations of my family have lived on this land for as far back as forever. But Alelo Kama was the first to clear some of the land to grow fruit to sell. Kama Farm was born. Alelo started with a simple roadside stand. Each year more land was cleared, until Alelo felt he had enough produce to sell to support his family. He also wanted to make sure he maintained and sustained the surrounding land. When my great grandparents took over Kama Farm, they opened a full roadside shop. My grandparents further developed Kama Farm by buying better and more efficient equipment. Kama Farm was large enough at that point that they hired workers to help harvest the fruit. So, it was a lengthy process for the farm to be what it is today. This is why this farm is so important to everyone in my family."

"I can certainly understand the years of hard work and determination." Derek stared down the path, only a bit of the original home peeked out. "Does anybody live in the home currently?"

Shaking her head, Leia replied, "No. The home is in complete disrepair. Plus, it was very rustic, with no running water or indoor plumbing. Noa, my dad, lived in it until he was six. He had to use the outhouse and everything. Then his parents built the front home you passed by on the way to the trailer. My parents live in that home now."

"Fascinating." Derek attempted to wave away the bugs buzzing by his face. "Maybe you and Kai could consider creating a farm tour, including a tour of the original bungalow. People could see and understand a little better what life was like for those who lived here for generations. Tourists love experiences where they feel immersed in the culture. The tour could end at the store. I would even include lunch where the tourists could sample the fresh fruits and anything else you grow here."

Leia pursed her lips. "I don't know, maybe." Gnawing on her bottom lip, she continued, "That would really be up to Kai and Alana. They are the ones who do this full time." Then she ripped the hairband off her wrist, placing it in between her teeth. Derek tracked her every movement as she gathered up the strands of her hair and pulled it back into a ponytail. Swiping at the sweat on her brow, Leia continued, "I know they threw around the idea a few years back, but it never really came to fruition. Kai might be open to considering it again."

Shifting, Derek glanced over his shoulder. "Where is Kai?" He peered down the dirt path behind them, seeing no sign of Kai. Derek wondered how long they had been chatting alone.

"I have no clue." Standing on her tip toes, Leia peered over Derek's shoulder toward the direction in which they last saw Kai. Lowering her heels back to the ground, Leia shrugged. "He's probably gone off to solve some problem on the farm. I think Kai left me to play tour guide." Leia wrinkled her nose at him, staring straight at Derek. "I guess you're stuck with just me."

Derek blinked. "I don't mind," he said, a tad too eagerly. Recognizing his error, Derek quickly added, "I mean you might mind more than me, but I'm fine continuing on with only you." Derek tugged at the neck of his shirt, due to its small size, the fabric dug into the skin around his neck.

Leia's lips twitched into a slow smirk. "I don't mind." With a smile, Leia added, "Lucky me." Then she swiftly pivoted forward, walking again.

Oh, Leia was flirting. With him. And boy did he like it.

Derek jogged awkwardly in his too big sandals to catch up to her. "You don't mind? You seemed to mind back at the trailer."

"It's okay …" Leia ran a hand over her hair. "You're growing on me."

Derek straightened his back, pulling back his shoulders. "I am? Why?" replied Derek.

Stopping abruptly on the trail, Leia flipped back around, facing him. Leia motioned a finger up and down his body. "It started when you put on that ridiculously small t-shirt of my ten-year old nephew without complaint. And you put on Kai's sandals which I know are probably about five sizes too big." Leia stared down at his sandaled feet. A blister had started to form between his toes the minute he put them on. "You can't be half bad if you were willing to do that," remarked Leia.

Derek pinched the restrictive fabric of his t-shirt over his abdomen. "Are you sure this is your nephew's? Why would Kai give it to me to put on?"

Her eyes twinkled back at him with mischievousness. "Kai was totally messing with you. It was a test, and I believe you passed. But don't take it personally, I think Kai wanted to see how easily you could go with the flow. His personality would never gel with someone who is overly uptight. He's messing with me too. I think Kai either thought I had a thing for you, or I was going to scratch your eyes out. Either way, Kai wanted to see it all play out."

Her words punctured the air.

Rubbing the stubble along his jaw, Derek replied, "Ahh, brothers. You've got to love them."

"Oh, do you have a brother too?" asked Leia.

"No. No," stammered Derek. "I—" Derek began to explain, but they were interrupted by Kai.

Neither had seen him approach, and Derek flinched when Kai slapped him on the back from behind. "I'm sorry about that. What did I miss?" Kai's glance skidded between them. "Are you two still trying to maul each other? Or did you work things out in my absence?" asked Kai.

Derek's gaze darted to Leia. Leia nonchalantly shrugged. Then in unison Derek and Leia burst out laughing because Leia had called it.

CHAPTER 3

With the tour of Kama Farm completed, Leia walked back down the path leading to the trailer. Derek and Kai were directly behind her, chatting. She had stopped following the conversation a few minutes back when they had started discussing college football teams. As much as Leia wanted to hate Derek, she couldn't. After spending the entire morning taking him on a tour of the farm, Derek proved to be kind and thoughtful. Leia wasn't thrilled the farm needed an investor, but if it had to be someone, Derek seemed like he might be the right fit. Leia always trusted her gut, and her gut told her Derek was a decent guy.

As they arrived back at the trailer, Leia lingered in front of the door and waited for Derek and Kai to join her. Once they halted, Leia said, "I think that concludes the tour …" her voice trailed off.

Kai slapped Derek on the back again, then held out a hand to shake Derek's hand. "It was great meeting you."

Derek shook his hand. "Likewise."

"Okay, Derek. You saw the farm. What happens next?" asked Leia.

Before Derek responded, Kai said, "First things first, Derek is coming to dinner tonight at Mom and Dad's. We need to teach

Derek about how welcoming Hawaiians can be, especially those you might potentially be going into business with."

Derek shoved his hands into the pockets of his slacks and smiled. "Kai said your mom is an excellent cook."

"Dad was the cook," remarked Leia as her throat grew tight. So much had changed since her dad's brain aneurysm. Her family's prior life was hazy. But one had to move forward and not linger on what was lost. If you didn't, you might forever be stuck in the past. "I mean Mom does okay, but ..." Leia glanced between Kai and Derek. "But what about the next steps for the business."

Kai wrapped his arm around Leia's shoulders, giving them a squeeze. "You don't need to worry about it, little sis. Derek and I will work it out. He'll be here over the next several days to do some more job shadowing. You can email him the financials, or we can set up a time for you to meet too. We won't decide anything until this trial period is up."

Leia gnawed on a fingernail. "I see," replied Leia.

Kama was slipping away from her. It was her own fault; Leia had opted to go to college to become a teacher. Her family had taken it okay, because the farm had been passed through the sons for so many generations. Since Kai was a child, he had shadowed Noa, walking the tight lines of fruit plants, learning the process of farming. When Leia went off to college, a few of her cousins stepped in to share the workload she should've taken on.

With Leia away, Kai thrived with the responsibilities he had on the farm. Leia's role shrank and shrank, which is what she wanted, but she didn't know it would make her feel so irrelevant. Like maybe she didn't belong at all.

For years Dad and Kai worked side by side in the business, and they seemed fine without her. They each had their roles. Eventually, Leia told Dad and Kai she wanted to stay connected to the farm too. Even if she didn't want to do it full-time, Leia wanted to contribute in some way, so she offered to help with the bookkeeping. But maybe Derek would suggest they hire a real accountant, not someone who took a few accounting classes in college. Her mood soured. Maybe Derek would buy his forty percent and push her out completely.

As Leia took a few steps away from them, she continued, "Okay then, I'll see you at dinner." Her eyes roamed over Derek's ridiculous appearance, though it only accentuated his nice physique. "It'll give you time to change."

Derek laughed, glancing down at himself. "What? Are you saying you don't want me coming in this?"

"Only if you feel comfortable, but you look …" Tilting her head to the side, Leia tried to think of the best word to describe Derek's state. "Hot."

Smugly, Derek cocked an eyebrow and said, "I'm hot?" He locked eyes with Leia.

Leia gulped. "You look hot …" she stammered, "as in warm." With a shaky hand, she swiped away a trickle of sweat rolling down her temple. *Stop talking. Stop.*

Derek grinned. "Since you pay such close attention to my appearance, I'll change just for you."

This guy was smooth … too smooth.

Acting nonchalantly, Leia tossed a hand up into the air. "Whatever, wear whatever you want." Leia stepped away from Kai and Derek, desperately needing to make an exit before she further dug herself into a hole.

Leia knew Kai would tease her about this entire interaction later. It didn't take a genius to pick up on Leia's attraction to Derek. Yes, Leia totally thought Derek was hot and not in the temperature way. But it was harmless. In a small amount of time Derek would leave, and Leia would stay in Hawaii where she belonged.

"Thanks, I will," replied Derek.

A twist on her feet, Leia said over her shoulder. "I'll see you both tonight." Leia didn't wait for a reply, but instead, she briskly walked away.

Her heart palpitated, and only returned to its normal steady beat with each step she took back to her apartment. Leia reminded herself Derek was here on business, and not just any business, the business of buying up nearly half of her family's farm. Her previous attraction for Derek dwindled. Suddenly, the line in the sand became clear again.

Leia went home, making sure to remove her dirty shoes before entering her small one-bedroom apartment. After doing some household chores like laundry and cleaning, Leia realized it was nearly time to head to her parents for dinner. With no real thought, Leia yanked a floral dresser off the hanger and changed into it. Before she exited her apartment to walk to her parents' house, Leia removed her hairband and shook her hair free so it could hang loose. Leia wasn't vain, but she knew her long dark hair was her best feature.

As she rounded the corner of her parents' house, Leia spotted Derek before he saw her. Derek sat on the front lanai in one of the wingback chairs facing the ocean, Dad sat in the opposite chair. Mom must have helped him out to the lanai to enjoy the view while she cooked, because it was only the two men alone. Slowing her approach, her feet crunched on the gravel path leading to the stairs up to the lanai.

Derek whipped his head in the direction of the noise. When he spotted her, Derek smiled and waved. "Aloha," greeted Derek as Leia climbed up the front steps.

"Aloha," repeated Leia.

Derek stood when she arrived on the lanai, adjusting his Hawaiian shirt. Her eyes couldn't help but roam over his tan body. His hair was still wet from the shower. Leia hated how her nostrils flared as she picked up his tangy aftershave.

Dang, Derek looked good. Real good. Leia never thought she'd have a thing for blond surfer boys, but her heart swooned harder than the best thirteen-year-old girl. His eyes matched the bluest blue in the sky. For a second, they paused in front of one another staring.

Derek gulped, and Leia watched his Adam's apple bob up and down. It took everything within her to keep herself from extending her hand and running a finger down his neck, but then Leia reminded herself she was being ridiculous.

Shoving his hands into the pockets of his dark khaki shorts, Derek finally said, "You made it."

Tucking her loosened strands of hair behind her ears, Leia replied, "I did." Pointing to the right, Leia continued, "I live in an apartment attached to the garage, so it isn't far."

Remembering Dad sitting on the lanai, Leia walked over to him and kissed him on the cheek. "It's good to see you, Dad."

Half of Noa's face curved up into a smile. Leia settled into the chair next to him.

Derek sat back down in the chair next to Leia, putting her in the middle of Derek and Noa.

Crossing her legs, Leia fidgeted with the hem of her dress brushing against her knees. "What have you two been doing?" Leia peered between Noa and Derek.

Leaning forward, Derek rested his forearms on his thighs. "Noa and I were enjoying the view." Derek shifted back, staring out at the view of the ocean. A clear blue sky with not a cloud in sight painted a beautiful backdrop against the turquoise water. "They don't call this place paradise for nothing. I see why your family has never left."

"I'm certainly not going anywhere." Leia tilted her head toward Noa. "Right, Dad?"

Noa gave a small nod. Since his brain aneurysm, Noa was limited in his speech. Though he worked tirelessly with a speech therapist, physical therapist, and occupational therapist, Noa's condition wasn't going to improve much more than it had. It had been a hard and arduous process for her whole family to accept.

In the beginning, they held out much hope that Noa would improve, but after a year, they knew Noa wouldn't be the same. Leia missed the many conversations she shared with Noa over the years, and especially his wise wisdom.

Leia patted the top of Noa's hand, giving it a squeeze. "How was your physical therapy appointment, Dad?"

"F-ine," replied Noa with a shaky voice.

Leia gave Noa's hand one more squeeze. "I'm glad to hear it." Then Leia removed her hand and sat back in her chair.

For a while, they sat staring at the ocean. A gentle ocean breeze filtered between them, making the humidity in the air more tolerable.

Finally, Leia broke the silence. Turning toward Derek, Leia rested her elbow on the armrest. Leia asked, "So, Derek, where did you get your Hawaiian shirt?" She allowed her gaze to slide down his frame. His damp hair had dried a tad, making his hair blonder by the minute.

Derek glanced down at his shirt like he had forgotten what he was wearing. He tugged at the collar. "I bought it from a little shop in Honolulu yesterday. I didn't think I'd ever actually wear it while I was here. Hopefully, it works for tonight." His cheeks reddened.

Leia remarked without hesitation, "I think you look nice." Unconsciously, Leia ran an unnecessary hand over her hair.

Derek added, "I like your dress." He gulped. "I mean, you changed too, right?" His hand gestured toward her body.

Raising an eyebrow, Leia replied, "Yeah, I changed." She half smiled.

Scratching his knee, Derek said, "I noticed." His blue eyes danced back at her against the blueness of the sky.

Noa coughed, breaking whatever spell Derek had managed to cast over her.

Leaning over her armrest, Leia asked, "Everything okay, Dad?" Their eyes met, and Leia caught his one-sided smirk.

Heat splashed her cheeks, and Leia patted his hand and uncomfortably squirmed in her seat. Though Noa couldn't communicate like he used to, Leia knew he caught the pulse of what was building between her and Derek.

Kai and Alana arrived, walking up the gravel walkway holding hands. Their children Malia and Hilo were squabbling with each other a few yards behind them.

Straightening herself, Leia crossed her arms. "Malia and Hilo, what are you fighting about now?" called out Leia.

Malia and Hilo guiltily paused in place. Then Hilo turned to Malia and announced, "I bet I can beat you inside." And off he bolted, brushing past Malia.

Hilo made it to where Kai and Alana were before Malia caught up with him. Malia yanked him back, taking the lead. The children raced up the stairs and into the house without even saying hello. The door swung shut behind them.

Alana rolled her eyes.

Kai laughed. "As you can see, we are totally nailing this parenting thing," he said to them as they climbed the front steps up to the lanai.

"I'm taking diligent notes for if I'm ever a parent," said Leia teasingly.

"Enough you two," said Alana, stopping in front of them on the lanai. "You don't want to scare off Derek with our unruly children and your sibling rivalry."

"Yes, of course," said Kai, wrapping an arm around Alana's shoulders. Kai turned his gaze to Derek. "Aloha, Derek."

With a warm smile, Derek replied, "Aloha."

Alana pointed. "I like the shirt."

Glancing down at himself, Derek replied, "Thanks. I wasn't sure what to wear."

Leaning into Kai's arm, Alana said, "We're pretty casual around here, so anything would have been fine." Then Alana bumped her hip against Kai's. "And sorry about Kai making you wear our son's t-shirt." Rolling her eyes, Alana gave Kai a pointed look. "Sometimes Kai forgets we aren't in high school anymore. He was the king of pranks then."

Kai smirked, overly pleased with himself. "I sure was, and that's why you fell in love with me."

Alana whacked Kai on his arm. "Fat chance. I thought you were a total goof off."

Wrapping an arm around Alana's shoulder, Kai glanced down at her. "But eventually you came around."

Elbowing Kai, Alana replied, "Because I thought you grew up."

Leia leaned over her armrest toward Derek, an inch between them, Leia made sure their bodies didn't touch. "Alana and Kai have known each other their whole lives," said Leia, feeling like she needed to give Derek a bit of their back story.

Meeting her gaze, Derek whispered back, "I think they are cute together."

Smiling, Leia said, "I do too."

Kai moved closer to Noa, crouching down in front of him. "How long has Mom left you out here, Dad? Are you ready to go back inside?" asked Kai.

Dad nodded.

Kai stood again and held out both his hands to Noa. Noa took them and slowly rose to his shaky feet. Derek jumped up, holding open the screen door. Leia rose too to give any assistance if needed. Kai and Alana helped Dad through the front door. They slipped off their shoes by the door before they continued down the hallway leading to the kitchen.

When Leia and Derek started to follow behind them, Alana said over her shoulder, "You two stay out on the lanai. We've got this." With her face full of amusement, her gaze flicked between them. "We'll come get you when dinner is ready."

Leia didn't dare look in Derek's direction. "Are you sure?" asked Leia.

Alana smirked. "Oh, I'm sure." Her voice was laced with innuendo.

Gnawing at her lip, Leia replied, "Fine."

They disappeared into the house. Leia and Derek stepped back onto the lanai. For a second, they paused, Derek gestured toward the chairs they had occupied. "Should we sit back down? You have an incredible view here. I could stay out here the entire day admiring it. And it seems like Alana wanted us to stay out," said Derek.

"I think you might be right," muttered Leia.

They walked back and sat down in their seats. The sun glistened across the water, and Leia took in the view she had enjoyed every day of her life. Yes, Derek was right. It never got old.

A comfortable silence settled between them. Derek turned his chin toward her. "You have a genuinely nice family. You're lucky." Shifting in his seat, Derek leaned way over his armrest. "I can feel the love you have for each other. It's …" His voice trailed off, and Derek peered back at the ocean again. When he continued, Derek kept his gaze fixed on the horizon. "It's beautiful to see a family like yours. I wish…" shaking his head, Derek continued, "I don't know what I wish."

She kept her gaze out on the ocean too, Leia ran a finger over her armrest. The wood was still smooth and slick. "I know I'm lucky, luckier than most." Around and around, her finger traced the wood. "How about you? What's your family like?"

His chest heaved, and Derek let out a long rattling breath. "My family is long gone. I was an only child. My dad died when I was in high school. Then my mom passed away some years ago. It's just me."

Leia's eyes dilated. "You don't have any family? Any?" Her chest pinched tight. Leia couldn't imagine being alone in the world, completely alone. "Not even an aunt or uncle? A cousin maybe?"

Derek shook his head, finding her gaze again. "I don't have anyone." His shoulders dropped. He leaned forward, resting his elbows on his knees. "I haven't for a long time."

His chest heaved while his gaze clouded. Leia had the strong urge to pull him into a hug, because his loneliness was palpable. No family, the thought was unimaginable to her. This town she lived in was full of all her family. Distant, but family. She had more cousins than she could count, aunts and uncles, who grew up loving her too. Sometimes Leia wanted less family not more, but when faced with the complete opposite option, gratitude slowly filled her heart.

Without reservation, Leia reached out and placed her hand on his forearm. "I'm sorry. I can't imagine. It must be incredibly difficult to feel so alone in the world."

Derek gulped, leaning the two inches closer, making their shoulders barely graze one another. "If I'm being completely honest, I sometimes wonder if I'll live alone my entire life. All I have is work."

"Leia! Derek!" bellowed a voice from inside. "Dinner is ready."

Leia flinched, immediately removing her hand from his forearm. Derek rubbed the back of his neck, standing. Holding out his hand to Leia, she took it, rising to her feet. For an awkward second, Leia forgot to let go. "Sorry." Leia jerked her hand out of his. Fluffing her hair unnecessarily, Leia asked, "Why don't you follow me inside?"

Smiling, Derek remarked, "It smells good."

"I wouldn't get overly excited." Opening the screen door, Leia held it open for Derek. He gripped the door, allowing them to pass inside. In the foyer, Leia continued, "From what I smell, I think my mom, Teresa, made loco moco. I don't think she had much time. You'll have to come over another time, and we can have kalua pork."

"I'll be grateful for whatever Teresa made," replied Derek. "I can't remember the last time I had a homecooked meal."

With a nod, Leia added, "My aunt and uncle have a little food truck down the road that sells excellent kalua pork. It's not homecooked per se, but delicious. You could go there to get kalua pork before you leave."

Shuffling his feet, Derek glanced down at them. He scratched his neck, bringing his gaze back to Leia. "Maybe we could go there together," said Derek.

Sweat trickled down her back. A commotion pounded in her chest. Leia flipped her hair over her shoulder. "Maybe," she managed. Her legs were heavier than before. Was Derek flirting with her? Or just lonely? "We'll see. You might not be here long enough for us to go together."

His hands plunged into the pockets of his shorts, Derek said, "Oh, I'd make time."

Leia gulped, twisting forward, somehow, she remembered how to walk. Wandering down the hallway, Derek followed behind her to the kitchen. They arrived at the threshold into the kitchen. The space to enter was tight since they both tried to pass through at the same time. Derek brushed up against her arm. Leia side-stepped to keep them from touching again, and they finally made it inside.

Leia guessed right, loco moco was on the menu. Kai and Alana had set the table minus the plates. They were sitting with Dad at the round eight top table in the breakfast nook. Leia imagined Malia and Hilo were off watching TV in the toy room. The kitchen wasn't large, nor did they have a separate dining room, but it worked for their family. They liked being in the same room where the food was being prepared, so nobody felt left out when they gathered.

Teresa glanced over from the stove. With a smile, Teresa greeted him. "Aloha, you must be Derek." Her voice was warm and inviting. Her glance rapidly slid over him, then Teresa shot Leia a knowing look.

Leia's cheeks warmed, making her clasp and unclasp her hands.

Derek moved closer to Teresa. "Correct, I'm Derek." He placed a hand over his heart. "Thank you for inviting me to your home. You have a wonderful family. You must be so proud."

As Teresa placed the meat onto a platter, she said, "I'm proud and lucky." She smiled over at Noa. "I should say *we're* blessed." Sidestepping closer to Leia, Teresa grasped Leia's arm. "Leia, could you help me plate the food?"

"Of course." Leia walked to the sink, flipping on the water to wash her hands. Over her shoulder, Leia asked, "What do you need me to do?" She finished washing her hands and dried them off.

Peering past Leia, Teresa asked, "Derek, do you want to help too? Then you can learn how loco moco is made. You never know who you might want to make it for when you return home."

"I'd love to learn." Derek stepped toward the kitchen sink. Leia moved as far out of the way as the restrictive space would allow. Flipping on the water, Derek washed his hands. Leia handed him a towel to dry them off. Their shoulders brushed up against each other again in the small intimate space. Leia caught a sniff of his coconut shampoo, and she hated that it made her knees a bit wobbly. Once Derek finished drying his hands, he neatly folded the towel back up and placed it on the counter.

His grasp tightened around the counter on both sides of himself and Derek asked, "What do we do first?"

"First, we put the cooked rice on each plate." Teresa pointed to the rice cooker on the edge of the counter. "Derek, can you scoop out a cup of rice and place it on each plate?"

Skillfully, Derek moved around Leia and replied, "Absolutely." He reached for the rice cooker.

Leia opened a cupboard, taking out the stack of plates. "I bet you didn't think you'd be put to work when you came over to eat," commented Leia.

Leia spread the plates out on the limited counter space still available.

After he opened the rice cooker, Derek snatched the rice scoop and placed a cup of rice in the center of the first plate. "I don't mind." Derek tilted his head toward Leia. "I used to bake sometimes with my mom, when I was young." He scooped out more rice, placing it on the next plate.

Leia shifted, leaning against the counter so she was facing Derek. "What did you usually bake?" asked Leia.

Ladle in mid-scoop, Derek said, "We usually baked cookies, brownies … that sort of thing. My favorite was my mom's chocolate chip pumpkin bread. She'd let me dump in a whole bag of chocolate chips into the batter."

"A whole bag?" Leia chuckled. "I'm sure that's why you liked it. It was half chocolate."

Teresa interrupted their exchange. "Leia, can you put the hamburger patties on top of the rice. I'm almost done with the eggs."

Twirling back around, Leia picked up the platter of cooked hamburger patties.

Derek finished scooping rice onto the plates. "What comes next?" he asked.

"Hamburger or the ground beef patties," replied Leia. "Then the gravy, last is the fried egg."

He leaned his hip against the counter, Derek causally folded his arms. "How do you make the gravy?" inquired Derek.

Before Leia could answer, Teresa piped up, "The gravy recipe is the one thing I can't give you. It's for family only."

From the table, where Kai and Alana sat next to Noa. Alana chimed in, "I can testify to that. Teresa wouldn't give me the recipe until after Kai and I had been married for two years." Holding two fingers up, Alana shook them.

"I wanted to make sure the marriage stuck." Teresa turned off the stove burner. Removing a ladle from the drawer, she dropped it into the pot with the gravy. "I didn't want you running off with Noa's family recipe. You should consider yourself lucky. Noa's mom didn't give me the recipe until we celebrated our ten-year anniversary." She ladled gravy on top of each hamburger patty.

"So, my only hope of getting the recipe is to marry Leia?" asked Derek.

Leia nearly choked on her own saliva. Kai who remained quiet until now, let out a long belly laugh. Leia's cheeks burned as she shot Kai a narrowed glance.

Teresa laughed too. Shrugging, Teresa said, "I guess that really is the only way."

Derek crossed his ankles, leaning back against the counter. "I guess then it's all decided. Though I'm sure Leia's boyfriend wouldn't take kindly to me proposing marriage for a gravy recipe."

Teresa quickly said, "Leia doesn't have a boyfriend." Leia's back stiffened. With the gravy plated, Teresa moved to the frying pan with the fried eggs. "She hasn't dated anyone for who knows how long." Teresa raised a knowing eyebrow.

A groan escaped her, and Leia covered her face with both her hands. "Mom," hissed Leia. "Please stop."

"It's okay little sis," said Kai. "We don't care you're single. There's no shame in it. You just haven't found the right person yet. We're only stating the facts."

Mortified, Leia groaned louder. Her cheeks burned. "Thanks for reminding me." She skillfully avoided looking in Derek's direction. "I— I—" stammered Leia.

Interrupting, Teresa announced, "The food's ready," like she hadn't singlehandedly embarrassed Leia. Edging closer to Leia, Teresa gave Leia's shoulder a squeeze. "Let's eat." Then Teresa motioned toward the plated food. "Derek and Leia, can you help bring it to the table?"

Derek quickly replied, "Sure thing." He found Leia's eye and smirked.

Alana rose and yelled down the hallway, "Malia and Hilo, it's time to eat."

The loud pitter patter of little feet sounded down the hallway, soon Malia and Hilo arrived, out of breath. Alana instructed them to wash their hands before sitting down at the table. Once Malia and Hilo washed their hands and sat down, Leia and Derek each carried two plates to the table. Derek returned for another set. Kai jumped up and snagged two more, while Teresa located some salt and pepper, placing it on the table. Once the plates of food were set in front of each place, they sat down. Leia sat between Derek and Teresa. Noa sat on the other side of Teresa with Alana and Kai next to their children. Kai quickly introduced his children to Derek.

Taking in the sight of the food, Derek said, "This looks delicious." He rubbed his hands together in anticipation. "I can't wait to try it. Thanks again for having me."

Teresa squeezed his forearm. "We're glad you're here. Even if you are here to buy half our family farm." The words ricocheted across the room, making the carefree banter of minutes before dissipate into thin air. Derek stared down at his plate. With a wave of her hand, Teresa said, "Please everyone *eat*." It wasn't a suggestion. "Before it gets cold." Teresa took her napkin and placed it on her lap. Next, Teresa tucked Noa's napkin under his chin, covering his shirt.

"You don't have to tell me twice." Picking up his fork, Derek dug in first, taking a bite. For a minute, everyone at the table paused, watching him eat and swallow his first bite. After taking a sip of water, Derek grinned, "Delicious." He wiped his face with his napkin. "I'm not kidding." He nudged Leia with his elbow. "Now that I know you're single. It might *really* be worth getting married so I can get the gravy recipe." He shook his fork over his plate. "I can see why this recipe needs to be protected."

Everyone laughed, but Leia. Her blood pressure simmered to near boiling point. Leia didn't find any amusement in his words. Tilting her head toward Derek, Leia found his gaze and glared. Derek shifted uncomfortably in his seat. Tugging at his collar, Derek focused on his plate. Slowly, Derek took a bite, swallowing it down with a large gulp of water.

After glaring at Derek sufficiently, Leia turned away and didn't talk directly to him for the rest of the meal. Nobody seemed to notice her quiet demeanor, at least that was the way it appeared to Leia who was more than ready to show Derek the door.

CHAPTER 4

The meal wrapped up. Derek pushed out his seat, standing. "Can I help with the dishes?" He carried his plate to the sink.

Everyone else at the table, minus Noa, stood too, bringing their plates and cups to the sink.

"I'd appreciate it," replied Teresa. After placing her dish in the sink, Teresa pivoted toward them. "Kai and Alana need to get home to get their children into bed." Walking back, Teresa rested a hand on Noa's shoulder. "Then I can help Noa get ready for bed." Holding out her hands, Noa took both.

Slowly, Noa rose. They left the kitchen.

Interlocking his fingers with Alana's, Kai gave them a squeeze. Peering over at them, Kai said, "Goodnight, Leia and Derek. Thanks for doing the dishes." Over his shoulder Kai said, "I'll see you tomorrow, Derek. Come on, kids."

Malia and Hilo gave Leia a hug before disappearing with their parents.

With a nod, Derek replied, "Until tomorrow."

Once everyone exited, the kitchen became eerily quiet, leaving him alone with Leia. Wasting no time, Derek flipped on the faucet. Gripping the sponge, he squeezed soap onto it.

Pushing off the counter, Leia came up beside him. Derek sensed Leia wasn't happy about him joking about marrying her. It wasn't like he was some love expert, but sometimes when Derek was nervous, he talked too much and forgot to use a filter. And Leia made him way more nervous than he'd ever been around any other woman. So, he rambled, stuck his foot in his mouth, and managed to act like a jerk. Well done. If he could go back, he'd redo the entire exchange. Maybe even make a comment about how the other men had gotten it wrong by not dating her. Something smooth and less Derek-like.

"I can help you load the dishes. I'll dry the bigger stuff that doesn't fit into the dishwasher." She removed a dish towel from a drawer, placing it on the counter. "Sound good?"

Feeling jittery, Derek rinsed the dish in his hands way more than was necessary. "It works for me," replied Derek. Turning, Leia leaned against the counter, facing him. Derek sensed she was studying him. With the dish done, Derek held it out to her. "Here you go."

Taking it from him, Leia popped open the dishwasher door, pulling out the bottom rack. She placed the rinsed dish on the bottom rack then leaned back against the counter.

For a few minutes, Derek scrubbed the dishes then handed them to Leia. Leia loaded them without a word. Both worked in near silence. Derek longed to think of something to say to engage Leia in a conversation. But his mind couldn't form a thought beyond *Leia's beautiful and you've already messed this up.* From the open kitchen window, Derek could hear the ocean waves. He tried his best to focus on the rhythmic crashing of the waves and not the skittish beat of his heart.

Derek moved onto the bigger pots and pans, scrubbing the pot vigorously. Finally, when he could no longer take the pulsating silence, Derek said, "I'm sorry about earlier." He flipped back on the faucet, rinsing the pot off. He held it out to Leia, and she took it for him with a towel in her hands.

Then, stopping mid-wipe, Leia asked, "What specifically are you sorry about?"

"I'm sorry I joked about marrying you for a recipe." Derek moved onto a pan, scrubbing off the stuck-on food at the bottom. Once he figured it was clean enough, he rinsed the soapy water off the pan. "Sometimes, I say things without thinking. It's one of my many flaws that I'm working on. I was totally out of line, and I apologize if I made you uncomfortable."

Leia bit her bottom lip. "I see ..." She finished drying the dish in her hand. Opening a cupboard near her feet, she placed the dish inside and shut the door.

Derek gulped, shutting off the faucet. Water dripped from the pan in his hands. He lightly tried to shake off the excess water. "I don't need another reason for you to hate me." He held the pan out to Leia.

Taking the pan from him, Leia methodically dried it. Sighing, Leia finally said, "I think you're too late." Opening the bottom cupboard, Leia placed the pan inside. "I was going to hate you no matter what. You're potentially buying half my family's farm. You were doomed to begin with, so I wouldn't worry too much about your marrying me comment. I'm over it. I can see you are a bit of a jokester."

His lips curled at the edges. Derek replied, "I can't help it. Life is too short and too difficult to take anything too seriously." Squeezing more soap onto his sponge, Derek reached for the rice pot and started to scrub.

Leaning against the counter, Leia crossed her arms and ankles. "So, mister jokester ... since you started it, have you ever been married?" asked Leia.

Derek froze. The soapy water dripped down the sides of his hands. With the back of his hand, he swiped at an itch on his nose. "How did you leap to asking me if I've ever been married?" He raised an eyebrow, meeting Leia's gaze.

Jutting up her chin, Leia replied, "I figured you haven't,

because if you had you wouldn't be able to joke around about it. You'd be ... tainted."

"Ahh." Derek flipped on the faucet, rinsing off his hands along with the soapy water on the pot. Once the water ran clear, Derek turned it off. "You're spot on. I've never been married." He tried his best to keep his voice even and undeterred.

Leia gave an almost indistinguishable nod. Derek handed her the dripping pot. Taking it from him, Leia quickly dried it and put it away. The dishes were done. Leia used the wet towel to wipe down the counters. Derek tried to make himself useful by scooting the chairs back in around the table.

With the kitchen clean, both leaned against the counter, their shoulders touched accidentally, and Leia shifted a few inches over. Derek wondered if Leia was waiting for him to leave. He listened to the ocean waves, feeling his heart tug within his chest.

Breaking the lull, Derek said, "I've come close a few times."

A look of confusion fluttered across Leia's face. "Come close to what?" Leia shifted, moving her hip against the counter instead of her back.

Derek stared out the kitchen window, away to the ocean. "To marrying. The first time was way back in my twenties. I even bought the ring and everything. But the night I was going to propose, she up and announced she was moving to England and wanted to break up."

Leia cringed. "Ouch. That's brutal." Shaking her head, Leia asked, "What did you do with the ring?"

Giving a forced laugh, Derek stated, "You mean the ring I spent my life savings on?"

Leia tsked, "Oh dear, tell me you were able to return it."

Folding his arms, Derek replied, "I couldn't take it back to the store. Trust me, I tried. I was outside of the return window, and they didn't care. They weren't budging no matter what, even when I tried to make them feel sorry for me. I don't imagine I was the first guy who was rejected and tried to get their money back. So, I sold it on eBay for a fourth of its value."

Lifting her brow, Leia replied, "eBay? Yikes. I'm sorry."

Shrugging, Derek said, "I guess it worked out for the best."

"How so?" asked Leia.

"I took the few thousand dollars I recouped from the ring and used it to start this very investment company with my best friend, Tyson." Unfolding his arms, Derek straightened himself. "Tyson added a few thousand of his own money to the pot, and together we've worked to build the company to what it is today. I know if I hadn't been rejected there's no way I would've taken such a chance on it. But at the time I thought I had hit rock bottom, so I had nothing to lose."

"Impressive." Leaning in closer to him, Leia asked, "What was the first thing you ever invested in?"

Her question caught him off guard. Usually, people asked how much his business had grown since then or about his latest investment ventures. "It was a gardening business. Our friend started it, and he needed a few thousand to purchase some more gardening equipment. Just enough for him to expand his business to where he could have people working under him."

"Did it work?" asked Leia.

Derek nodded. "He expanded his business, and we tripled our little pot of money. It helped us get started toward other business investments. Little by little Tyson and I built this investment company to what it is today."

"Wow, that's wonderful." Leia gripped the counter on both sides of herself. Staring out the window too, she paused, then finally said, "You said you came close to marrying a few times, who else broke your heart?"

His throat grew tight. "My girlfriend just broke up with me through a text message. Like literally right before I came here. I thought I was going to propose when I returned from Hawaii. I hadn't bought the ring yet, so I guess I dodged a bullet," said Derek.

Leia placed a hand over his own. "I'm sorry. I'm glad you hadn't bought the ring yet." She removed her hand.

Running a hand through his hair, Derek said, "I guess that's my silver lining in this whole thing." They both stared out at the ocean. Silence enveloped them with only the sound of the ocean filling the space. Finally, Derek said, "Truth is, I'd probably been trying to hang onto something that hadn't worked for an extraordinarily long time. But I never thought I'd be this age and not married."

Derek didn't know why he was spilling everything to Leia. But he liked how she listened and didn't interrupt him. It gave him some time to work through his emotions. Most women he dated never gave him a chance to get a word in edgewise. Leia was different. She asked thoughtful questions.

"I'm sure you'll make it happen someday," said Leia.

Lost in his train of thought, Derek tried to catch up. "Make what happen?" asked Derek.

Straightening herself, Leia ran a finger over the top of the slick countertop. "The getting married. You'll find someone."

"Ahh ... but apparently not anytime soon," said Derek.

Leia pursed her lips together, glancing toward the front door. After a little lull, Leia said, "Thanks for coming to dinner and for helping with the dishes."

Derek took that as his cue to leave. He probably had way overstayed his welcome. Pushing off the counter, he said, "Thank you for having me. I enjoyed spending the evening with you and your family."

With a smile, Leia said, "Thanks. I don't want to keep you." Leia moved toward the exit of the kitchen. "I'll walk you out."

Derek followed behind Leia down the hallway to the front door. Her hair swung back and forth across her shoulder blades, and Derek found himself mesmerized by how it glistened under the overhead lights.

Once at the front door, Leia opened it and held it for him. "Where are you staying while you're here in Oahu?" asked Leia.

Through the open door, Derek shifted back to face Leia. "I have an Airbnb I rented up the road." He moved his shoulder in the correct direction. "I walked here because it's not far. It's maybe five to ten minutes on foot." He took a sidestep.

Nodding, Leia stepped further out onto the lanai. Putting a hand on her hip, Leia looked out at the water. Tracking her gaze, Derek took in the breathtaking view of the ocean. Soothing sounds of the ocean waves relieved the stress in his body. The moon lit up the night sky, casting a glow on the water. Derek understood why people lived here forever. Why would you ever leave a view like that? No wonder Leia's family was so protective of their land. If he had a choice, he'd stay here too.

Folding her arms against herself, Leia said, "I guess I'll see you soon." She peered down at her feet then back over at him. "I'll try and work on the books tonight and make sure everything is up to date. Then I'll email them over to you."

He shoved his hands into their pockets, Derek said, "If you don't mind, can you send them to Tyson too? It makes it easier than forwarding everything on to him."

Unlocking her arms, Leia tucked some loosened strands of her hair behind her ears. "Of course, no problem."

Derek forced himself to look away from her, because he didn't want her to catch him staring. "Thanks," he said.

Derek and Leia stared out at the ocean. With only a foot between them, Derek caught the scent of her perfume. His stomach swam, making heat slowly crawl up his neck and cheeks. Forcing himself to move, Derek took a step away, moving toward the stairs.

"I already know you're an early riser." Derek shuffled back and forth on his heels. "Do you try to make it to bed early?"

Shrugging, Leia scratched her elbow. "When I'm teaching, I make more of an effort to go to bed at a decent hour. Especially, when I know I'm going to be in a room full of kids, and I'll need to be patient. But I'm on a short fall break, so it doesn't matter when I go to sleep."

"Makes sense." A slow smile crept across Derek's face. "I'm sure the kids love you though." Derek rubbed the back of his neck. He knew he was prolonging their conversation, but Derek couldn't force himself to leave. The casual back and forth between them was a positive change to what he was used to. His ex-girlfriend spent most of her time taking pictures of herself to post on social media. With a little bit of distance from his ex, Derek was starting to see how wrong they were for each other. "I happen to remember most of my grade school teachers fondly. I'm sure your students feel the same way about you."

Folding her arms, Leia rubbed her biceps like she was attempting to stay warm from the slight breeze. "It's fun to run into some of the students I had years ago and see them all grown up." Leia tilted her chin toward him and added, "I'm sure you were a top-notch student."

"Guilty," laughed Derek. "I was a total teacher's pet and a major nerd."

Leia flashed him a sideway glance and tsked. "I believe you were a teacher's pet, but I don't believe you were a nerd. I'm sure you were some cool California surfer boy."

He straightened his shoulders, Derek said, "I mean, I do know how to surf..."

Dang, Derek wanted to impress her.

Leia's gaze roamed over him. "I assume that's why you thought you were a strong enough swimmer to go out into Shark's Cove alone."

With a nod, Derek replied, "I did overestimate my abilities. I tend to do that often. It's one of my many flaws."

Playfully, Leia shoved his arm. "Again, with the flaws." Her lips twitched at the corners. "I want to see you surf."

Derek knew he shouldn't have mentioned his surfing skills. With how strong Leia was as a swimmer, he could only imagine she dominated surfing too. If they did go surfing, Derek would no doubt become a total joke to her.

"I haven't surfed in years." Derek almost mentioned the last time he surfed was before his mom died. "I imagine I'm very rusty."

"You're in Hawaii. You must go surfing," said Leia.

"I wouldn't even know where to go." Derek tapped his shoulder once against hers. "And I don't have a surfboard."

Leia smirked. "You're in luck." Though they weren't touching, Derek swore he felt her heat radiating off her body. He forced himself to swallow. "We have plenty of surfboards to share. I've lived here my entire life, and I know the best spots. One morning this week," she pushed a finger into his chest. "I'm taking you surfing."

"Ahh." Derek rubbed the back of his neck. "I'm immediately regretting mentioning I surf. You're going to put me to shame. I can tell by the smug look on your face that you are an expert surfer."

Leia jutted her chin and whipped her hair over shoulder. "I don't have a smug look on my face," said Leia matter-of-factly. Straightening her shoulders, Leia continued, "I think perhaps you're scared, because maybe you don't surf at all." She cocked an eyebrow. "And I caught you in your lie?"

"Is that what you think?" Derek laughed, loosening the pent-up nerves building in his chest. "I surf."

Throwing her hands down at her side, Leia said, "I can meet you on Thursday morning, six o'clock, meet here. We can take my parent's truck to fit the surfboards. I'm taking you to Pipeline Beach."

Derek knew he should refuse. His carefully guarded business

boundaries were going out the window. In the past, Derek always kept business strictly business. If he became too involved with his clients in their personal life, it made it impossible for him to think clearly.

More importantly in this situation, Leia would no doubt surf in circles around him. And Derek hated to lose, but on the other hand, he rarely backed down from a challenge. Redemption would be his.

"Then it's settled." Derek stared directly back at Leia. He paused, waiting for her to rescind her offer. Leia didn't bat an eye. Taking the front steps, Derek said over his shoulder. "I'll see you later then." At the bottom of the stairs, Derek twisted back around. "You better be ready to eat my dust."

Smirking, Leia replied, "Oh will I? You're on."

Derek laughed and left. Leia remained on the lanai, watching him walk toward his Airbnb.

~

His blaring alarm woke him up early in the morning. Quickly, Derek dressed in his board shorts and a T-shirt, remembering to bring his towel, wetsuit, and wallet on his way out the door.

As he approached Leia's house, Derek spotted a truck idling in the driveway. Leia appeared walking down the driveway, carrying a surfboard under one arm. Her hair was thrown up in a messy bun. Dressed in shorts and a tank top, Leia's swimsuit straps were poking out.

Derek gulped, extra aware of his attraction to Leia. The thought of seeing her in a swimsuit made his nerve ends simmer.

When she spotted him, Leia smiled brightly. "Aloha, Derek." She slid the surfboard into the back of the truck.

Derek finally remembered how to speak. "Hi, Leia." He stopped at the back of the open truck bed, a few feet from Leia. "Can I help you load anything else up into the truck?"

The windows of the truck were rolled down, blasting out Hawaiian music. He tossed his towel and wetsuit into the back of the truck.

"I only need to load up the surfboard for you." Moving back toward the garage, Leia waved him on. "Maybe you should come pick one out. We need to find one that is the correct size for you." Over her shoulder, Leia added, "I don't need you claiming you didn't surf well because you had the wrong size board."

Derek forced a laugh. "Absolutely. You're completely right."

After he filed around the truck, Derek followed Leia back to the detached garage at the end of the driveway. It was filled with beach stuff: beach chairs, surfboards in every size imaginable, coolers, umbrellas, and piles of sand toys.

Shimmying her body sideways, Leia squeezed through a small path to the wall with the surfboards. She cradled one, meeting Derek's gaze. "Let see what board will work." Leia glanced between him and the surfboard. "You need it extra-long, right?" she grinned.

With an eye roll, Derek replied, "Hilarious." Weaving his way through the mountains of stuff, Derek stopped in front of the array of surfboards lining the side of the garage wall. Leia rifled through a few, and Derek did the same. Finally, he found one that he thought would work. Snatching it, Derek said, "Can I use this one?" He pulled it all the way out from the rack.

Leia peered around the surfboard toward Derek. For a few seconds, Leia's gaze slid up and down Derek and the surfboard. Biting her bottom lip, Leia finally said, "I think it will work. That's the board Kai usually uses, and he's an excellent surfer."

As he scrutinized the board, Derek asked, "Will Kai care that I'm borrowing it?" Somehow, he had managed to get off on a good foot with Kai, Derek didn't want to jeopardize their rapport with one another by using his prized board without permission.

"Kai hasn't surfed in a long time. He won't care at all." Leia unhooked a wetsuit from where it hung on the wall. "Come on.

Let's head out." Then Leia walked to the side of the garage. Derek followed her with the surfboard in his arms. She stopped in front of a keypad to the left of the garage door and punched in a code. Slowly, the garage door lowered. "Are you ready to be creamed?" asked Leia, as she gave him a sideways glance.

His back stiffened. Something told him he was about to make a complete fool of himself. "Are you?" he countered, though he felt extremely far from the confidence he was trying to exude.

Her lips puckered together, and then Leia scoffed. "I guess we'll see who's bluffing soon enough." Leia stepped toward the truck. "Let's hit the road."

Both walked down the long driveway, Hawaiian music blared back at them. Derek loaded the surfboard into the back. Leia tossed in her wetsuit and towel, closing the tailgate. Then they both walked around to their respective sides and climbed in.

After they settled into the cab of the truck, Leia turned down the music a tad. "I purposely had Hawaiian music playing for your arrival," stated Leia. Her lips twitched in an incredibly cute way. Derek forced himself to look out the windshield. "I needed you to hear *good* music."

Derek laughed. "Okay, enlighten me." Turning his body toward hers, he asked, "Who should I be listening to?"

To reverse the truck, Leia rested her arm along the back of the bench. Slowly, she backed her way out of the driveway, turning on to the road.

"Umm, what do you think of this song?" Leia reached forward, turning the music up a little louder.

Leia drove down the road. For a minute, Derek concentrated on the words and melody of the song. He liked the rhythm and beat, finding it soothing and cathartic like music he'd want to listen to if he was out on a catamaran, sailing.

Finally, when the song ended, Derek remarked, "I like it. Who sings it?" He fidgeted with the end of his boardshorts, caught himself and placed his arm along the back of the truck bench.

"Kolohe Kai," replied Leia. Tilting her head nearer, she continued, "He beats Tom Petty. No contest."

His hands went up in defeat, Derek said, "We don't need to fight. We can like different artists, but I like the sound of this artist's voice. Can you play another one of his songs?"

They made a left onto the two-way highway, Leia flipped through two songs until she landed on another song by Kolohe Kai.

The words of the song were displayed across the dash, Derek read them out loud, "Cool Down."

Shifting in his seat, Derek glanced at Leia. Her gaze held steady on the road, but Leia seemed more at ease, relaxed in a way Derek hadn't seen before. Without even thinking, he tapped his fingers against the grey fabric of the truck bench.

Leia bobbed her head to the beat. "Listen …" She glanced out her window, staring at the ocean then back at the road. "This might be my favorite song he sings." Her lips curled up at the corners, forming a half-smile, like she was trying to hold back her enthusiasm. It made Derek like her even more.

Intently, he took her instructions. Derek listened to the not-quite-reggaeton beat. As he stared out the window at the ocean, he admired the view as the sunrise sneaked above the water. Golden light dripped in through the window, casting a captivating glow on Leia's face.

Derek scratched his chin. "What's ohana?" He allowed himself to further study the silhouette of her face. "The song says, 'Go grab your ohana'. I'm just wondering about the meaning."

After she readjusted the rearview mirror, Leia double checked it. Then she flashed him a quick gaze, before staring back through the windshield. "Ohana means family. So, grab your family is what it's saying."

"Oh, duh." Derek tapped the heel of his hand against his forehead. "I should know that by now. I've heard it a lot. I guess I never took the time to ask or find out." He placed a hand over his chest. "I apologize."

Leia shifted in her seat. "You don't need to apologize. You asked." Her lips twisted into a full, heart-stopping smile. Geez, Derek could live off that smile for who knows how long. "And now you know."

Heat hit his cheeks. Derek forced himself to look away out toward the ocean. More light creeped into the truck. Taking the sunglasses which hung from the top of his collar, Derek put them on. Leia flipped down her visor and a pair of sunglasses came tumbling down. Impressively, Leia seized them with one hand without them dropping to her lap. She put hers on too.

Next, Leia rolled down the windows. They seemed to be getting more comfortable with one another as each mile passed. Derek let his arm hang out the window on his side. They listened to the music of Kolohe Kai the entire way to Pipeline Beach. As they pulled into the parking lot, Derek leaned forward to fully take in the sight of the beach. He gulped. The waves were bigger than he normally surfed. Seeing he had years of absence from the sport, Derek started to question his judgement in agreeing to come.

Moisture tickled Derek's brow, and he swiped at it. As Derek pointed toward the waves, he asked, "How tall do you think those waves are?" He rubbed his jaw.

After she turned off the ignition to the truck, Leia traced the length of his arm pointing to the ocean. "I don't think they're unusually high. Maybe nine feet. You should see it when the waves are like twenty feet. It's too dangerous for me to even try it." Leia tapped her shoulder against his as amusement filled her eyes. "Why? Are you nervous?" asked Leia.

The stubble on his jaw suddenly felt itchy. Unconsciously, he scratched at it. Derek replied, "Me?" He gawked. "Never." He tried his best to give her a flat look, though he knew Leia saw right through him.

Leia laughed and unbuckled her seatbelt. "You're such a liar." Her finger circled his face. "You happen to have fear clearly written all over your face." With a smirk, Leia added, "I like it."

Removing his sunglasses, Derek tossed them on the bench in between them. "You like how much I'm flipping out right now?" asked Derek.

In one swift movement, she perched her own sunglasses onto the top of her head. Leia reached out and touched him on the forearm. His churning middle settled. "It's okay." Lowering her voice, and without a hint of sarcasm, she said, "I'll be with you the whole time. I won't let anything happen to you."

Derek stared into her captivating eyes. A great calm replaced his previous terror. "I believe you." Unbuckling his seatbelt, Derek continued, "You saved me once. You might have to do it again. But let's go before I talk myself out of this whole thing."

With a quick nod, Leia removed her hand, climbing out of the truck. Derek followed.

CHAPTER 5

In the parking lot, Leia walked to the back of the truck and opened the tailgate. First, she removed her sunglasses from the top of her head and placed them on the bed of the truck.

Soon, Derek joined her and asked, "What's the plan?"

His intense attention on her made heat slowly creep up her neck. "I— I—" Leia stammered. Leia tried to remember what to do first.

With shaky hands, Leia grappled with her wetsuit. Derek snagged his too, mirroring her movements. Why was she acting so skittishly? Leia surfed at this beach too many times to count. Was she worried about looking like a fool in front of Derek? Nah, she had no doubt she'd surf in circles around him. The thought made her straighten her back. But the facts were, Derek and his totally ruggedly good-looking body, were one foot from her and Leia was about to see it ... again. *Simmer on down. Simmer. Down.*

Suddenly, the rhythmic crashing waves on the shore matched the staccato beat of her heart. Leia fumbled with the zipper on her wetsuit, zipping it all the way down. "Let's get our wetsuits on, and then we can get the surfboards out." Her voice almost sounded normal, not foreign, and weird like another person was talking.

Derek stripped off his shirt without a word, tossing it into the back of the truck in one long smooth movement. The sight of his trimmed abs and waistline made her pause in place. Yeah, she saw his hunky body the first day they had met, but today was *different*. More intimate.

Shaking her head, Leia forced herself to glance away. Derek placed his foot into one leg of the wetsuit then after wiggling around, he stepped into the other leg and pulled the wetsuit up to his waist. Leia shifted her body further from him. After she hung her own wetsuit off the tailgate of the truck, Leia removed her shirt and shorts. Swiftly, she tossed them inside the truck bed, Leia wished she didn't feel so vulnerable and exposed, but then she reminded herself Derek saw her in a sports bra and shorts.

A loud honk from behind them, made Leia jump. A truck barreled past them into a parking space three spots up.

Leia's gaze darted to Derek. He shrugged. Then Derek scratched his head and averted his eyes toward the beach. Leia's hair from her updo came loose. Yanking the hairband out of her hair, she placed it on her wrist. As she held out her wetsuit in front of herself, Leia managed to slip her foot into one hole and then the other. Being tight, she struggled to bring it up and over her hips. Finally, she shimmied her arms into the top of the suit.

Once done, Leia tried a few times to reach the zipper. Exasperated, she sighed and asked, "Could you help me zip up the back?" She twisted her back to him.

His head whipped back toward her, Derek ran a hand down his face. "Sure," he partly croaked. Derek stopped inches from her. Leia felt his breath against her back, spreading goosebumps across her skin. She wondered if he noticed. Swiping her long dark hair over one shoulder, Leia held it away from the zipper with both hands. Derek fingered the zipper, bringing it up halfway until the resistance was too tight to easily zip it up. "You might need to drop your arms, so I can zip it up the rest of the way," said Derek.

"Oh, right." Leia lowered her arm, doing her best to bring her entire hair over her shoulder. She dropped her hands by her sides. "Please be careful of my hair, I don't want it getting caught in the zipper."

Derek tugged at the open sides of her wetsuit. Leia tried to glance over her shoulder to see what was taking him so long. "Head forward please," commanded Derek. "Like you said, I don't want to get any of that beautiful hair of yours caught."

Leia obeyed.

Finally, Derek brought the zipper to the top of her wetsuit. His hands lingered on her shoulders. Then in what seemed like an afterthought, Derek brought her hair from in front of her shoulder to the back. Leia sucked in air as his fingertips grazed her hair. Derek stumbled a step back.

For a moment, Leia waited for the thunder in her temples to subside. Once she could hear normally again, Leia shifted to face him. Bringing a hand to her hip, Leia asked, "Do you want me to zip yours up?"

His lips twitched as he stared down at his still bare chest. Derek nodded. "I'd appreciate it." Pulling the dangling half of his wetsuit up, Derek pushed his arms through the sleeves. He wiggled his arms for a minute, until the suit fully covered his broad shoulders. "Okay, I'm ready." He took a backward step toward her, stopping a mere two inches from her.

Leia's fingers trembled as she clasped the zipper. Her fingers slipped for a second and grazed Derek's back. Immediately, goosebumps sprawled across his skin. Knowingly, Leia smiled, zipping it up the rest of the way. Leia was satisfied that the feeling of attraction was mutual.

Unable to resist, Leia patted the top of his wetsuit covered shoulders, Leia said, "There you go." She removed her hands, and

Leia took a few steps away in a need to widen the gap between them.

First, he stretched his arms above his head, Derek said, "Thanks." Then he twisted from side to side then bent forward, no doubt trying to get his wetsuit to form to his body.

Taking her hairband off her wrist, Leia put it between her teeth, gathering her hair into a bun. Once she smoothed out the top, Leia replaced the band. With a wink, Leia said, "Let's do this."

"Umm." Derek scratched his head and finally said, "I guess there is no time like the present."

At the back of the truck, Leia pulled out her surfboard. Derek followed suit and removed the other surfboard. After rearranging their items, Leia closed the back of the truck.

In tandem, with their surfboards underneath their arms, they walked to the edge of the water. Soon, the warmish saltwater ran over the top of their toes. Leah pushed her toes into the sand, allowing the gritty mixture to wiggle in between the empty spaces around her feet. Water nipped at her ankles.

As she glanced across the water, Leia took in the scene of the turquoise water, the brightest blue sky, and a smattering of other surfers. Leia loved it here. It had been ages since she had surfed. Making a promise to herself, Leia vowed to come here more often. As she took a few steps forward, Leia let the water soak into her wetsuit around her calves. Slowly, her body adjusted to the temperature of the water, making her brave enough to move further out into the water.

Leia raised an eyebrow and found Derek's gaze. "Are you ready?" she asked.

With a wide grin, Derek replied, "I was born ready." With his free hand, he scooped up a handful of water with the upcoming tide, tossing it in her direction. Leia shrieked and jumped away as the cool water seeped into her wetsuit. His lips twitched mischievously. Derek continued, "You know you talk a lot of trash, and now I want you to prove you aren't all talk."

Leia jutted her chin and puffed up her chest. "I don't talk trash." Leia kicked water at him. "I can't help it if I happen to be good at most things."

"Oh, I know …" Derek splashed her again. Leia attempted to use her surfboard to block herself from getting hit. After a long pause, Derek remarked, "I like it, Leia. I like it a lot." Their eyes locked, making her breath catch in her throat.

Warmth flooded her middle as she kicked more water toward him, Derek leaped out of the way. "What do you like?" inquired Leia.

Playfully, Derek scooped up another handful of water, tossing it at her. She shrieked again as the cool water landed in the center of her back, trickling down the length of her wetsuit.

Grinning as if he had won, Derek said, "I like your confidence. In fact, I think I like everything about you."

"Is that so?" Leia suddenly felt anything but confident. "I— I —" stammered Leia.

Derek's uncanny gaze rocked her. "You know you can just say thank you," said Derek without breaking eye contact.

Unconsciously, she chewed on the inside of her cheek. Leia said, "Then thank you." The playfulness from moments before whisked away with the ocean breeze. Leia smacked Derek on the arm. "Quit trying to flatter me to get out of surfing." She hoped to bring back the flirtatious energy pulsating between them.

Holding up a hand, Derek replied, "I'm not trying to get out of anything. I only speak the truth."

For a second, they stared back at each other, Leia wondered if he was going to kiss her, which was an absurd thought. Derek was here in Hawaii to buy half her family's farm not to try and date her. Her back stiffened. The playful mood from before seeped right out of her.

Leia looked away first, taking in the vast wide ocean. "Let's surf."

She'd show him. Leia wasn't all talk.

Without hesitation, when the next wave crashed on the shore, Leia walked further out into the water with her surfboard under her arm. She didn't stop until the water hit her waist. Dragging the surfboard beside her, Leia swam once she could no longer touch the ocean floor. Derek soon appeared next to her. Matching her stroke for stroke with his long broad arms, Derek kept up with her brisk pace. It took them a few moments to make it out past the breaking waves. They swam until the water smoothed out.

Once in calm waters, Leia brought herself up onto her surfboard, straddling the board with one leg on each side. A glance over her shoulder confirmed Derek was only seconds away. Once next to her, he used his strong muscular arms, to bring himself up and onto his board, straddling his too.

A few minutes ticked by as they sat on their boards, waiting for a wave big enough for them to surf. Contentment filled her being, as Leia took in the beauty surrounding her.

Derek broke the silence. "How old were you when you learned to surf?" He kept his gaze straight out at the water.

Swiftly, she brought her hands to each side of her board and dipped her fingers into the water. Spreading her fingers apart, she let the water lace in between her fingertips. "I don't remember." Leia kept her eyes on the waves too. "I simply remember always knowing how. How about you?" She allowed herself one peek at him, taking in his strong square jawline.

Derek ran a wet hand through his hair, smoothing it out. The water made his blond hair dull to a light brown. "My dad taught me. I think I was maybe six or seven years old. It was a wonderful day being out on the water with him." He smiled to himself, making the lines around his eyes scrunch up.

For a second, Leia thought he'd continue, but he didn't. "What made it so great?" asked Leia.

Tilting his head toward her, Derek met her eyes. "I remember being with my dad. And I remember feeling happy and loved."

His voice faded away, and Derek turned back toward the ocean. "Do you think we should try and catch this next wave?" He pointed.

Leia glanced out at the ocean. The wave coming was only a couple hundred yards away. With a shrug, Leia said, "Sure. I think it looks like a good one."

The wave came near. Leia paddled away from him and ready herself on her board. As she concentrated on the approaching wave, Leia assumed Derek was doing the same. Seconds away, Leia held her breath as the perfect moment to catch the wave came. Up she sprung on her surfboard, riding it perfectly the entire way to the shore.

Once on the safety of the shore, Leia glanced out at the water looking for Derek. He must have waited for a different wave because she didn't spot him. Then out of nowhere, Leia noticed him, riding the next wave like a champ. He wasn't a liar. Derek did surf. And well. Leia's insides did a somersault.

Derek reached the water's edge, finding his footing, he made his way toward her with his surfboard under his arm. Running a hand through his hair, Derek shook his head, freeing some of the water from it.

Once within earshot, Leia asked, "Were you trying to show off?" She laughed. "Why didn't you take the wave I did?"

Water cascaded down his temples. Derek swiped at it and replied, "I know. I decided to take the next one. I didn't want you to see me if I failed to get up."

Pursing her lips together, Leia replied, "I see."

"Honestly," Derek walked further up the sand, plopping down his surfboard beside him. "The wave you took was taller than I thought. I knew it was above my abilities to ride it, so I waited until I saw one, I thought I could ride."

With a shrug, Leia said, "I thought you rode that wave remarkably well."

His face lit up, sending a zing down her spine. "You did?" asked Derek.

He looked so sincere, so satisfied with her simple compliment. Leia knew she'd chase that expression repeatedly like an addicting thrill.

"I did." Shifting toward the water, Leia raised an eyebrow. "Now, are you ready to ride another one? You can't stop with one."

Derek picked up his surfboard again. "I'm ready but go easy on me. I think the last wave was only a bit of beginner's luck. Who knows what I'll look like on the next one."

"Nonsense," said Leia. "Stop being humble." Shoving him playfully with her free hand, Leia added, "Now show me what you've got."

With a few steps, she moved further into the water. Then Leia waited for Derek to join her. Together, they swam out past the breaking waves again. Once to the calm water, they sat back on their surfboards, waiting for a good wave to come along. One approached; they rode it back to the shore. They repeated this several times without talking. Leia couldn't remember when she had enjoyed herself more. The comfort of Derek's presence, the blissful feeling of salt water against her skin, the rush of adrenaline when she stood up on her board, somehow, she wanted to live in this day forever.

After a ride to shore, Derek shook out his dripping hair. Rubbing at his eyes, he asked, "Are you getting hungry? I'd love to take you to breakfast." He walked out of the water and onto the dry sand of the beach. Plopping his surfboard down, Derek swiped water off his temples with the heel of his hand.

Joining him on the soft, dry sand, Leia placed her surfboard down next to his. Saltwater stung her eyes. Leia used the wrist of her wetsuit to swipe at them. Once the sting subsided, Leia gently tugged her hairband free from her hair.

"I could eat," remarked Leia.

"Then let's head out," said Derek.

Sticking her hairband between her teeth, Leia found his gaze. Gathering up her wet messy strands of hair, she replaced her hairband. Next, Leia reached for the zipper on the back of her wetsuit but struggled to reach it.

Without skipping a beat, Derek closed the space between them. "Here, let me help you." He motioned for her to turn around. Leia obeyed, shifting her back to him. Derek tugged the zipper the entire way down. "Do you know anywhere good to eat around here?" Derek dropped his hands, stepping away from her.

She wiggled her arms out of the wetsuit, Leia pulled it halfway down to her waist. "There's a place only a few miles down the road. They have fantastic banana macadamia nut pancakes." Her stomach growled at the suggestion.

A warm grin spread across his face. "My mouth is watering already. Sounds great," said Derek.

Derek seized the edge of his zipper without any difficulty. He unzipped it, tugging it down to his waist. Removing the sleeves of his wetsuit, Derek let it hang down around his waist. Leia forced her glance away up toward the parking lot when she caught herself staring at his perfect physique.

"Pancakes it is," said Leia.

They both bent down and picked up their surfboards, walking back to the parking area. After they placed the boards in the bed of the truck, Leia gripped one hand on the vehicle while she used her other hand to tug down the rest of her wetsuit. Soon, she stepped out of it, Leia tossed it into the back of the truck. Derek struggled to get his wetsuit off. Hopping on one foot, he eventually managed to rid his body of the restrictive material.

With an exasperated look, Derek swiped at his brow and asked, "Why are wetsuits always so much harder to get off than on?" His curious gaze landed on her.

Nonchalantly, Leia shrugged. "I didn't have any trouble

getting mine off." Puffing up her chest, she put both hands on her hips. "I think it might just be you."

"Oh, it's me. Is it?" Derek took one step closer to her. "I find that hard to believe."

Leia gulped as the air thickened. "Believe it," she replied, with a quiver in her voice.

Suddenly, Leia realized she was standing in front of Derek in nothing but her dripping wet swimsuit. It took everything within herself to stand straight and not agonize over whether Derek found her appealing or not.

Leaning casually against the truck, Derek folded his arms. "I think you happen to be one of those people that everything comes easily to."

"I disagree," countered Leia.

Derek blinked, glancing out toward the ocean. "Everything comes hard to me, but you— you looked fierce out there. I couldn't take my eyes off you." Leia opened her mouth to speak but didn't know how to respond. Straightening himself, Derek reached into the truck and rifled through his pile of stuff in search of his towel. "I'm impressed. You're impressive." Finding his towel, Derek wiped his face off.

Locating her own towel, Leia pulled it out of the truck and patted her face dry. "I don't think you should be impressed because I rode a few waves. You need to see the professionals. They are the ones who are impressive." Leia ran the towel down her dripping legs.

Running his towel over his bare chest, Derek caught Leia staring at him. "I'm sure they're good, but they aren't the ones I'm interested in seeing."

Boom. His words ricocheted between them, making heat wiggle its way up her spine.

Dang, this guy was good.

Too good.

Too smooth.

Leia forced a laugh, whipping her towel at his arm. "You're such a sweet talker. I'm sure you say that to all the ladies." She tossed her towel into the back of the truck.

"What ladies?" Shaking his head, Derek placed his towel in the bed of the truck too. Sadness splashed across his face. "I was dumped, remember? I'm obviously so *not* a sweet talker."

Leia didn't know how to respond, so she gave him a flirtatious shove. "Give it time. I'm sure in no time at all you'll be right back out there on the hunt for your next girlfriend."

"I highly doubt that," muttered Derek.

Leia took her shorts out of the truck. Attempting to shove her leg through the first hole, Leia stumbled, hopping around to find her equilibrium.

Quickly, Derek's hands found her waist and steadied her. His fingertips pressed into her sides.

Her skin sizzled. "Thanks," croaked Leia. "I think I've got it now."

Derek let go. Their eyes locked. Then Derek broke eye contact first and rifled through the things in the truck until he located his T-shirt. With boardshorts on, Leia watched him pull the shirt over his trimmed abs. Her pulse thundered, making her mind muddled. Leia quickly reminded herself to keep things professional, to simmer her eager little heart down. Clearly, Leia hadn't been around a man in far too long. She was mistaking kindness for interest. With shaky hands, Leia snatched her tank top, shoving it over her head. With her swimsuit still wet, her shirt stuck to it. She put on her flip flops right as Derek did the same.

Clapping his hands together, Derek rubbed them back and forth. "I'm ready for pancakes."

Leia closed the back of the truck. "I am too." Her hand trailed the slick painted truck as she walked toward the driver's side. Leia opened her door and took her place behind the wheel. Derek climbed in on the opposite side. Inserting her keys into the ignition, Leia paused, "Oh wait, I left my wallet at home." Her cheeks burned. She didn't want to assume Derek would pay for her breakfast, not when he may be bailing the farm out of financial ruin. Leia didn't want him thinking she had personal money problems too. But maybe this was a date? Was it?

Derek gave her shoulder a squeeze, and said, "I've got you covered." He pressed the window button, lowering it the whole way down. Derek let his arm hang out the side. "Besides," Derek shifted toward her, "this is a date, and I don't care what anyone says, I always pay. I'd let my dad down if I did anything different."

A date? Her middle pooled with a warm swimming sensation.

Leia smoothed out the top of her hair. "A date?" She flipped the key in the ignition, revving up the engine. "Is that what this is?"

With a wink, Derek smiled. "You bet it is." He nodded toward the radio. "Now, would you mind turning back on that Hawaiian guy—something Kai. I want to hear more from your favorite singer, because I, for one, plan on becoming an expert on all things Leia."

Pressing the power button on the dash, the music came blaring out of the speakers. Leia cued it to another Kolohe Kai song. Casually, Derek bobbed his head to the beat. Slowly, Leia backed out of her parking space, driving toward the pancake house a few miles down the road.

CHAPTER 6

With his arm hanging out the lowered car window, Derek let the balmy air flow between his fingertips. Smiling, he couldn't remember the last time he felt this relaxed and free. Glancing over from his place on the truck bench, Derek admired the silhouette of Leia. The entire morning, he had flirted shamelessly with her. Though he knew he needed to knock it off, Derek couldn't. Everything about Leia mesmerized him, her grace, beauty, and confidence. He didn't know spending time with someone could feel this easy.

Most likely, he was walking his way into dangerous waters. Everyone knew the first rule of business was to never mix business with pleasure. But here he was doing exactly that.

His pocket buzzed multiple times. Derek knew it was messages from Tyson, his friend and business partner, but he didn't want to look. Nothing was going to ruin this perfect Hawaiian morning, especially not the demands of Tyson.

Derek and Tyson were opposites. Tyson wanted investment deals that were fast. Get in and get out was Tyson's motto. Derek, on the other hand, took his time studying the potential investments out at every angle. Their different approaches served to balance each other out. Tyson was all risk. Derek was all caution. Then together they were magic. A combination which made them successful in the growth of their investment company.

Tipping her head in his direction, Leia asked, "Do you need to get that?" Her gaze skidded to his buzzing pocket then back to the road. "I don't mind you answering it."

Pulling his arm back into the safety of the truck, Derek pressed the window up button. Rolling it back up, he stopped it an inch from the top. "I'm okay. I know who it is." He shifted his shoulders toward her. "And I'm in no hurry to answer it."

"How can you know who it is? I haven't seen you check your phone once, and it's buzzed probably twenty times in the last few minutes." Leia double checked the rear-view mirror then over her shoulder before exiting the two-lane highway. "Whoever it is, they certainly seem impatient to touch base with you."

Derek sighed, making his chest heave. "It's got to be Tyson, my business partner." Tension crept back into his neck and shoulders. "Only *he* would text me a bazillion times in a row."

Raising her perfectly plucked eyebrows, Leia asked, "Are you sure it's not that ex-girlfriend of yours?" Derek paused, and when he didn't reply, Leia continued, "Maybe she's come to her senses and realized the error of her ways. Maybe she's come crawling back." She pursed her lips together.

Rolling his eyes, Derek shook his head. "Nah, it's not her. Promise." His pocket buzzed again. "She was very clear she was done with me."

"Check it." Leia pulled into the parking lot of the pancake house. "The suspense is driving me batty." She parked, turning off the engine.

Reluctantly, Derek slipped his phone out of the pocket of his board shorts. With a tap of his finger, the screen lit up. Unbuckling his seat belt, Derek scanned the extensive list of messages from none other than Tyson. As he suspected, Tyson had texted him multiple times asking for an update on the potential farm investment. Before Derek left for Hawaii, Tyson had voiced his hesitation to invest in the farm. Tyson didn't believe it was worth their time when the potential investment would take years to recoup. Derek had started to move forward on the initial meeting without Tyson's full support, because he believed the farm could be profitable again.

Tyson wanted Derek's final decision, and Derek didn't have one. Not yet. Derek shot Tyson a quick text letting him know he'd call him later with an update. Immediately, Tyson texted back, giving him a time by which he needed a report.

His jaw clenched as he slid his phone back into his pocket. Derek said, "Sorry about that." He cranked his neck back and forth, to rid it of tension. Unbuckling his seatbelt, Derek reached for the door. "Are you ready to eat? I'm starving."

"Me too," replied Leia.

Leia unbuckled her seatbelt, climbing out of the truck. Derek exited and went around the front of the truck to join Leia. Once together, they wandered to the front of the pancake house. Derek held the door open for Leia, the wafting smell of bacon and pancakes came tumbling out. His stomach growled.

Leia pointed at his stomach and said, "I heard that," she laughed.

They walked to the end of the line of people waiting to order.

Placing a hand over his abdomen, Derek rubbed it. "I guess I worked up an appetite." He smirked, then bumped his shoulder against hers. "I was trying to keep up with a beautiful surfer I know."

Leia shuffled her feet, peering down at them for a second. Red splashed her cheeks, making Derek's pulse gallop.

Leia stammered, "I— I—" She twisted her hair around one of her fingers.

A voice from behind them, interrupted Leia. "Hey, are you

two lovebirds in line or what?" The woman encroached on their space, breathing down their necks.

Derek flinched. With a swift peek over his shoulder, he caught the glare of the disgruntled person. Derek smiled. "We're in line. Sorry, we'll move up. We didn't notice it had moved." Derek exchanged a conspiratorial look with Leia.

Leia's lips curled up at the corners into a half smile. They shuffled forward up the line.

Once properly in the correct spot in line, Leia pointed up at the menu on the wall behind the cash registers. "I always order the banana macadamia nut pancakes." Leia then looped her thumb around one of her empty belt loops.

Rubbing his jaw, Derek scanned the menu. "Banana macadamia nut pancakes, you say? I can't say that I've ever had them before."

As Leia leaned a bit closer to him, he felt Leia's breath on his neck. It sent a shot of adrenaline down his spine. "I think you'll like them," said Leia. "Unless you don't like banana," Leia paused then added, "then you'll probably hate them."

He tried to peruse the menu some more but found himself distracted by Leia's nearness. Derek spoke slowly, "I don't mind banana." Derek couldn't decide.

"Everything here is good." Leia gestured toward the menu. "I don't want you feeling like you *have* to get the banana pancakes, just because I suggested it. I know people can have strong opinions when it comes to banana." Leia nibbled on a fingernail.

Was Derek picking up on some nervous energy from Leia? Leia always came across super confident. Derek loved seeing her a bit vulnerable. The line moved again. They shuffled forward.

Because he couldn't resist, Derek wrapped an arm around Leia's shoulders, giving her a squeeze. "I'll get the same as you. You've been here before, I trust your opinion," said Derek.

Her face lit up. "I think you won't be disappointed." Leia swiped at her forehead with the back of her wrist.

Forcing his arm away from her shoulders, Derek stepped forward. Soon, they arrived at the front of the line. Derek ordered them both banana macadamia nut pancakes and two drinks. Afterwards, they found an empty two-top table in the small, crowded restaurant. They sat down across from one another.

Fiddling with the salt and pepper shakers on the table, Derek forced himself to stop. Randomly, Derek asked, "Do you eat breakfast before your long runs?"

After learning Leia was training for a marathon, Derek spent the last evening researching about what it would take for him to get back into shape to run a marathon himself. It was still something he was vaguely interested in completing, but Leia was springing him into action.

"No," Leia tilted her head to the side, studying him. "I mean I don't eat a full breakfast, maybe a banana or half a bagel with a gel."

"Gels," Derek took a sip of his soda. "Are those the little packets of goop that taste horrible and make you gag?"

Leia laughed. "Yep." She nodded, resting her elbow on the table. "When I first started using them on my runs, they made me gag every single time. I finally found one type that tastes okay. I have to take them or I'll hit the dreaded runner's wall. Then I can't finish my run." She ran a finger down the length of her silverware sitting on top of a napkin.

Shifting forward in his chair, Derek said, "It sounds like you are speaking from experience."

"Unfortunately, yes." She removed her hand from her silverware and rubbed it across her thighs. "Once, when I first started training for long distances, I literally left my house with nothing other than water. I hadn't even eaten anything before starting. I hit mile ten, and my body started to shut down. I sat down on the ground and called my mom to come pick me up. I don't know what I was thinking, but I've learned a lot about running since then."

Derek forced himself to take another sip of his soda. "I bet." Derek leaned back in his chair, faking a casual state. "You've inspired me to get back into running. But I don't even know where to start. I can't even run a mile anymore. It's pathetic."

Leia placed a hand over the top of his. "You aren't pathetic." Her voice oozed compassion. "Start with one minute then add another minute. Just go slow. Everybody must start somewhere. I believe in you."

"Th—thanks." Derek blinked, trying to remember how to speak. "It means a lot."

They were interrupted by the delivery of their food. The server set their plates down and left. Wafting off the plate, the delicious tantalizing smell of pancakes made Derek's mouth water.

As he stared down at the pancakes, Derek chuckled. "These are huge." He gripped his fork and placed his napkin in his lap.

Leia smiled. "You said you were hungry." Picking up the little cup of syrup on the corner of the plate, Leia poured some over her pancakes. "But you did order us the triple stack." She picked up her fork too and cut into the pancakes.

Derek muttered, "I didn't realize they were the size of a serving platter."

Taking a bite, Leia waited until she swallowed then said, "I'm glad, because I'll probably polish these off. I worked up an appetite trying my best to show off."

Derek poured syrup over his pancakes. Shaking a fork at her, Derek said, "I knew you were trying to impress me," he winked.

After she finished a sip of her soda, Leia gave a single nod as she took another bite. Finally, Derek tried a piece of the pancake. As the sweet, spongy texture hit his tongue, he sighed with delight.

"Mm." Derek pointed to his mouth. "These are delicious." He couldn't help but lick a drip of syrup off his bottom lip.

Smugly, Leia said, "I told you."

For a few minutes, they ate in silence. Both enjoying the pancakes after a morning out in the waves.

Breaking the lull, Derek commented, "My mom used to make me pancakes every Sunday morning when I was a kid. I have very fond memories of waking up to the smell of pancakes and bacon."

Sadness washed over him. The deep ache in his chest bubbled up to the surface, and Derek missed his mom all over again.

Wiping her face with her napkin, Leia fiddled with her fork for a moment, before she asked, "What were your parents like? Did you get along with them?" Without taking her gaze off him, Leia cut into her pancake.

Derek rubbed the back of his neck with his free hand. "Oh, are we getting all personal now?" What he intended to be flirty came across as harsh. A lump formed in his throat. Derek forced himself to take a sip of his soda. Even after swallowing, it remained.

"I apologize. I thought you bringing them up meant you were okay to talk about them." Leia's back stiffened. She took another small bite and looked away. "I was only trying to make conversation. We don't have to get *personal*."

Lightly, Derek touched her bicep. "I'm sorry. That came out all wrong." He let go, rubbing his stubble with one of his thumbs. Sitting up straight, Derek exhaled then continued, "As you can see, I'm a bit rusty at flirting." He took a deep calming breath and found her glance as he said, "My mom made everything magical. Dr. Seuss day, she made green eggs and ham. On the fourth of July, she decked herself out in red, white, and blue from head to toe. My dad was quieter and more reserved, but I knew he loved my mom and would do anything for her. My dad went along with all her outlandish plans, over the top parties, and extensive list of itineraries on family vacations. I know they had their problems like any couple does, but I always knew they loved each other. I realize now what a gift that was to see day in and day out. Two people who despite their own faults and misgivings, choosing to look past the imperfections and simply love each other. I hope someday to find what they had."

Slowly, Leia licked her fork and set it down on her plate. Her forearms resting on the table, Leia asked, "If you could pinpoint one thing, what do you think they had that made their marriage work?"

"Love." Derek had the strongest urge to lean in and kiss her, which was absurd. With a jittery hand, Derek forced himself to pick up his soda and take a sip. Setting his soda back down, he added, "They had love. And it was enough."

Wistfully, Leia sighed. "Love, it always comes back to that, doesn't it?"

His neck stiffened. "Too bad it can feel impossible to find," remarked Derek.

Leia's mouth opened, but then she closed it. She dug into her pancakes and took a bite. Once done chewing, Leia waved a dismissive hand. "Enough about love." She did a head tilt toward his empty plate. "I can see you enjoyed your pancakes."

Lazily, Derek stretched. "They were delicious, and now I could use a good nap." He laughed, wishing he hadn't demolished an entire platter of food without stopping.

Leia slid out of her seat. "We should go." Pulling out her phone from her pocket, Leia checked the time. "I know you're meeting with Kai in an hour." Slipping the phone back into her pocket, Leia gathered up her trash and tossed it into a nearby bin.

"Correct." Stumbling to his feet, Derek gathered up his trash. "I don't want to be late."

After their table was cleared of everything, Derek headed for the door, holding it open for Leia. Leia passed through, heading toward the truck. They walked in silence across the parking lot. Derek wondered when he'd see Leia again. He hoped it would be later that day. His pocket vibrated again, making his shoulders tighten. Reality hit him, Derek was only in Hawaii for a short time and here on business. Who was he kidding? There was zero point in getting wrapped up in Leia.

They climbed into the truck on their respective sides. After double checking his phone, confirming it was another text from Tyson, Derek put it back into his pocket without responding. Tyson could wait.

Leia started the truck, pulling out of the parking lot. Hawaiian music played, but Derek didn't hear any sound, only the thundering of his pulse in his temples. Over and over, Derek tried to remind himself Leia lived here, he lived in Los Angeles, and there was an entire ocean in between them. He needed today to be the last time he saw Leia socially.

But even after his practical self-talk, Derek broke the silence and asked, "Am I going to see you again this afternoon?"

Leia turned down the music, so it was barely audible. "Could you say that again?" She double checked her rearview mirror before glancing over her shoulder, merging into the other lane. "I couldn't hear you."

Derek cleared his throat. "Will I see you this afternoon?" he boldly asked.

Leia shot him a fast sideways glance. "I don't think I need to be there when you meet with Kai again." Her knuckles turned a tad white from gripping the steering wheel. "I'm going to spend the rest of the morning getting the receipts from the store in order to email to you and Tyson."

"Oh." Derek slumped down in his seat. "I see." He stared out his passenger side window. Maybe the morning had been all in his head?

"But …" Leia's cheeks slowly reddened. After a long pause, Leia said, "Why? I could see you later tonight, if you needed me. I don't have anything planned."

Straightening himself, Derek blurted out, "Do you want to go with me tonight to that food truck your aunt and uncle own? The one with the kalua pork." He clasped and unclasped his hands.

"Kai might offer to take you there for lunch," said Leia.

With his pulse in his throat, Derek emphasized, "I don't want to go with Kai. I want to go with *you*."

Nibbling on her bottom lip, Leia questioned, "Why?"

"I thought that was pretty obvious." Puffing up his chest, Derek continued, "You're way better to look at than Kai."

Leia laughed. "Am I?" Pulling off the highway, Leia slowed their speed.

"Yep," replied Derek. "So, Leia, are you free for dinner tonight?"

"I don't know …" Her voice faded away. Leia shook her head. "Isn't it bad to mix business and pleasure? Sounds like it could get messy."

"I like messy," said Derek.

"You live in Los Angeles. I live in Hawaii," said Leia like that was the end of it.

"I know, but it's only dinner." Derek held up a single finger. "One dinner to be exact … at a food truck. That's something you can do with people you barely like."

A chuckle escaped her. Leia said, "Fine, one food truck dinner. Derek, I don't need …" Her voice trailed off, and Leia didn't finish her thought as she put the truck into park in her parents' driveway.

He unbuckled his seatbelt and said, "I guess I'll see you tonight."

Some unruly hair fell into her eyes, and Leia pushed it behind her ear. With a nod, she answered, "I guess so."

CHAPTER 7

"Come in!" bellowed Leia from her bedroom. "I'm back here."

Leia heard the screen door creak open then slam shut. Teresa's footsteps squeaked on the wood floors down the hallway to Leia's bedroom. Standing in front of her closet mirror, Leia tilted her head to the side, scrutinizing her appearance. She wondered if her linen shorts and black top looked okay.

A moment later, Teresa appeared at the threshold of her bedroom door. Leaning one shoulder against the door frame, Teresa's gaze roamed over Leia. "You look nice." Teresa raised an eyebrow. "Are you going somewhere?"

After she slid the closet door open, Leia dug out a pair of strappy leather sandals. "I'm going with Derek to Aunt Aria and Uncle Kalon's food truck." Sitting down on the edge of her bed, Leia didn't glance over at Teresa as she buckled the back strap of her sandals.

Her voice raising an octave, Teresa commented, "You don't say." Teresa smirked. "I knew there was something there."

Snapping her head toward Teresa, Leia said through a clenched jaw, "It doesn't mean anything."

Leia wondered why she was getting so defensive. As a grown

woman, she could go to dinner with whoever she wanted without explanation. Though she knew her family enough to know everything was everyone's business. Especially with her going to Aria and Kalon's food truck, her appearance would no doubt send shockwaves through the family phone tree.

Teresa scoffed and folded her arms. "Sure, okay. Just keep telling yourself that, and maybe eventually you can convince yourself you aren't attracted to Derek."

With a huff, Leia stood. "So what if I am?" She smoothed out the front of her top. Wandering into her attached bathroom, Leia continued, "It doesn't matter. Derek leaves soon enough, and I'll go back to my life being boring and predictable. He's a nice distraction. That is all." Her brain was scattered, and Leia tried to remember what else she needed to do to get ready for her date.

Teresa followed Leia into the bathroom, sitting down on the closed toilet seat. Leia opened a drawer, pulling out her makeup bag. Unzipping the bag, Leia pulled out her mascara, twisting the top off. Leaning forward toward the mirror, Leia applied a layer of mascara on her top eyelashes.

"Makeup, huh?" Teresa laughed. "You might like him more than I thought. I haven't seen you wear makeup in years."

With her mascara wand in hand, Leia whipped her head in the direction of Teresa. "I wear makeup," Leia said defensively. "Sometimes ..."

"No, you don't." Teresa crossed her legs, resting her hands on the top of her knees. "You don't even wear it when you teach," said Teresa smugly.

"The kids don't care what I look like." Leia applied a layer of mascara to her bottom lashes.

As Teresa tapped her bottom lip with her pointer finger, she asked, "But Derek does?"

Twisting back on the cap of her mascara, Leia tossed it back into her makeup bag. Next, Leia took out her blush. After she flipped it open, she removed the little applicator brush. "No. I mean I don't think so. He knows what I look like. Besides I'm not even putting on that much, only some mascara, blush, and lipstick." She swept the blush across her first cheek.

Teresa held up both hands in defeat. "Ok. I think it's nice you're trying." With one hand over her heart, she continued, "I, for one, like Derek, I think he's a nice guy. Kai told me today about his ideas to make the farm more successful. But he lives in Los Angeles, you might be—"

Interrupting Teresa, Leia pursed her lips together and asked, "Was there a reason you stopped by?"

Abruptly, Teresa stood and brushed a piece of lint off the front of her top. "I only came by to see if you wanted to watch a movie with Dad and I, but I can see you have other plans for the evening. I'll let you get to it." Taking a step to leave, Teresa said over her shoulder, "Remember, Leia, never kiss the guy on the first date. You need to make them work for it."

Leia playfully hit Teresa on her arm. "Mom! Nobody is kissing anyone."

Teresa cackled while she continued down the hallway. Her laugh trailed behind her echoing in Leia's being. Eventually, the front door creaked open and closed.

With Teresa gone, Leia finished applying her makeup. Since Leia still had a few minutes to spare before Derek arrived, she decided to curl her hair. Once her entire look was complete, Leia took in her image. Staring back at her reflection, she wondered if she should wipe off the makeup. Did it look like she was trying too hard? A tapping at the door left Leia no time to change her appearance.

Swiping her purse off her bed, Leia slugged it over her shoulder. Teresa had left the door open, but the screen door closed. Leia spotted him first. Derek wore khaki shorts, sandals, and a plain blue cotton tee that made his eyes pop. Shifting, Derek saw Leia wandering down the hallway. He smiled and held his hand up in a wave.

"Good evening," said Derek.

Leia pushed the screen door open. "Hey, Derek," she said with a quiver in her voice. "You look nice."

Derek's gaze skidded over her, making her middle do a weird flip turn. Scratching his jaw, Derek said, "Thanks, but, Leia—wow." He shuffled his feet, glancing down at them then back at her. "You look fantastic."

Leia couldn't hide the smile spreading across her face. "Thanks." There was a beat of silence while they both stared back at one another. Leia fiddled with her hair before forcing herself to stop. "Should we head out?" asked Leia.

As he took a step backwards, Derek tripped on a potted plant next to her door. "Yea, sure." He reached down and picked the plant back up, placing it back where it was. "Is it close enough to walk?"

Closing the door behind her, Leia replied, "It's about a mile down the road, but I know a path that cuts through the farm and twists around to their property. I don't mind walking. What you think?" Catching his gaze, she raised an eyebrow.

Shoving his hands in his pockets, Derek said, "I'd love to walk. It'll give me a chance to see even more of the farm."

Gesturing toward the path, Leia said, "Sounds good. Let's go."

They started down the dirt path, worn smooth from years of walking on it. Her Kama ancestors had lived on the land for generations. Leia didn't know the story of how they arrived, only that they had always been here. Generations lived in harmony with one another, sharing the fruits which grew freely on the land. Any excess crop was traded with other local families. As the Kama family expanded their fruit crop, increasingly more and more each year. A portion of the profits were poured back into Kama Farm. By the time her dad Noa took over, the farm had expanded to grow a wide variety of fruit.

Dense plants, native to Hawaii, lined both sides of the path. Leia pointed out a few to Derek. Ohelo, which was a shrub with edible berries, lama, a tree with white flowers, and naio, a shrub with pink flowers. Derek listened intently as she explained that ninety percent of the plants on the farm were only found in Hawaii.

As he halted in front of the naio, Derek gently touched one of the pink flowers. "How do you remember the names of all of these plants?"

Shrugging, Leia started walking again. "My grandma taught me the names. I guess I've always known them."

"Impressive." Derek strode to catch up with her. Shoving his hands into his pockets, Derek peered at the plants as they passed by them. "This place is beautiful, magical really."

"It's why I'll never live anywhere else." Leia let out a wistful sigh. "I belong here." Tilting her head toward him, she caught Derek's gaze and smiled.

"You sure do." Derek bumped his shoulder against hers. "It's probably nice to feel so at home here."

Leia didn't know how to reply, so she remained silent. Soon the plants thinned out, giving way to her extended family's property. A small cluster of homes came into view. Some of her cousins lived there with Aria and Kalon and their own families.

"We're almost there," said Leia. "Aria is my aunt and my dad's sister. Aria is married to my uncle, Kalon."

"Oh, I see. That's nice you all live so close to one another. And you were right. This isn't far at all," remarked Derek.

Derek walked beside her. Their arms brushed multiple times. The physical contact drove her batty. Leia wondered if Derek was feeling the same connection. She stole a glance at him, but his eyes remained glued on the homes ahead.

"The food truck is past these homes toward the road." Leia pointed in the proper direction. "It's nice. They have some tables and umbrellas set up."

Taking in a deep breath, Derek said, "I can already smell it. It's making my mouth water." He smiled wide at her.

"You can always smell it before you see it." Leia tucked her unruly strands of hair behind her ears. "Aria inherited this half of the property when my grandparents passed away. My dad received the other half which had Kama Farm on it. Aria wasn't interested in the farm, so it worked out, because she was able to open the food truck on her property."

Soon, they arrived at the food truck. They wandered around the side of it, getting in line behind the others waiting to order. Leia fidgeted with the end of her shirt. Catching herself, she cupped her opposite arm's elbow.

A big menu was on the front of the trailer, Leia pointed and said, "I think we should order the kalua pork plates. It'll give you a taste of the pork with the traditional sides."

The line moved up without Leia noticing. Gently, Derek placed his hand on the small of her back, gesturing for her to move up. Her body buzzed. Nearly stumbling, Leia took some steps forward, breaking their touch.

Once they stopped again, Derek rubbed the back of his neck. "It sounds fantastic to me. I'll get that," replied Derek.

Then someone from her side wrapped an arm around her shoulders. Leia's eyes traced the length of the arm, settling on her Aunt Aria.

"Leia, your mom let me know you were heading over." Aria gave Leia's shoulders a squeeze. "What are you doing standing in line? Come on around to the back, and we'll get you whatever you like." Aria directed her away from the line. Derek followed too.

"I didn't know you were working tonight." Leia gnawed on the inside of her cheek. The family phone chain wasted no time. "I guess I should've known my mom would give you a heads up." They continued to the side of the food truck.

Aria glanced around Leia toward Derek. "And who's your friend?"

Leia unconsciously fluffed her hair with one hand and

pointed with a thumb toward Derek with the other. "This is Derek. He's visiting from California." Leia didn't want to divulge her family might be bringing in an outside investor. The less Aria and Kalon knew the better.

"Really?" Aria's gaze flashed between Leia and Derek, before landing directly on Derek. "You don't say." She raised an eyebrow.

Derek held out a hand. "It's nice to meet you." Aria shook Derek's hand. Derek continued, "Leia told me you have the best food, so I insisted she come eat it with me."

"Thanks," Aria warmly smiled. Playfully, Aria nudged Leia with her elbow. "So, is this a date?"

Leia's cheeks burned, and she avoided Derek's eyes. "I— I—" Leia gnawed on her bottom lip.

Without hesitation, Derek said, "It's a date." He wrapped an arm around Leia's shoulders. Twisting toward Aria, he asked, "Leia said we should get the kalua pork plates. What do you think? Or do you recommend something else?"

Walking a few feet, Aria reached for the screen door on the side of the trailer. "I agree with Leia." She half stepped into the trailer and shouted into it, "Two pork plates please. It's for Leia and her *date*."

Someone from inside shouted back, "My cousin Leia? She's not on a date." Then out poked the head of her cousin, Kale. His gaze roamed over Leia and Derek. Kale smirked, meeting Leia's gaze. Then Kale leaned back into the trailer and shouted, "I'm wrong. Leia is on a date with a blond guy."

Leia covered her face with her hands and groaned. Derek gave her shoulders a squeeze before dropping his arm. Sweat tickled her brow. Mortified, Leia didn't dare look at Derek when she removed her hands.

"With a blond guy?" bellowed Uncle Kalon from inside the trailer. "I need to see this." Seconds later, out popped Uncle Kalon. He took one look at Leia and laughed. "I guess Kale wasn't lying." Doing a head tilt toward them, Kalon asked, "Leia, who's your guy friend?"

With aprons, gloved hands, and crocs on, Kale and Kalon took one step down onto the trailer stoop.

Derek held his hand up in a wave. "I'm Derek."

"Like I told Aunt Aria, we're here to eat." Leia swiped her sweaty palms on the sides of her shorts. "I told Derek, you have the best kalua pork this side of the island."

"I can't argue with you there." Kalon held up his gloved hands. "I would greet you properly, but I need to get back into the kitchen. I'll bring two plates out to you." He shifted toward Kale. Speaking to Kale, Kalon said, "Kale, find them a couple drinks. They can eat at the picnic table behind the trailer. The shade is better back there plus it's secluded." Kalon entered the trailer without another word.

Kale nodded toward the back. "Go on and sit around back. Leia, I'll bring you your drinks." Then Kale disappeared into the trailer.

Aria gave Leia a hug. Smugly, Aria said, "I'm glad you stopped by. Go on now." She shooed them toward the back.

Derek pulled out his wallet. "How much do I owe?" He opened it and pulled out a few twenty-dollar bills.

"No way. Leia's family." Aria waved her hands in front of herself. "It's on the house."

After hesitating a second, Derek put the money back and shoved his wallet back into his back pocket. "Okay, then." He put his hands down at his sides. "Thank you."

"Any time," said Aria.

Then Aria opened the food truck door and slipped inside.

Leia pivoted on her feet and waved Derek on. "Follow me."

Derek obeyed, trailing next to Leia around back. They settled at the picnic table, sitting on opposite sides of the table from each other. Leia wondered what he thought about being bombarded by her extended family. Her family was a lot, but she loved them.

"So …" said Leia.

"So …" repeated Derek. Leaning forward, Derek stated, "I like your family. They're nice and friendly."

Leia rested her elbow on the table, cradling her chin with one hand. "I thought you were going to say overly loud and pushy. And way too much."

Derek laughed, easing the pit in her stomach. "Nah, nothing like that." He caught her gaze and smiled. "You're lucky to have so many people who care about you. That's what I was thinking. I can't say I have one person—"

Kale interrupted Derek with his arrival. "I have your drinks." Kale set down two canned sodas. "The food will be done in about five minutes."

With a smile, Derek picked up one of the ice-cold canned sodas and said, "Thanks."

Kale lingered beside the table. Leia gave him a pointed look, but he didn't take the hint to leave.

Loudly, Leia cleared her throat and said, *"Thanks,* Kale." Her eyes widened.

Kale rubbed his hands together. "I'll go check on the food." He walked around to the side of the trailer and entered.

Popping open the top of his soda, Derek took a long swig. Leia stared, watching his Adam's apple bob up and down. The sight was mesmerizing. It took everything within her to not reach out and run a finger down it. Ridiculous, yep.

Suddenly, Derek stopped mid sip, catching her jaw-dropped stare. Embarrassed, Leia fumbled with the top of the other soda until it finally popped open.

Setting his can back down on the table, Derek said, "This drink is fantastic. I don't think I've ever had papaya guava soda." He twisted the can a bit, reading the back side of the label.

"I know, it's pretty good stuff." Leia examined her soda can. "I have kiwi strawberry." Taking a long swig, Leia let the fruity bubbly goodness coat her taste buds. Once she swallowed, Leia smacked her lips together. Placing the soda back down, Leia folded her arms resting them on the table. "I like the papaya guava, but I think the kiwi strawberry is better. Do want a taste?" She picked her soda back up and held it out to him.

Grinning, Derek reached for the soda. "Sure." His fingers grazed hers as he took the soda from her, sending a tantalizing zing down her spine. After taking a sip, Derek glanced down at the can and back at her. "I agree, that's delicious."

Pushing up her chin, Leia said, "See, I told you I was right."

Handing the soda back to her, Derek said, "I believe you."

Both stared back at one another. With each passing second, her pulse picked up its pace. Tension grew, practically palpable in the air they breathed. Leia wondered what kissing Derek would feel like, and if he had ever thought about kissing her.

Almost on cue, Derek reached into his pocket, pulling out his Chapstick. Slowly, he applied a coat to his lips before shoving it back into his pocket. Leia forced herself to look away, to squelch her earnest desire to hook his collar and tug him across the table toward her.

Derek broke the silence and asked, "Did you run today?"

The question caught her off guard. "No. I was surfing with you, remember?" She cocked an eyebrow.

Smacking his forehead with the heel of his hand, "Duh? I can't believe that was this morning. It feels like I've already lived three lives since arriving here." Derek took another sip of his soda. "How far do you usually go?" Setting his soda back down, he rested his hand a mere inch from hers.

Leia's skin itched to be touched. His fingers so near hers without skimming hers drove her batty. "Usually, I only run seven to ten miles." She took another casual sip of her soda, eyes locked with Derek. "I go longer on the weekend."

Derek whistled. Leia laughed then shoved her hair over her shoulder. "Never," Derek wagged a finger, "use 'only' when you say you ran seven to ten miles. Geez. I'm impressed." He grinned, further unwinding the nerves in her stomach, relaxing her.

With her arms outstretched wide, Leia enthusiastically said, "I know, I'm amazing." Then Leia rolled her eyes.

Aria arrived beside the table with a plate in each of her hands. Placing a kalua pork plate in front of each of them, Aria reached into her pocket and pulled out some disposable bamboo utensils in paper sleeves. "Here you go." Aria gave Leia's shoulder a squeeze. "I hope you enjoy the food." She directed her glance to Derek. "Please come back anytime."

"Thank you." Derek peered down at the plate of food then over at Aria. "This looks and smells delicious." He smiled warmly back at Aria.

"Thanks, Aria," added Leia.

Taking a step away, Aria said, "Stop by and say goodbye before you leave." She turned, walking around to the trailer door.

Both removed their utensils from the paper sleeves, Derek picked up his fork. "Now, tell me what is on my plate." His fork hovered over his food.

Leaning way over the table, Leia pointed out the different items on his plate, the poi, pork, macaroni salad, rice, and salmon poke. Once done explaining to Derek about the different items, Leia straightened herself and speared a piece of the pork. "Go ahead and try something." She shoved a bite of the pork into her mouth.

"Here goes nothing." Derek dug into the pork, taking a bite. After chewing and swallowing, he said, "Delicious." Next, he pierced some macaroni salad and popped a bite into his mouth.

They continued to eat. Derek gave the proper compliments. Leia wanted to find some fatal flaw that would dampen her attraction to him, but she came up short. As the meal finished, Leia found herself wondering when she'd see Derek again.

With a licked clean plate, Derek patted his stomach. "This was delicious. Thank you for bringing me here."

Leia fiddled with her hair. "The people you really need to thank are Aria and Kalon."

"Absolutely, you're completely right," replied Derek.

Cupping her ear, Leia teased, "Can you repeat that a little louder?"

Derek's eyes twinkled around the edges. "I'll be right back." He swung his legs over the picnic bench. "Give me a second." Derek walked to the trailer side door.

While Derek went to go talk to them, Leia rose too and gathered up the trash and threw it into the nearby bin. Then she joined Derek by the trailer. Kalon was at the long metal counter scooping out macaroni salad onto a plate. Aria was busy speaking to a customer through the service window. Kale was nowhere to be seen. Once they finished with their tasks, Derek gave them the proper thanks.

Aria said, "My pleasure. Come by anytime. We hope to see you again, Derek." Finding Leia's glance, Aria added, "Make sure you say goodbye to Kale." She pointed out the service window. "He's wiping the picnic tables down."

"We will," Leia tugged Derek away from the door. "Thanks again," said Leia, leading Derek a few feet away. Whispering, Leia said, "We need to make a run for it, or we are never getting out of here."

"I don't mind." Derek reached out and ran a single finger down her forearm. "I don't have anywhere else I need to be."

With his finger on her arm, Leia reminded herself to breathe. Never had a man's touch made her feel so completely out of control. Flustered, Leia forced herself to focus on finding Kale. Pinching his shirt sleeve, Leia tugged him toward the picnic tables in front. "Come on. Let's find Kale."

They walked to the front of the food truck where the picnic tables were set out on a grassy area facing the road and ocean.

Her gaze landed on Kale as he wiped down a table, Leia pointed and said, "He's over there." Without thinking, Leia clasped Derek's hand. He quickly interlocked his fingers with hers before she had time to realize her error.

As they approached, Kale stopped mid swipe. Clocking their hand holding, Kale smirked and folded the rag in his hands. "Are you two lovebirds out of here?" Kale shuffled around the picnic table to the opposite bench and wiped it down.

Sweat trickled down her back. Kale would no doubt run back to his parents and report seeing them holding hands. Suddenly, she felt like a teenager all over again. The phone would be buzzing and by the time Leia arrived home tonight everyone in her family would know.

Derek spoke up before Leia and said, "We are, and I appreciate your hospitality. It was nice meeting you, Kale." Letting go of Leia's hand, Derek held it out to Kale.

Kale took a step closer, shaking Derek's hand. "I hope to see you again," said Kale, moving toward Leia.

He held his arms out to her for a hug. Leia hugged him.

As they walked away, Kale added, "Take care of Leia. She was my favorite babysitter when I was little. She let me stay up late and eat all the candy I wanted."

Leia scrunched up her nose. "I can't believe you remember I let you do that," replied Leia.

Kale shook his rag at her and said, "I remember so much." He glanced at Derek. "I've a ton of dirt on her if you ever want to hear about it."

Rolling her eyes, Leia said, "Good *night*, Kale." Leia tugged on Derek's sleeve, pulling him away.

They reached the dirt path which weaved back to her parents' property. A few paces into the path, Derek reached for her hand again, interlocking his fingers with hers. They walked hand in hand with only the sound of the ocean behind them. Leia wondered what any of this meant. Derek was leaving soon, too soon. And here she was acting like she was having a summer fling but not in actual summer. They'd spend a few memorable days together, then what?

"I'm back to teaching on Monday," remarked Leia between the ticks of her pounding pulse.

"Fall break, right?" asked Derek. Leia nodded. He scratched his head with his free hand. "I should've asked sooner when you were headed back."

Swiping at a trickle of sweat on her temple, Leia continued, "I don't have any more breaks until Thanksgiving."

They didn't speak for a while. Her feet tickled from the dust of the dirt being kicked up by her sandals.

As the path curved, Derek asked, "Are you glad you're a teacher?"

They passed by the cluster of homes Aria and Kalon's families lived in. Out front a few of her cousins were playing a game of kickball. She waved and they waved back, but Leia and Derek kept walking.

"I like being a teacher, and I like helping at the farm. I'm glad I can do both. I enjoy the kids and the challenge. Being a teacher means I have every summer off, which in Hawaii is not half bad. The breaks let me enjoy everything Hawaii has to offer. And as for my family's business, I'm as involved with the farm as I want. It wasn't ever my passion, not like it was for Kai. He grew up walking the fields with my dad. Kai lives and breathes the land. He understands it and cares about it more than I ever could."

Soon the edge of her parents' home peeked out, Leia prayed they weren't outside on the lanai to witness them walking hand in hand. It would only embarrass her further.

The million-dollar question rolled around in her head. "When do you go back to Los Angeles?" asked Leia.

"I'm— I'm not sure," said Derek without glancing over at her. His eyes were glued on the path back to her apartment. "I hope to stay here for a little longer than I originally thought."

Leia was living in a dream world. One she didn't want to leave anytime soon. This thing, fling, whatever it was, would abruptly end … soon. If Leia was smart, this would be their first and last date. Too bad the rat-a-tat of her heartbeat begged to differ.

They arrived in front of her apartment. Leia dropped Derek's hand, digging into her pocket for her keys, pulling them out. Though the muggy air from earlier was replaced by the cool and sweet night air, Leia's brow was slick.

The keys in her hands jangled as she fidgeted with them. Leia said, "Thanks for taking me out tonight. I had a wonderful time. I like being around you, Derek."

With a nod, Derek gulped, "I hoped you'd say that." Taking a step closer, Derek moved inches from her. "I like you too, Leia, and more than as my client's sister."

His body heat warmed her up as the intoxicating scent of his cologne danced at her nostrils. The smell made her dizzy, Leia stumbled a step back until her body found the door, she rested herself up against it.

With a nervous laugh Leia said, "Then we are in agreement, we like each other."

His gaze boldly found hers, and for a second, they stared back at one another. Unconsciously, Leia moistened her lips.

Nerves bubbled up inside her, and with a shaky voice, Leia asked, "Now what?"

Leaning in slowly, Derek palmed the door on the right side of her. His other hand moved to her hair, weaving his fingers into it for a second before he finally swept it over her shoulder. Leia sucked in air. Her lungs refused to fill with oxygen. *Dang, this guy had moves.* His eyes flickered between her eyes and her lips. *This was happening.*

After an eternity, Derek stated boldly, "And now, I kiss you." He waited for her to respond. "Unless you object."

Without any reservation, Leia reached out and traced a finger along his exposed collar bone. "Is that what's going to happen?" asked Leia.

Derek gave an almost indistinguishable nod. Leia gulped. Derek moistened his own lips. Then ever so slowly, he moved closer, giving Leia a moment to grant permission. When the tension was more than she could bear, Leia gripped a fistful of his shirt and tugged him forward. Their lips collided, making a fire light up in her gut.

Immediately, Derek wrapped his arms around her waist bringing her closer, supporting her upright. Leia's hand plunged into his hair, raking his temples in the process. His lips danced with hers. She couldn't remember the last time a kiss felt this good, this complete, this perfect. Leia had already known they had some sort of brewing chemistry, but kissing Derek was unreal.

The rhythmic waves of the ocean mixed with her galloping pulse. As his lips skated across hers, Leia didn't worry about the future. Deepening the kiss, his lips parted, allowing her to taste more of him. His scent radiated off him, filling her lungs and encapsulating her with its tingling satisfying aroma.

With their lips still brushing against one another's, Derek whispered, "I knew you would taste good. I just didn't imagine you tasting this good." He kissed her again.

Half laughing and half kissing, Leia asked, "My lips like your lips too."

Leia looped her hand around Derek's collar, bringing him nearer. Wasn't the saying tomorrow would worry about tomorrow? Because apparently, it was Leia's new motto. If this was going to be the only time she ever kissed Derek, Leia wanted it to last forever.

CHAPTER 8

Derek nearly floated back to his Airbnb. Never in his wildest dreams did he imagine the evening would end with a heart-stopping kiss. Sure, a guy could dream, but he hadn't thought it was within the realm of possibility. Walking back, Derek glanced to his left taking in the view of the dark night sky against the ocean. A full moon reflected against the water. Taking a minute to enjoy the beauty, he breathed in the salty air. His being was lighter than it had been in years. And it was all because of Leia.

Leia. Leia. Leia.

A startling vibration in his pocket brought Derek back to earth. Tugging his phone out of his pocket, Derek peered at the screen. His shoulders drooped. Running a hand down the length of his face, Derek cleared his throat before he clicked accept. Placing the phone to his ear, Derek said, "Hey there, Tyson. What's up?"

Tyson shrieked, "What's up? WHAT'S UP?"

Derek flinched. Sure, he had ignored Tyson's phone calls when he was out with Leia, but he hadn't anticipated Tyson to lose it on him. "Calm down. I was out. I'm here now. What do you want to discuss?"

"Were you out with *her*?" asked Tyson. "The client's sister?"

Sweat gathered on his brow, Derek swiped it with the back of his palm. "I was, but she's not part of the deal. My financial dealings are with Noa and Kai. They own the business. Leia only helps with the books for the fruit shop. She doesn't have any claim to the farm. So, I'm not technically breaking any rules."

"She lives on the property, doesn't she?!" Tyson half screamed and half questioned.

Derek knew he was in the wrong. He had no right to start something up with Leia for a myriad of reasons. Every line existing between business and pleasure, Derek was crossing. "I know, but I thought we discussed earlier today that you didn't think it was smart to invest anyways. You said we wouldn't make any money. I think we can, but we are at an impasse," said Derek.

"We aren't investing in the farm," stated Tyson. His voice evened out a tad, the edge disappearing. "So, you need to get yourself back to Los Angeles. I have another potential investment in Boston. A cranberry bog which I believe will reward us both handsomely. I want you out there as soon as you can make it there."

Derek groaned. In the past, he never minded the travel. With no family of his own, being home felt, well, lonely. His business dealings rarely left him in one place for exceptionally long, which was how Derek always liked it. So, why did the thought of leaving make him suddenly queasy?

He knew why.

Leia.

Leia was in Hawaii, not Los Angeles or anywhere else for that matter. What had he done by getting involved with her? And kissing her, he knew, was major mistake, practically a catastrophe.

Halting in place, Derek stared out at the beautiful, dazzling water. The smattering stars against the big ole moon settled the pounding of his heart.

"I'm not ready to walk away from the farm," said Derek firmly. "I think I need another week to finish analyzing everything."

And another week with Leia.

Pausing, Tyson groaned. "Another week? I don't know what you'll learn in a week that you don't already know now."

"I'll know if there's a way to invest in some better equipment to streamline the harvesting of the fruit." Derek scratched his chin. "I also want to explore the idea of farm tours. It would make the farm a tourist destination and people love doing things out of the ordinary on their vacations."

"I thought the family was against starting tours of the farm," replied Tyson.

"They were, but I think there is a bit of wiggle room. Kai's coming around to the idea," said Derek.

After a long pause, Tyson said, "Fine." He let out a long breath. "You need to find out the potential costs of starting the farm tours and how much potential revenue it might bring in. I'll give you two days. If the numbers don't show potential or if the family is against it, it's time to move on," said Tyson.

"I agree with you. I'll discuss it with Kai," said Derek. There was a long pause. Derek double checked the phone screen to make sure he was still connected. "Are you still there?"

Slowly, Tyson replied, "I am," another pause, "I hope she's worth it."

"Worth what?" asked Derek.

"Worth throwing away fifteen years of tried-and-true business analysis," stated Tyson. "Throwing away a sound mind, because you're completely wrapped up in being Romeo."

Derek forced a laugh. "I'm far from being Romeo."

"Uh huh … okay. You keep telling yourself that, but I'm not investing a dime in something that is going to fail," said Tyson.

Rubbing the back of his neck, Derek stared out at the ocean

waves crashing against the shore. "I understand, and you're right. We'll be in touch," said Derek.

Then Tyson ended the call. Derek slipped his phone back into his pocket. His euphoric mood from minutes earlier soured.

Early the next morning, Derek woke to the vibration of his phone. Groggily, he swiped at his eyes, attempting to read the message displayed across the screen. Seeing it was from Leia, he quickly sat up.

> Are you ready to start that marathon training you've been alluding to? Or are you all talk?

Throwing the covers off himself, Derek chuckled. His fingers zipped across his phone screen.

> I thought my surfing proved I'm not all talk.

> True. I'm out running. Text me the address of your place, and I'll run on by and you can join me for as long as you can stand it.

> You're on.

After he texted Leia the address of his Airbnb, Derek quickly rose to change into running clothes and brush his teeth. While tying his running shoes, his phone buzzed.

> I'm outside. You better not keep me waiting.

Derek slipped his phone into his pocket, charging out of his place to where Leia was waiting out front. She wore black running shorts and a tank top. Her hands flew to her hips at his arrival.

With a half smirk, Leia asked, "Are you ready for this?" Her eyes glided down the length of him, and instinctively, he straightened his back.

Derek stepped toward her. He wondered what the proper protocol for greetings when you kissed once but weren't anything official. High five? Hug? Kiss?

Without over analyzing it anymore, he went for a hug.

Leia gave him a loose hug back. "I'm already sweaty." Her eyes darted away from him. "But I guess you will be too in a few minutes, if you stick with me long enough."

As he let go, Derek said, "I can only promise I'll make it a mile."

Leia tsked, "A mile?" She nudged him with her elbow. "Can't you do better than that, surfer boy?"

His lips twitched into a smirk. Derek asked, "I've moved up to surfer boy?"

Leia gave him a playful shove. "Enough chitchat. Let's go." Then she darted down the road.

Leia didn't glance back but bolted out ahead. Derek ran to catch up with her. The pounding of his feet hitting the pavement competed against the thundering of his heart.

"What pace is this?" Derek managed to ask between two shaky breaths when he finally came up beside her. "Isn't this a little fast for a long run?"

Seamlessly gliding along, Leia wasn't struggling a bit to maintain her running pace. "It isn't that fast." Her voice came out smoothly without an ounce of struggle. "But I'll slow down."

Leia slowed down a tad, enough for Derek's breath to even out without his voice shaking while he spoke. "How far are you planning on running today?" asked Derek.

Shrugging, Leia replied, "I'll see how I'm feeling." She tapped her shoulder against his. "Or more importantly how you're handling the run. I've already run two miles."

They ran side by side on the wide shoulder against the

oncoming traffic. Leia hugged the side closest to the ocean while Derek was nearest the traffic lane. For a long time, neither spoke. They just ran. And ran. Derek wondered how far he had gone, because if Leia wasn't beside him he would've quit five minutes ago.

After a curve in the road, Leia broke the silence. "Let's stop up there." She pointed to a grassy area overlooking the beach. "There's a drinking fountain next to the restrooms. I didn't bring my water with me."

Derek welcomed the respite. "Sure, whatever you want," he tried to sound casual though nothing sounded better than a break.

Slowing their pace, eventually Leia stopped running and walked across the grassy area which led to the drinking fountain. The park was empty. Once in front of the drinking fountain, Leia bent down, taking a long swig of water. Done, she wiped her face with the back of her hand and stepped to the side so Derek could access the drinking fountain. Derek took a few big gulps then straightened himself.

"Don't you usually wear one of those running belts that holds water bottles?" asked Derek.

"I do," said Leia. "But I didn't feel like carrying the weight, and I know enough stops along the way to get water. It isn't ideal, and if I was running over ten miles, I could never do it without a water belt. But I don't have enough time this morning to go that distance."

His eyes glided over her sleek form. Derek resisted the urge to pull her close, wrap his arms around her waist and kiss her for a second time. Bringing a hand to his hip, Derek used his other hand to swipe the sweat trickling down his temple. "Because of me? Am I slowing you down too much? If you need to run ahead, go for it."

Leia shook her head. "No. It's not that." Glancing down at her watch, Leia pressed a button he assumed was tracking their distance and time. "I don't have very much time this morning, because Tyson emailed me about the farm's financial reports. He kept telling me it was urgent, and he needed them by late morning."

Derek froze. "Tyson contacted you." His jaw tightened.

Looks like Tyson wasted no time. Derek didn't appreciate Tyson going behind his back. Derek had promised he'd get Tyson the information he needed, but Tyson hadn't even given him any time to do it. Anger seeped into his veins. In all their years together, Tyson had never contacted a client without his knowledge. He always made sure to cc Derek onto every email.

Leia replied, "Last night. Tyson gave me a list of things he needed me to email over to him. I was a little confused, because I had told him most of those things Kai had, not me." Leia shrugged.

He formed fists on both sides of his body, Derek spoke slowly, "I can't believe Tyson emailed you," he remarked, through an almost locked jaw.

Leia tilted her head to the side, studying him. "Am I missing something? Are you and Tyson at odds with one another?"

To dissipate the tension formed in his neck, Derek cranked it side to side. "No," he said much too quickly. "I'll sort it out with Tyson today. I don't know …" Derek waved it off. "I'll talk to Tyson when I get back this morning. I'd love to see the report too, so if you don't mind sending me a carbon copy of the email."

"Absolutely. I'll was already planning on it." Pushing a button on her watch, Leia glanced at Derek then back at the street. "Are you ready to go? We'll run another mile then head back if that works for you."

Eager to work off his pent-up anger, Derek said, "Yes, let's do it."

They ran back to the road, following it up another mile before turning around and heading back to Derek's Airbnb. During the rest of the run, Derek remained distracted. His mind ruminated on Tyson emailing Leia. Though he had every right to contact Leia for the financial records, the entire thing rubbed him the wrong way. It seemed like Tyson didn't trust Derek, and if they didn't have trust with one another, how could they continue to be in business with one another?

Leia slowed their pace, stopping in front of his Airbnb. Derek was shocked the run was over. He had been so lost in his thoughts, for a few miles Derek hadn't even noticed he was running. Maybe this was why people ran? To sort out their problems?

Lingering in front of his place, Leia asked, "Will I get to see you today?" She bit down on her bottom lip.

"Of course," replied Derek. He took a step closer to her, capturing her by her waist, bringing her body against his own, sweat and all. "Tonight, if I don't see you at the farm sometime today."

There he went again, muddling business with whatever this thing was—bad idea.

"Tonight then. I want you to come over to my place for dinner. I'll cook you something," said Leia.

For the briefest second, Derek hesitated. Dinner at her place? It felt way more intimate than dinner at a food truck with her family popping in and out of nowhere. Rubbing the back of his neck, Derek said, "Could I buy you dinner somewhere instead? I don't want you to have to cook for me."

Kissing him quickly on his cheek, Leia said, "Nah, you can take me somewhere tomorrow night."

Laughing, Derek remarked, "Are you already planning tomorrow too?"

Tucking some loosened strands of hair behind both her ears, Leia asked, "Yeah, aren't you?"

For a second, Derek stared back at Leia's challenging gaze like she was calling his bluff, if he was in fact bluffing. Fire raged in his gut. Derek wasn't bluffing. He liked Leia. A little too much.

But soon, he'd be gone. And if he left not investing in the farm, Derek would be leaving with Leia cursing his name. The thought made him break out in a cold sweat.

Finally, Derek said, "I want to plan every available minute I have with you." He tugged her closer, wrapping a sweaty arm around her waist.

Though they were both sticky and slick with sweat, Leia managed to smell intoxicatingly delicious. How did she do that?

"Okay, until tonight." Leia gave him a quick peck before untangling herself from his arms. "I need to get those financials out." As she twisted toward the road, over her shoulder, Leia said, "Later." She ran away at twice the pace she had been running with him earlier.

"It's a date," yelled Derek to her image as it drifted further and further away.

Before Derek could wonder if Leia heard him, she held up a hand without turning around. Derek waited until she was completely out of sight before going inside to his Airbnb.

CHAPTER 9

Seated at her desk inside the trailer, Leia swiveled in her chair to face Kai. "Did you receive the financial report I sent to Tyson? I sent a copy to you and Derek also," said Leia.

Kai shifted forward, moving around his mouse. His computer screen lit back up. "I reviewed it item by item with Derek earlier." Scanning the document, Kai leaned back in his chair and faced Leia. "I don't know what he is thinking, but I have the feeling Tyson isn't as welcoming of the idea of investing in Kama Farm as Derek is." Kai crossed his ankles and cradled the back of his neck with his hands.

"Because he asked for the financial report?" questioned Leia. She wasn't privy to all the conversations happening between Kai and Derek.

Shaking his head, Kai said, "That's only part of it. Earlier today, I had a conference call with Tyson and Derek. Tyson flat out stated he wasn't eager to invest unless the numbers showed a bigger rate of return for them."

Her stomach dropped. With a constricted throat, Leia asked, "What's going to happen if they don't invest?"

"I don't know." Kai shifted forward, snatching a stress ball off the corner of his desk. He squeezed it in one hand. "We'll probably have to sell off sections of land to subsidize the farming. The fact of the matter is we aren't making enough from our small fruit stand. With both dad and mom unable to work, I had to hire other people to replace them. And that is making it impossible to turn a profit. Alana has stepped in when she can, but she, too, can only do so much. Something must be done." He switched the stress ball to his other hand and squeezed.

"I don't want to see the farm sold off in sections. You need to do whatever it takes to prevent that from happening, because the land surrounding the farm is what makes this place so special. We need to save all of it, not only the farm." Leia's mind spun. Before, she didn't understand the full picture, but now the reality was staring her in the face. An outside investor wasn't ideal, but losing the land or the farm would be devastating. "Did Derek talk to you more about the farm tours?" Leia clicked her mouse, opening her email again. She read through the email thread, looking for anything she might have missed. "It might make the farm profitable again."

"Leia," said Kai. "I don't know. I'm not even sure where to start or if it would only be a last-ditch effort to save something that can't be saved. I'll discuss it with Alana further, because she'd be taking on some of the extra workload too." He squeezed his stress ball tighter, making his knuckles white.

Leia had never seen Kai this concerned. Usually, Kai was carefree; not much upset him or stressed him out. Maybe Kai didn't see a way out if the investment money didn't come in. Her throat burned with bile.

Gulping, Leia asked, "What does Mom say?"

"You know I can't trouble Mom with any of this. She's already at her max, taking care of Dad. Mom's main concern is making sure she and Dad can live out the rest of their days on this land and in their home. They thought they had years left to work Kama before handing everything over to me. I certainly thought I had more time too so I could be trained properly to take everything on. But now, I only I hope I can give them their wish to keep Kama."

"We all want the same thing too," said Leia. "None of us want to live anywhere else."

Raising an eyebrow, Kai said, "Are you sure about that, little sis? Last I heard, you might be announcing you're moving to California to be with a washed-up surfer boy." Kai tossed the stress ball on top of his desk.

And Kai was back to his usual self.

Leia scoffed. "He isn't a washed-up surfer boy." Pushing up her chin, she continued, "We're almost the same age."

Kai crossed his arms against himself. "Exactly," he smirked.

"Watch it," warned Leia. Wagging a finger in his direction, Leia added, "Remember, Kai, don't dish what you can't take."

His hands flew up in defeat, Kai said, "I'm not. Geez. No need for you to get all testy. I'm only reporting that Aria and Kalon said you two were awful cozy with one another last night at their food truck for dinner." He tsked, giving her a pointed glance. "Come on, Leia, I thought you were smarter than to bring a guy on a first date to a place where he'd be on full display. A rookie mistake, because now the entire family knows about your budding relationship."

"I'm not in a relationship." Her cheeks warmed. Leia swiveled in her chair, turning away from Kai. The less he knew about her developing feelings for Derek, the better. She wiggled her mouse around to reveal the computer screen. "But, if you must know, I had a nice time." Leia shrugged nonchalantly. "I think Derek did too."

Rubbing his hands together, Kai said, "So, my sister is finally having her summer fling."

"It's fall," countered Leia.

"True, but I mean the essence of a summer fling is exactly what you are doing with Derek. People come to Hawaii to escape their lives. A whirlwind romance is practically in the tourist pamphlets for visiting Hawaii." He waved a hand. "Hence your fling."

Sharply, she swiveled her chair to face Kai. Leia said defensively through a clenched jaw, "It's not a fling."

Kai reached out and squeezed Leia's shoulder. "Sorry little sis. It is just that. Derek is going back to Los Angeles, you'll stay here. But I get it, everyone deserves a little fun now and then."

His words knocked the wind out of Leia. Leia shook her shoulder free from Kai's hand. Pushing up her chin, Leia narrowed her eyes at Kai. "I'm not discussing Derek any further with you." Leia swiveled back and faced her computer. With a shaky hand, she forced her fingers to find her keyboard.

In a much softer voice, Kai said, "I only don't want to see you get hurt. I think you might like the guy. But remember, tourists always go back to where they came from."

Kai was right. And Leia hated it. Derek and she had zero chance of being together, so she was having a fling. So what? Her mind only had one image in it, and it was of her and Derek kissing. Her lackluster romantic life was dismal, and for once she was having a bit of fun having her flirty exchanges with Derek. But Leia knew what this thing was, and she couldn't make the mistake of letting herself care too much.

Kai and Leia worked in tandem silence. When Leia finished up the loose ends on the bookkeeping, she stood and stretched. When she checked the time, Leia was disappointed Derek hadn't stopped by at some point. With school starting back up next week, Leia couldn't stick around any longer, she had things she needed to get ready for Monday.

With no choice, Leia reluctantly gathered up her purse, pushing in her chair. "I'm off," said Leia.

Kai stopped typing on his keyboard, glancing over at her. "Are you sure about that?" He double checked his watch. "Derek is coming by in ten minutes. He's bringing some proposals about the farm tours."

Defensively, Leia crossed her arms and said, "I thought you told me earlier to stay out of it."

"I know, but I've had a little longer to stew over it. I'd like you to stay and hear Derek out so you can give me a second opinion," replied Kai.

Dropping her purse next to her desk, Leia sat back down. "I'll stay. But I can only be here for another hour. I need to run to the grocery store and clean my apartment."

Raising an eyebrow, Kai said, "Since when do you go to the grocery store? You usually just take fruit from the fruit stand and eat whatever Mom makes you."

"You make me sound like a child," replied Leia.

"Is that what I did?" asked Kai.

Their conversation was interrupted by the squeaking of the screen door. Derek popped his head inside. His gaze skidded to Leia, and Derek smiled warmly at her. Heat flooded to her middle, making her hands shaky.

As he stepped inside, the screen door slammed behind him. "Leia ..." Her name dangled in the air. Derek added, "Hello, Kai."

Kai clocked Derek then Leia and knowingly smirked.

Leia rolled her eyes at Kai, giving him a pointed look before she returned her gaze to Derek. "Kai asked me to stay. He said you're giving him some information on starting farm tours," stated Leia.

Scratching his chin, Derek strode the rest of the way inside with a messenger bag slung over his shoulder. His appearance was significantly more casual than their first business meeting together. Derek wore a plain blue T-shirt and khaki shorts with leather flip flops. The only thought that popped into her mind was dang, *she kissed that!* No wonder she wasn't worried about the future.

As he lowered himself into the chair facing Kai and Leia,

Derek replied, "Great idea. You can give me your opinion too." He set his messenger bag down beside his chair then dug out his laptop and placed it on his lap.

After Derek was settled, he shot Leia a sizzling glance. The air crackled with palpable energy. Leia forced herself to look away because she was hot and flustered.

Slamming a hand on top of his desk, Kai said, "You two kissed. Didn't you?" His gaze darted between the two of them. He wagged his finger back and forth. "There's a weird energy thing going on."

Clumsily, Leia shifted in her seat then jutted her chin. "I don't think that's any of your business." She folded her arms protectively across her body.

Derek's eyes dilated. "I don't know how to respond." He flashed Leia a panicked gaze.

Kai rolled his eyes. "I knew it." He threw up a hand. "I knew there was something between you guys." He pointed at Derek then Leia. "Everyone deserves a little fun now and then but," he pointed at Derek, "we need to keep things professional, okay?" Kai raised an eyebrow.

"Of course." Derek cleared his throat, making his Adam's apple do that mesmerizing bobbing motion. "Should I show you my presentation about the farm tours now?" His hands lingered on top of his laptop.

Casually, Kai leaned forward. "Let's see it."

After Derek scooted his chair closer to their desks, he placed his laptop on the corner of Kai's desk facing them. The screen displayed a PowerPoint presentation already cued up. Derek dove into explaining everything to them. The first slide had a list of their lost revenue over the past several years. Leia cringed at the numbers, doing their books, she wondered how she had been so blind to their financial situation. But Leia had only made orders for supplies, cut checks for the employees, and tallied up the daily sales from the store. Kai hadn't ever asked her to compare expenses to revenue. Kai needed a real accountant.

Onto the next slide, Derek explained how the farm tours could help to recoup the loss and make the farm successful again. He walked through the startup costs, time frame, and other practical parts of making it a possibility.

Kai interjected and asked, "How many tours a week will we need to have in order to make the farm profitable again?"

Rubbing his chin, Derek replied, "I believe one tour a day with ten to twenty guests, where the guests get to pick some of the fruit and eat a meal prepared with the things grown on the farm. I believe it would be enough to get you out of the red and into the black." He gestured toward Kai. "Now, if you up that to say maybe three or four tours a day, I believe that would give you enough profit to eventually become successful enough to hire more employees, maybe even pay off my company's investment so you can completely own the farm again on your own."

"I like the sound of that," said Kai.

"I don't know," piped in Leia. Shaking her head, Leia continued, "I worry about the amount of traffic this would create through the farm. I fear it might damage the surrounding native plants, and the whole place will become crawling with people."

"I'm glad you mentioned that, Leia." Derek clicked to the next slide. "I do believe we need to be careful to maintain the integrity of the land. That's why I would suggest smaller more manageable groups of ten to twenty people max. Most people come with their families, so you would only have maybe three families and cars parked at a time. Then you aren't overwhelmed with visitors. In addition, the smaller groups help to create demand while preserving the land."

Derek then explained the actual tour, cost, time, and everything else involved. After clicking to the last slide, Derek closed the PowerPoint presentation and asked, "So, Kai, what are your thoughts or questions?"

Blinking, Kai glanced toward Leia. "What do you think, little sis?" asked Kai.

Leia leaned forward and said, "Is this something your business partner Tyson is willing to do? From my emails with him, he made it seem like your investment firm wasn't willing to invest the amount you mentioned."

Derek tugged at his shirt collar. "I think Tyson will come around and come to see the farm could be a profitable investment."

Holding up a hand, Kai said, "But Tyson isn't on board with any of this now?" He shot Derek a pointed look.

An exhale made Derek's shoulders drooped. "No," shaking his head, he continued, "Tyson wants me to leave as soon as possible and start on a different potential investment." Sitting straight, Derek said, "But I'm not ready to give up on the farm. Give me a few more days, and I'll convince Tyson to invest." He raised an eyebrow. "I mean, are you ready to move forward with the farm tour idea?"

Kai glanced at Leia. Leia shrugged. "It's up to you, Kai. This is your life, your family's livelihood, not mine."

"But you live here too, and more importantly this is about Mom and Dad too," said Kai.

"And what do you think Dad would tell you if he could voice his opinion?" asked Leia.

Without hesitation, Kai said, "He would tell me to save the farm at all costs."

With a nod, Leia said, "There's your answer."

Kai turned back toward Derek. "Ok. Let's move forward with your investment and farm tour idea. I guess that's if your business partner Tyson comes on board."

Firmly, Derek stated, "He will." But Leia noticed the shakiness in his hands as he moved to place his laptop back into his messenger bag.

She wondered if he wasn't revealing everything. Maybe

Derek would go to Tyson, and Tyson would say no. If that happened then Derek would leave, the farm wouldn't get the money it needed, and everything would fall apart. Her head started to spin.

Sweat trickled down her back. Bile bubbled up her throat. Forcing herself to swallow, the acid burned. "When will you know for sure?" asked Leia.

As he tugged his shirt down, Derek said, "Tyson's out for the rest of the day on a family matter. I'm scheduled to speak with him first thing tomorrow and then we can go from there."

Nodding, Kai said, "Until tomorrow then." He stood, pushing in his desk chair. "I need to go fill in for Alana at the store for a few hours. She's taking the kids to their various sports activities." Walking to the door, Kai twisted back toward them. "Keep me posted, Derek."

"Of course," replied Derek. "We'll talk soon."

Kai exited, leaving the screen door to slam shut behind him.

Leia stood, walking around her desk. Sitting down on the corner of her desk, she palmed the surface on both sides of herself. "What happens if Tyson won't pass off on the investment for the farm?" asked Leia.

Derek scratched his jaw. "He will," replied Derek.

"But what if he doesn't?" asked Leia. "Then what will my family do? They could lose the farm and everything they've worked hard to build."

His gaze shone with reassurance. Derek interlocked his fingers with hers giving them a squeeze. "I'm not going to let that happen," said Derek. "Promise."

Leia wanted to believe him, trust him. But the truth was she had only just met Derek. Maybe he was only telling her what she wanted to hear? If Tyson said no to the investment, Leia didn't see how Derek could do anything about it.

Leia shook his hand away and folded her arms across her body. "How can you promise that? You don't know the future."

Her voice cracked. "And no matter what you'll be gone soon." Leia cast her gaze away, refusing to look at Derek.

Yanking Leia into a standing position, Derek wrapped his arms around her, and she mirrored his movements. He leaned in. "I'm here now. Everything will work out. I don't want you to be stressed out about this anymore," whispered Derek into her hair, making her neck tickle.

With her head against his chest, Leia listened to the steady thump of his heartbeat. His spicy aftershave filled her lungs, making her reasonable self conveniently forget about the implications of their fling. Leia was being foolish, and she knew it. If she was smart, she'd end this little thing right now. But she couldn't bring herself to do it. If she only had tonight, maybe tomorrow, or only a few more days, Leia wanted to spend them with Derek.

Eventually, she slackened her arms around his hips, Leia tilted her chin back enough to find Derek's gaze. "I'm putting my trust in you," said Leia.

"You won't regret it." Derek swiped some of her unruly strands of hair from her forehead, tucking them behind her ear. For a second, they stared at one another. Finally, Derek gulped, "Are we still on for dinner tonight?"

Up on her tiptoes, Leia kissed Derek quick on the lips. "You bet. I'm cooking for you. Remember?" said Leia.

"Are you sure you don't want me to take you somewhere for dinner?" asked Derek.

Shaking her head, Leia replied, "No, I'm making you dinner. Then I want to take you to my favorite place in the entire world."

His hand cupped her neck. Slowly, Derek leaned an inch from her lips. "I'd be honored." Then he kissed her worries away.

CHAPTER 10

As Derek faced the ocean from his back lanai, he stretched out his legs and propped them on the outdoor coffee table. With his phone to his ear, he said, "Tyson, I'm sorry to interrupt you on your family thing, but I was wondering if you had a chance to review the PowerPoint information I presented to Kai." He rubbed the back of his neck then cranked it both ways to release the tension in between his shoulder blades.

"I saw it," replied Tyson.

Radio silence followed. Derek double checked his connection, bringing his phone back to his ear. "And?" asked Derek.

Clearly annoyed, Tyson scoffed, "You already know what I'm going to say."

A groan escaped him. Derek shifted forward, placing his feet back on the ground. "You don't want to invest in the farm," stated Derek.

"You saw the numbers. We'd be lucky to come out of this thing making one or two percent of our investment. I won't risk the capital. It's too tight a margin," said Tyson.

"I disagree," said Derek, though the pit forming in his stomach, begged to differ.

With his voice full of irritation, Tyson said, "I don't have time to go the rounds with you on this. I'll call you tomorrow morning. We have a lot of things to discuss besides this particular investment."

Sweat formed on his brow, Derek swiped it away with his free hand. "Okay, until tomorrow."

Derek ended the call, placing the phone down on the loveseat cushion next to him. Anxiety bubbled through his veins. Only an hour earlier, he promised Leia they'd invest, and he'd take care of the farm. Now he was nothing but a liar. Tyson was right. The margins were too tight, the risk too great. He couldn't gamble away what they had worked years to build. It wasn't worth it, no matter how captivating he found Leia.

The picturesque scene before him, Derek welcomed the gentle ocean breeze that cooled him off. Derek breathed in the salty air. Geez, it was beautiful here. He saw why people paid the exorbitant prices to stay here. How was he ever going to leave this view? How was he going to leave Leia? Derek couldn't stay, and Leia couldn't leave. Nothing would come of their little rendezvous, and the thought fully depressed him. Loneliness washed over him as he thought of returning to his empty place in Los Angeles.

Shaking off the impending doom, Derek forced himself to gather up his laptop off his coffee table and work on some other assignments until dinner time. In the middle of his work, Leia shot him a text instructing him to wear good walking shoes and comfortable hiking clothes. He wondered where she planned on taking him.

Eventually, the time to leave approached.

After he changed, Derek walked over to Leia's apartment. Knocking on the door, Derek stepped back, waiting for Leia to answer.

Leia yelled, "Come on in. The door is unlocked."

Obeying, Derek opened the door and announced, "It's Derek.

Where are you?" Clasping and unclasping his hands, Derek peered around the small tidy living room waiting for further instructions. It had a brown leather sofa facing a TV.

Leia poked her head out doorway behind the wall with the sofa pushed up against it. "I'm in here." Waving him in, Leia disappeared again. "I have something on the stove, and I don't want it to burn," she called out to him.

He walked the rest of the way to the kitchen and lingered in the door frame. Leia flipped the sizzling meat on her skillet.

"Smells good," commented Derek.

At ease, Derek rested his shoulder against the doorway. He watched as Leia puttered around the kitchen, opening and closing various drawers. Derek admired Leia at home in her own space. She looked relaxed and comfortable. And dang, she was gorgeous. His throat grew tight when he thought of leaving her. He yanked at the collar of his shirt.

Then Leia caught him staring. Heat splashed her cheeks. Leia paused then said, "I hope you like spam." Picking up her spatula, Leia flashed Derek a smile before returning her attention to her skillet.

A whiff of the meat aroma made his stomach growl. Derek said, "I can't say I've ever eaten spam."

Leia flipped the meat again with her spatula. "Like ever?" asked Leia.

A single head shake, Derek said, "Nope."

Leia tsked, "It's a staple here." Turning off the burner, Leia reached over and opened the top of her rice cooker. "I hope you like it. I've eaten it all my life, so I'm used to the taste." Next, she opened a pack of what looked like seaweed.

Straightening himself, Derek stepped into the intimate space of the kitchen. "Can I help you with something?" He moved up close to her.

"Umm …" Leia selected two white plates out of her cupboard to the right of her stove. She placed them on the counter. "Nah,

I'm almost done. This is the easiest dish to cook." Picking back up her spatula, Leia said, "I never said I was a good cook, but I thought you needed to try another Hawaiian staple before you return home." Leia stalled in place.

Boom. Her words splattered right between them, dangling in the air. Words which perfectly punctured whatever may or may not be growing between them.

Derek bypassed the awkward pause. Casually, he twisted, leaning his back against the counter to face her. "You say it's easy to cook. How do you make it? Or is this another one of those family recipes I have no chance of getting?" A sudden urge to run a hand down the length of her arm overtook him. Derek forced himself to plunge his hand into his pocket.

First, she placed a green sheet down on each plate. Next, Leia scooped out some rice and placed it on top of each sheet. "Spam musubi is only seaweed, rice, and spam. But I promise it's better than it sounds." Taking a step to the stove, Leia used a spatula to place a piece of spam on top of each pile of rice.

"And what is spam exactly?" Derek scratched his head. "I feel embarrassed even asking."

Wrapping the spam and rice with the remaining ends of the seaweed, Leia said, "It's pork and ham processed together then canned."

Derek replied, "I can't wait to try it." He tried his best to sound enthusiastic, but Derek didn't like seaweed or the sound of spam. But he'd choke the stuff down if he needed.

As Leia laughed, she slapped him playfully on his arm. "You don't sound very convincing. If you don't like it, we can stop and get some shave ice after our hike."

"Hike? Spill. Where are you taking me?" asked Derek.

Wagging a finger back and forth, Leia said, "Nice try. It's a surprise. I'm not telling you until after dinner."

Rubbing his hands together, Derek said, "Fine, dinner first."

Their gaze caught and Leia smiled as she handed him the plates. Her head motioned to the small two-top table in a breakfast nook. "Can you take those to the table? I'll fetch the silverware."

"Sure." Derek took the plates from her, walking the few steps to the table. After setting them down, Derek twisted back toward Leia. "Do you need me to get anything else for you?"

The drawer squeaked open, and Leia pulled out silverware for them. She held them out to Derek. "Here. Then I'll get the drinks."

Derek took the silverware from Leia and walked it to the table, placing it down beside each plate.

Peering into her fridge, Leia ducked around the open fridge door. "What can I offer you to drink? I have more of those fruit sodas you liked. Does kiwi, mango, or papaya soda sound good to you?" asked Leia.

"Um." Derek paused in place. "How about mango."

"Good choice." Leia reached in and pulled out two mango sodas, bringing them to the table. "Are you ready to try some spam?" She set the sodas down on the table and settled into her seat.

Derek sat down across from her. "Are you kidding me? I was born ready."

Gesturing toward his plate, Leia said, "Then dig in." She picked up her fork. Derek did the same.

After getting a fork full, Derek said, "There are firsts for everything. It smells good. So, here goes nothing." Shoving the bite into his mouth, he chewed. Leia hadn't taken a bite yet and instead was studying him intently. The texture was not his favorite, but it wasn't terrible. Derek swallowed. "Wow. It's amazingly simple but so good." He popped open his soda and took a swig.

A look of relief washed over Leia's face, and she cut into her food with her fork. "I'm glad. I was nervous. I wasn't sure how adventurous you were with trying new foods." She took a bite of her rice and spam.

Another bite later, Derek asked, "So, where is this favorite place of yours?"

Leia bumped her shoulder against his own. "I can't tell you. Where is the fun in that?" Her eyes twinkled back at him mischievously.

"I'm not a surprise kind of guy." Derek rubbed his jaw then took another sip of his soda. "I like to know what's coming, because then I can be prepared."

Teasingly, she shoved Derek's arm, Leia said, "Loosen up." Taking another bite, Leia waited until she swallowed to continue. "I can tell you the place is on my parents' property." Pushing up her chin, she added, "Now you have one hint."

Derek couldn't resist her cute appeal. He leaned over and kissed her quickly on the temple. "I'll try to go with the flow." Derek winked. "But thanks for the hint."

They finished up their meal. Derek helped wipe down the counters and load the dishwasher. Once the kitchen was clean, Leia said, "Let me go find my shoes and then we can head out." Leia left the kitchen and disappeared into the back room, which Derek assumed was her bedroom.

Derek went back to the living room, sitting down on the sofa to wait. Glancing around, Derek admired the view of the ocean from her side window. It peeked through various plants and trees, but offered a beauty many would give anything to see. He wondered if he would ever want to live here, permanently. His work certainly kept him on the road a lot so moving his home base from California to Hawaii wouldn't be too terribly inconvenient. Whoa, what was he even thinking? Moving here for Leia? They'd only just met. He shook off the entire ridiculous idea.

Luckily, a few seconds later, Leia appeared with running shoes on, and her hair tossed up into a messy knot on top of her head. With a hand on her hip, Leia asked, "Are you ready to go to the most beautiful place in the world?"

As he stood, Derek replied, "Absolutely." He strode next to her, taking the liberty to wrap his arm around her waist. "I don't know what will be more beautiful, you or the location." He squeezed her waist.

Her cheeks tinged pink. Dang, Derek loved making her blush.

"Umm … stop." Leia laughed. "That's a tad too cheese ball for me."

"You mean you don't find my awkward middle school pick up lines endearing?" Derek waggled his eyebrows at her.

"I mean," Leia's lips twisted playfully, "no," she said with a huge grin.

Derek chuckled.

"Alright," Leia waved him forward. "Let's go. Before we lose the sunlight." Then Leia held up a finger. "We need flashlights in case it's too dark on the way back." She strode five steps to a hall closet, opening the door. Digging around for a second, she then produced two flashlights. Handing one to Derek, Leia said, "Here. Then we each have one. Better yet let me get a backpack."

"I don't mind carrying both," replied Derek.

Shaking her head, Leia popped back into the closet then produced a backpack. Unzipping it, she held it open. "Here, let's put them inside. I'll get two water bottles too." Leia dropped her flashlight inside, followed by Derek's.

Leia stepped back into the kitchen, removing two water bottles from the fridge. Once everything was inside, she zipped the backpack closed and swung it over one shoulder.

Derek stopped her, taking the backpack off her shoulder. "Let me carry it," said Derek. "You cooked me dinner. Now you're taking me to the most beautiful place in the world, according to you. The least I can do is carry the backpack."

Halted in place, Leia found his gaze. "Are you sure? It's pink checkered."

Adjusting the backpack on his back, Derek replied, "Pink happens to look great on me."

Leia giggled, holding both her hands up. "I mean, I agree." She walked to the front door and opened it. Over her shoulder, Leia added. "But then again, you'd look good in anything." Her gaze slid down his frame. A slight pause, then Leia waved him over. "Come on. We might only have tonight together, and I for one want to make every minute count."

Leia's words ricocheted back and forth through him. Derek walked through the open door, hoping secretly they had more than tonight. If Derek was being truly honest, he hoped they had forever.

CHAPTER 11

With Derek, Leia weaved around the back of her apartment, making their way to the dirt path which cut across her parents' property. After their arms brushed for the second time, Derek laced his fingers through hers, giving her hand a squeeze. They walked for a while in silence, passing by the tight, even rows of different fruit plants. The air reeked of manure. Unconsciously, Leia waved her free hand back and forth in front of her face to mitigate the pungent aroma.

"It usually doesn't smell this bad," commented Leia. She pinched her nose for a few seconds, but it didn't help. The smell wasn't going away, and Leia needed to force herself to smell it so eventually she'd get used to it. "This is definitely still fresh, and I'm remembering why when I gave you a tour of Kama, we never got this close."

Derek shrugged. "It doesn't bother me."

"You'd think it wouldn't bother me either after all of these years, but I guess I have a bit of a sensitive nose," said Leia.

Derek ran a single finger down the slope of her nose. "But it's a beautiful nose." Leia gave Derek a playful tap against his shoulder. "Anyhoo, when does school start for you tomorrow?" asked Derek.

A groan escaped her, and Leia dramatically dragged her feet, kicking up dirt. "It starts at eight. So, I'll be up at five to go for a long run before I head in to work. I must be to the school by seven forty-five."

Leia couldn't remember dreading her return to teaching this much, but then again, she hadn't spent any of her prior breaks with a hunky guy. Part of her didn't want tomorrow to come, because it meant Derek was that much closer to leaving her for good. Then what?

"Can I join you for your run?" asked Derek. "At least for the first few miles. I don't think I'll see you tomorrow if I don't go."

Leia looped her hands around his elbow. "Hey, I thought you promised me dinner tomorrow night." Raising an eyebrow, Leia continued, "I expect you to take me some place spectacular if it's really our last night together."

Derek wrapped an arm around her waist. "Oh, you remember that part, do you?" asked Derek.

A single finger landed firmly in the center of his rock-hard chest. "I remember everything." Leia meant for the words to come off playfully, but the air grew thick between them. Instantly, she regretted revealing how deep her new feelings were for Derek.

Forcing herself to look away, Leia dropped her hand from his elbow, picking up her pace a bit. Derek reached out, running a hand down the length of her arm. Slowing down, Leia twisted to glance up at him.

Their eyes caught. Derek pursed his lips for a moment then said, "I remember everything too, everything that has to do with you." He blinked.

His words whizzed through her. Even if Derek did claim to remember their time together, maybe that's all it would be … memories.

Soon, they left the rows of fruit plants of Kama Farm behind. The clearing along the dirt path squeezed tighter. On both sides of the path were luscious green plants and myriad flowers in every color under the sun. Kama's acreage was left further and further behind them as the quiet stillness of nature surrounded them.

"In the summers, I used to always run back and forth on this path with my cousins." Leia pointed at a small path to the right. "If you follow that path it leads to a small watering hole where we would swim, until the sunshine dried it up until the next summer."

"Sounds idyllic," replied Derek. "Most of my summers, I was stuck in summer day camps because both of my parents worked. I never knew any of the other kids, and I always kept to myself. It was long and boring. By the time summer ended, I was grateful to go back to school. At least at school, I knew the kids from the previous years and could see my friends again."

"I— I'm sorry that was your experience." Leia couldn't imagine a life without it being filled with family. "I know I'm lucky to have so much family. When we get together for birthdays or weddings, it's one big party. It's loud with Hawaiian music and more food than anyone could ever finish. If you stick around long enough, you'll see what I mean." The words tumbled out before she had a chance to process them. "I— I—" Leia fiddled with some loosened wisps of her hair, forcing herself to tuck them behind her ears.

Stopping, Derek shifted closer to her. "I'd love to see it." His hand found hers, and he continued, "I'd be honored to go, and I wish I'd be here to go with you."

His words settled in the uncomfortable spot in the pit of her stomach. Leia tried to ignore the nagging feeling building inside of her.

Tugging Derek forward, Leia said, "Come on. Enough about

things we shouldn't worry about right now. We're getting close to my favorite spot, and I don't want to be in a sour mood."

Derek obeyed, matching her step for step as the dirt path curved upward. Climbing for a few minutes, Derek gripped his chest dramatically. "Thanks again for reminding me once again how out of shape I am," commented Derek.

Leia rolled her eyes and whacked Derek on his arm. "Stop being so hard on yourself."

Soon, the path evened out. Leia led him to an opening above the tops of the trees. Both halted to catch their breath. Up here they took in the view of Kama Farm and her parents' home nestled in the distance. Then the earth gave way to the miles of seemingly endless ocean.

Derek stared out unflinchingly at all of it. Finally, Derek exhaled and said, "Wow. This might be the most beautiful view I've ever seen."

Leia squealed and clapped her hands together. "I knew you'd love it." Her hand found his, and Leia led him to a grouping of flat rocks. "Let's sit for a minute." She tapped the screen of her watch. "We have maybe a half hour until sunset." She sat down on a rock big enough for them to sit side by side.

Derek lowered himself next to her and said, "I see why this is your favorite place in the whole world." He stared out at the view. Slowly, he removed her backpack, placing it on the ground by his feet. After a little lull, Derek knocked his knee against hers and asked, "Do you bring all your boyfriends here?"

Leia laughed, rubbing her hands rapidly over her thighs. "What boyfriends?" She raised an eyebrow, catching Derek's side glance. "Honestly, I can't remember the last time I've come here." Slowly, she let out a loud exhale. "Or even why I wanted to bring you here."

Derek brought his body closer to hers, wrapping an arm around her shoulders. Leia leaned into the warmth cascading off his body. Derek whispered into her ear, "I'm glad you did. I consider it a privilege." His words tickled her neck, sending goosebumps down her spine. He kissed her temple. "Thank you."

A lump formed in her throat. Leia wondered why his words pierced her so deeply. She liked having someone who cared about her, wanting to be with her. Yes, she had family, tons of them, but she didn't have this, a person next to her with whom she could share her life. For so long, Leia figured her time had passed, but then Derek came waltzing in, making her remember what it was like to have someone who was just yours.

A lump formed in her throat. Leia croaked, "My pleasure." Then she tilted her head, making it fit perfectly in the crook of his neck.

They sat in the stillness of the evening, watching as the sun dipped lower and lower. With each passing minute, Leia wondered how much time she had left to live in this fantasy world. A world with Derek, where the future didn't exist, and today was all that mattered. Finally, the last stray stretch of gold submerged below the water, replacing the sky with a dark blue. A smattering of stars slowly appeared against the rising of the moon.

Much too soon, Leia forced herself to untangle from Derek's arm. Once free, Leia stumbled to her feet. "We'd better go." After she dusted off her backside, Leia held out a hand to Derek. He took it. "It'll be pitch black on the path back in a few minutes. I worry about one of us tripping."

Derek reached down, nabbing the backpack. In a swift movement, Derek unzipped the top and held it open for her. Leia dug out the two flashlights. He zipped it closed, swinging it onto his back. She handed him one of the two flashlights, clicking hers on. Derek did the same.

As they started down the path, Leia said, "Let's take it slow." She kept her flashlight pointed down, illuminating the next few steps on the path. "I don't want to slip and get injured. I'm not as young as I used to be."

With a laugh, Derek said, "Then I must be ancient, because I'm older than you."

Whacking him on his arm, Leia said, "You know what I meant."

Though it was dark, Leia caught the mischievousness in his glance. "I know." He smirked. "You're way too fun to tease."

Rolling her eyes, Leia said, "Okay, Derek." Leia reverted her gaze to the path in front of them.

They walked, taking care with each step not to rush. It was quicker back to her apartment than the way up. Eventually, Kama Farm came into view. Manure tickled her nostrils as they walked by the rows of fruit. When they passed by her parents' house, Derek wrapped an arm around her waist, giving it a squeeze. "This has been an incredible evening. I'm so glad I shared it with you."

With him near, Leia picked up his distinct manly scent, making her skittish. "I'm glad we had today too. We might not have many more times together." Her voice faded off, and she darted her gaze away from him and toward her apartment.

"I know," Derek's voice cracked. "I don't know how to remedy that."

Leia didn't have an answer either, so she remained silent. Her fall fling was ending, and she hated where that would leave her, alone.

They arrived in front of her apartment. Derek dropped his arm from her waist, taking a step back. "Five, right? Bright and early?" asked Derek.

It took Leia a second to process what he was asking. "Are you talking about running with me?" asked Leia.

Nodding, Derek wrung his hands. "We might only have tomorrow to run together. I'd like to join you one last time if you don't mind."

Gnawing on the inside of her cheek, Leia tried to sound casual. "Sure. I'm running twelve miles. So ..."

"So, I'll join you for the first five," said Derek.

Then they stared back at one another. Leia wanted him to pull her tight against his body, in an embrace and reassure her this week wouldn't be it. But Derek already felt distant, like though he was here physically, he was already gone. Part of her wanted to say, forget it, don't bother, tonight can be our last night together. But Leia still longed for more time.

So, Leia took a step toward Derek. Once close enough, she interlaced her fingers through his, giving them a squeeze. "I'll see you tomorrow." Her eyes caught his. "And if we only have tomorrow, then you'd better make it good."

Derek tugged her body closer, wrapping his arms tightly around her waist. Tipping her chin up, Leia rose to her tiptoes and kissed him on his cheek.

His fingers found her hair and slid through the long silky strands, continuing down her back. He held his hand firmly there. "I think we can do a little better than that," commented Derek.

Slowly, he leaned in, cupping his other hand behind her head. Gently, his lips slid across hers. And the thoughts of tomorrow whisked away with the ocean breeze.

CHAPTER 12

After a fitful night of sleep, Derek was grateful for the blaring sound of his alarm clock to end his misery. He dreaded his upcoming conversation with Tyson. Tyson was right, investing in the farm with such slim margins of return wasn't in the best interest of their investment company.

His stomach clenched into knots. Caring for Leia and her family beyond a normal business relationship had been a mistake. Why had he muddled the lines of business? And now he'd have to face the empty promises he had made. Derek wanted to back out of his morning run with Leia, but it had been his idea.

Quickly, Derek dressed, pulling on his running shorts, shirt, and shoes. Leaving his Airbnb, Derek jogged toward Leia's place. The plan was for them to meet halfway, then he'd run with her for five miles before she continued the rest of her run. In the darkness, Derek spotted Leia's running lights on her shoes and waist. Slowly, she came close enough for him to make out her face.

Derek waved and bellowed, "Good morning!" His voice carried down the road.

"Good morning," Leia called back. Soon she came up beside

him, gesturing up the road without stopping. "Let's keep running in this direction, then we can turn around." Derek started running beside her, and Leia continued, "And I'll drop you before I continue further in the other direction past your place."

"I'll follow your lead," said Derek.

Digging into the side pocket on her black spandex shorts, Leia pulled out a clip-on light. Holding it out to him without slowing her pace, Leia said, "Here, clip this onto the edge of your shirt so cars can see you."

Derek took the clip-on light from her. Turning it on, he then attached it to the hem of his shirt. "Thanks. It is pitch black out here. There's not a porch light to be seen," remarked Derek.

Peering to his left, Derek took in the view of the ocean. The moon shone across the water, but besides its light and a smattering of stars, there was no light. Calm serenity enveloped Derek. His worries from moments prior eased out of his being. Derek knew he'd continue running on his own when he returned to Los Angeles. If he kept up with his training, then maybe he could return and run the Honolulu marathon with Leia. There he went again, planning a future he had no claim to, and after Leia found out about his empty promises, she wouldn't want to ever see him again.

His shoulders drooped, but he made himself listen to what Leia was saying.

"I know. But I like it. I find it peaceful to be out here before everyone else is up," said Leia.

His breathing became labored. Derek struggled to maintain the quick pace Leia was running, but he didn't dare ask her to slow down. "I— I could see that." Derek managed to say in quick spurts.

Laughing, Leia replied, "Should I slow down?" With a side glance, she raised an eyebrow.

"Nah … don't slow down on … my account," said Derek with a shaky voice.

"I like your confidence and your refusal to admit when you're struggling." Leia paused then added, "it reminds me of myself." Though she didn't say anything, Leia slowed enough for Derek's labored breathing to even out.

"I don't believe that for a second. You're confident because you have every right to be. You excel at everything you do." Derek flashed his eyes toward Leia. "I have a more 'fake it until I make it' approach to life."

"I don't excel at everything …" Leia's voice faded off, and she darted her glance to the road in front of them.

Scratching his head, Derek asked, "What don't you think you excel at?"

"Relationships." Leia shook her head. "I'm not good at them which was why I stopped trying years ago."

"I think perhaps maybe you dated a bunch of losers. Please don't give up on all of us because you've had a few bad experiences," said Derek. "You're not the problem. You're incredible and any guy would be lucky to have you."

"Thanks," said Leia. "Though I appreciate your encouragement, but you'll be gone soon, too. You'll go back to where you came from … and once again …" Her voice faded off. "I'll be alone right back at square one."

Derek wanted to argue with her and tell her he wasn't going anywhere. He'd stay right here in paradise, living in this dream world if she'd have him. But he remained silent. His gut twisting itself, impossible to ignore. Leia wouldn't want him to stay, not after she learned the truth about his investment firm's plans.

They ran another mile before turning back toward Derek's Airbnb. His feet pounding against the pavement competed against his heavy breathing. His mind was miles away as he thought about breaking the news to Kai, Leia, and her family. A pinch between his shoulder blades made pain radiate down his back. Abruptly, Leia came to a halt. Derek stopped running and was shocked to see they were only a few feet from his place.

Out of breath, Derek leaned forward cupping his knees with his hands. He tipped his chin up enough to make eye contact with Leia. Managing a smile, Derek said, "Have a wonderful day at work."

Leia didn't stop but waved and said, "You too. I'll see you tonight."

Derek had completely forgotten he had promised to take Leia to dinner. He paused for a second, "See you tonight," he replied. "Do you care if we drive to Ko Olina for dinner?"

Leia twisted, backpedaling. "Sounds fun. Later, Derek." Pivoting back, Leia continued down the road.

Lingering in front of his door, Derek watched Leia's form slip further and further away until she completely disappeared from his view. Then with heavy steps, Derek opened his door and continued inside.

After he showered, Derek took his laptop out to the back lanai to enjoy the view of the ocean while he reviewed the financials for the farm again. He hoped there was some blaringly obvious mistake that would magically correct the numbers to his favor. But to no avail. Tyson's concerns remained valid. They couldn't invest in the farm and make enough money. And Derek knew if they didn't invest, Leia's family would probably be forced to sell the farm outright.

With a sigh, Derek leaned back in his seat, cupping the back of his neck with his hands. In his mind, he reviewed the idea of the farm tours. Honestly, Kai could start the tours with little to no investment. If Kai knew enough locals, they could advertise it at their various businesses, on their personal social media accounts, and through word of mouth. Maybe there was a way for Kai and his family to save the farm without any investment. Then Derek wouldn't be a man of broken promises. It could work. But it didn't resolve the repayment of the bank loan the farm owed.

His phone ringing broke his train of thought. Swiping it off the coffee table, Derek glanced at the screen before hitting accept. "Good morning, Tyson."

"Hi, Derek. I've been over the financials again— only due to your insistence," said Tyson.

Derek cut him off. "I know we can't invest."

"It was a waste of time to have you even go out there," stated Tyson. "I don't know what we were thinking. We should've taken a better look at the earning potential of the farm before flying you out to Hawaii. We usually aren't this far off when it comes to the potential profits margin. What a mistake" he sighed loudly.

Running a hand through his hair, Derek replied, "It wasn't a total waste." Derek almost added he met Leia and that was something. "I'm glad I came."

"I'm not following. We wasted money by having you travel out to Hawaii," said Tyson. "Money we can't recoup."

"I'll count it as my vacation." Derek shifted, sitting up. "I won't charge any of my expenses to the company."

"That's certainly generous of you." Tyson paused. "Does this have anything to do with that girl?"

His eyes locked on the crystal blue waters in front of him, Derek said, "Leia." Tilting up his face, Derek let himself bathe in the sunlight. Light seeped into his being.

"Yeah, Leia," said Tyson with a voice full of annoyance. "I think you're forgetting you leave tomorrow. I mean come on. You had a fling, fresh off your new break up with Heather. You were vulnerable. I still happen to think you and Heather have a chance to reconcile."

"That's never going to happen," replied Derek. His jaw tightened, making a pinch between his shoulder blades. "She broke up with me through a *text* message. Heather didn't even dignify our relationship with a face-to-face conversation." He ran a hand down the length of his face. "I can't believe I thought I was going to marry her," muttered Derek.

"She'll come around. Once Heather realizes she walked away

from the best thing that happened to her, she'll come crawling back," said Tyson.

"In her text, Heather said she met somebody else. She isn't coming back." Derek sucked in the air. Through gritted teeth, he asked, "Can we stop talking about Heather?"

"Fine. But I'm only saying this Leia was a distraction for you. A nice one no doubt, but Derek it's just that. It's time for you to come back home to Los Angeles. I have several potential investment opportunities I want to review with you. It's time to get your head out of the clouds and back into the game," said Tyson.

Home. Where was his home? Was it in Los Angeles? Or was that simply where he lived because he had always lived there? Derek had no family. No ties anywhere. Half his time was spent flying here and there. Before Derek wanted to travel, he welcomed the act of never being anywhere too long. Surely, Heather had tired of his constant avoidance of anything real and tangible. When things became difficult, Derek hopped on a plane and headed out of town. Naively, Derek always believed time and distance would repair whatever wasn't working in his relationships. He never learned.

"I'll come back tomorrow," said Derek. "There's nothing left for me to do but leave."

Derek wished the thought didn't depress him like it did. As the crystal blue water sparkled before him, Derek couldn't remember the last time he felt this at home. Like this place was where he always belonged. But then he remembered how vacations were a glimpse into a dream way of living not a reality. One had bills, obligations, and work which made the vacation a welcome respite from the mundane.

"I'm glad we're back on the same page. I'll see you soon," replied Tyson.

Derek said goodbye to Tyson, ending his call. Promptly after hanging up, Derek booked his return flight to Los Angeles. Once his flight was booked, Derek gathered up his things, shoving his laptop into his messenger bag. He now had to let Kai know about his decision. Standing, Derek slugged the bag over his shoulder and headed out of his place, walking to the farm.

As he came up the gravel driveway, Noa and Teresa were sitting out on the front lanai. Derek waved and for a second, he hesitated, wondering if he should head directly around the house to the office trailer to meet with Kai as planned. But something about the leisurely view of Leia's parents sitting in their wingback chairs, holding hands, gave Derek pause.

Instead of weaving around the house, Derek climbed the front steps. With a smile, Derek greeted them, "Good morning." He readjusted his slipping messenger bag. "You both look extra comfortable this morning."

Teresa met Derek's gaze. "We are enjoying the beautiful view." She motioned to the empty chair beside her. "Come sit with us a while."

Double checking his watch, Derek wondered how much Kai would mind if he was late to their meeting. "I have a meeting with Kai." Derek rubbed the back of his neck, glancing between Teresa and Noa. "I don't want to keep him waiting."

Waving his comment off, Teresa motioned to the seat again. "Sit. I'll text Kai and tell him to come up to the lanai. Whatever you must discuss with him, you can do it in front of us. This place has been in Noa's family for too long to count. We're more anxious than anyone to know how we can save the farm."

"Okay, then." Derek lowered himself into the empty chair beside Teresa.

Teresa pulled her phone out of her pocket. Her fingers zipped across the screen. Moments later, her phone dinged. She tapped on the message. "Kai is coming up to the house, so relax." Teresa stood, slipping her phone into her dress pocket. "I'll go get something for us to drink."

Waving the suggestion off, Derek replied, "Please it's not necessary, and I don't want to be a bother."

"You aren't. I'll be right back," said Teresa. Then she disappeared into the house.

Derek and Noa sat alone. Only the sound of the ocean weaved between them. Derek knew Noa's speech was limited, but for whatever reason Derek started talking. "You have a wonderful family, Noa. One most would be envious of, even I'm envious of what you have here with them." Derek glanced over at Noa. Noa gave a small nod. "You have this beautiful place, on this magical island. I don't want you to worry. I'm going to make sure you get to keep it all. I couldn't let Leia lose this."

Peering out at the view of miles of endless ocean, Derek's breath caught in his chest at the beauty of the blue sky blending into the turquoise sea. He understood why generations of people lived here and why they never left. This place meant more, it meant everything.

Noa cleared his throat, and slowly said, "Th-an-k y-ou."

Two words only, but they were spoken with such sincerity. It pierced Derek's soul. If he could help Noa and Teresa, Leia, Kai … all of them, then this trip wasn't a waste. It was far from it. This trip had changed the very fiber of himself.

Kai appeared in the walkway, making his way up the gravel path. Teresa came back from inside the house with a tray of sodas, handing Derek a guava one. Derek popped the top, taking a long swig, hoping the bubbly carbonation would settle the nerves in his stomach. Kai climbed the stairs to the lanai, sitting down in an empty chair next to his parents.

After Teresa gave Noa and Kai a soda too, she settled back into her seat between Derek and Noa. Once everyone had taken a few sips of their drinks, they focused their attention on Derek.

Setting the soda on the side table, Derek leaned forward resting his forearms on his thighs. "I'm going to give it to you straight. Our investment firm will not be investing in the farm." He let the words land.

Teresa sucked in the air. Noa flinched.

Kai's eyes narrowed as his jaw tightened "So, you're like all the rest of them." He shook his head and rolled his eyes. "And I thought we could trust you."

Derek sat straight, holding up a hand. "I know, and you can, but you don't need our investment money. I think you can save the farm on your own. If you start the farm tours like we discussed, I believe it'll bring in the needed revenue to get you out of debt in two to three years. After that you'll start to bring in a nice profit, and the most important part is you'll remain the sole owners of the farm."

"But what about the loan due at the bank?" Teresa exchanged a glance with Kai, before staring back at Derek. "The bank told us we need it paid back by the end of the year. We don't have two to three years," said Teresa.

"True, that's where I've been thinking. I'd be willing to give you a personal loan. You can use the funds to pay back the bank. Then slowly with the profits you earn from the tours, you can pay me back. Once you pay off my loan to you, I'll go away, and you'll keep a hundred percent of the farm," said Derek.

"I thought you said your firm wasn't investing in the farm," stated Kai.

"My investment company is not investing in the farm." Derek scratched his chin. "I personally would front you the money from my own account."

Teresa reached for Noa's hand. "Isn't that incredibly risky for you?"

"Probably," said Derek. He shifted, resting his ankle across his opposite knee. "But I have the money, and I want to help. I can't let you lose the farm or this place. So, take the money, pay off the bank loan, and then pay me back."

Derek knew he was breaking all reasonable rules of business. But he cared too much, this time it was nothing but personal.

"Do you do this often? Invest your own money when your business partner says no?" asked Teresa.

"This would be a first," replied Derek.

Kai took a swig of his soda. "At what percent of interest?" asked Kai. "Maybe you just want us to default on the loan to you and then you'd take everything."

"I can do it for two percent," said Derek. "And I know you won't default on the loan. After spending the last few days with you and your family, I know you're honest and hardworking people. I trust you'll pay me back."

"Yes, but this is still a huge risk for you if the farm tours don't work out. We could still lose the farm along with your money," said Kai.

Squirming in his seat, Derek lowered his leg back down. "I'm aware of the risk, and I'm okay with it," replied Derek.

Kai raised an eyebrow and asked, "Does Leia have anything to do with this offer?"

"She has everything to do with it." His gaze skidded between them. Derek scratched his jaw. "One more thing. Leia can't know about me paying off the bank and our arrangement."

"Why not?" asked Teresa.

"Because I don't want that to be a factor in how she feels about me," said Derek. "I want Leia to want me for me, and not for anything else."

CHAPTER 13

With a shaky hand, Leia applied the last sweep of mascara to her bottom lashes. Her first day back to teaching had left her exhausted and overwhelmed. Leia received a new student who had a myriad of behavior problems and learning difficulties. It wasn't anything Leia hadn't faced before, but for whatever reason, this student challenged her in ways that made her feel out of her depth and control. On top of that, thoughts of the future of the farm whirled around in her head. The reality that Derek was leaving didn't help either.

Leia tossed her mascara back into her makeup bag, zipping it closed. Leia wondered where Derek was taking her. More importantly, she wondered when Derek was returning to Los Angeles, because she knew with a big ocean in between them, they would be done.

With nothing left to do, Leia left the safety of her bathroom, flipping off the light as she exited. On second thought, Leia shot Derek a text, telling him she'd walk up to her parents' house, and he could pick her up there.

As she placed her purse over her shoulder, Leia straightened her sleeveless cotton dress before exiting her apartment. The gravel path crunched under her feet as she walked. Leia heard Kai's voice in the distance, most likely he was on the back lanai of his bungalow. His voice became clearer as she approached, but she remained hidden from his view behind the thick plants and bushes lining the path that wove by his bungalow toward her parents' house. Alana said something that Leia couldn't make out.

Leia didn't mean to eavesdrop, but for whatever reason, she kept her presence hidden by not calling out to them.

Clear as noonday, Kai said, "Derek told us not to tell Leia. That's part of the deal."

"I see," replied Alana.

Freezing in place, behind the safety of the plants, Leia crunched down.

"I think he needs to tell her. I don't understand the secrecy of the whole thing," said Kai.

"I agree, but you promised and now you have to leave it alone." After a long pause, Alana continued, "someday she'll find out. Things like this never stay hidden, no matter how much someone wants them to."

"She's going to get hurt," said Kai. "I hate that part. I wish …"

Leia had heard enough. Springing upward, she walked toward the back lanai. Soon the edge of Kai and Alana's back lanai, came into view. "Kai! Alana! Are you back there?" asked Leia in a loud and booming voice.

"Yes," they replied in unison.

Alana leaned over the railing of their lanai and waved.

With wobbly knees, Leia walked closer to them, waving back. Kai came up next to Alana, leaning over the railing too.

"Where are you off to, Leia?" asked Kai. "You're dressed way too nice to be heading to Dad and Mom's."

Stopping by the side of their back lanai, Leia glanced up to them. "You mean I'm not in my normal lounge wear," she stated.

Alana whacked Kai on his arm. Clearing her throat, Alana said, "You look pretty, Leia. Are you going somewhere with Derek?"

"Dinner," said Leia. "I guess some place in Ko Olina."

"Derek goes home tomorrow," said Kai. "But I'm sure he already told you."

Derek hadn't told Leia, but again she hadn't asked. Leia knew he wouldn't stay forever, but the announcement of his for sure immediate departure made her stomach clench and bile trail up her throat.

Instinctively, Leia jutted her chin and replied, "I know." She shrugged, but her hands trembled. Maybe this was the piece of news Alana and Kai had been discussing? "It's fine. He'll go home to Los Angeles, and everything will go back to the way it was before."

Kai raised a skeptical eyebrow and asked, "Are you sure about that, little sis?"

Alana squeezed Kai on his forearm. "I hope you two have a nice time." She gave Kai a pointed look, before shifting back to smile at Leia.

With a forced smile, Leia said, "Thanks. I will. Have a nice night." Swiftly, Leia walked past their back lanai toward her parents' home.

As Leia approached her parents' front lanai, Derek stood from where he sat alone, waiting for her arrival. Her parents must have been gone for the evening, maybe they had ventured to Aria and Kalon's house for dinner? If she had known, Leia wouldn't have asked him to wait there for her.

Derek had on the same khaki shorts and Hawaiian shirt he wore to her parents' house for dinner. Taking the steps down two at a time, soon Derek arrived in front of her. Before she had time to think, Derek brought her tight against his body in a warm, inviting embrace.

"Leia," said Derek. His voice tickled her neck, sending a shiver down her spine. "You look beautiful."

Closing her eyes for a moment, Leia tried to remember the strength of his arms, the smell of his shampoo, the rustling of his stubble against her cheek. If this was the last night she spent with him, Leia cared to remember every little thing about him.

Finally, Leia broke their embrace, stumbling a step backward. While she regained her footing, Leia pinched the front of his Hawaiian shirt. "Let me guess, this is your new favorite shirt." She let go of his shirt, glancing up at him to meet his gaze.

His hands glided down his abdomen, and Derek said, "I know you like this on me—so I wore it—again." He shuffled his feet. His cheeks reddened with each passing second. *Dang, he looked cute.*

As Leia cupped his cheek, she said, "I'm only teasing you."

Derek gulped. "Ok." He scratched his jaw.

Her lips twitched into a smirk, and Leia said, "I think you look good— really good."

A huge grin lit up his face. Derek wrapped his arms around Leia's waist, tugging her closer again. He kissed her quickly on the lips. "I hope you like shrimp," said Derek.

"I love it," said Leia.

Unwrapping his arms from around her, Derek's hand glided down the length of her arm until his fingers intertwined with hers. "Great, because I have it on good authority there is a fantastic restaurant in Ko Olina that makes the best shrimp and macadamia nut pie. Plus, I heard the view is unreal."

For a second, Leia almost brought up her knowledge of Derek's departure tomorrow, but she didn't want to ruin the evening. Instead, she interlaced her fingers with his own. They walked hand in hand to Derek's rental car parked in the driveway. Derek opened the passenger side door, holding it open for Leia. Leia slid into the seat.

For a second Derek paused and gripped the corner of the

door. Slowly, he swallowed. Leia stared as his Adam's apple bobbed up and down. "I'm leaving tomorrow," sputtered Derek. He met her gaze. "I should've told you earlier. If you don't want to go out with me tonight, because I'm leaving, I totally understand."

"I know," said Leia. She broke eye contact, staring out the windshield. "Kai and Alana told me." She paused, her heartbeat rapidly building. Shifting her gaze back toward Derek, Leia stated, "I don't care. I mean I'm not happy you're leaving, but I knew the end was inevitable. But I still want to spend tonight with you."

Derek released his grip on the door, moving it back to the handle. "Then let's make it a night to remember." Then he closed the door.

They drove from the north shore down to Ko Olina, arriving as the sun slipped a little further. The sun's rays stretched out across the water in a glittering dazzling white. Derek found a spot in the public parking lot next to the Ko Olina Marina. Once out of the car, they walked toward the path wedged between the beach and the resorts. A light breeze made the salty air dance around them as he took her hand. They walked the paved walkway weaving around the Ko Olina lagoons and resorts.

Back when Derek was a child, he had vacationed with his parents in Ko Olina. It was a memory tucked way back in his psyche, but as he came around the bend on the path and saw the resort where he had stayed at as a child, Derek halted in place. Leia nearly tripped at his abrupt stop.

Derek stared back at the resort as a wave of happy memories washed over him. He missed his parents and being a part of a family. His voice cracked as he pointed up toward a tall tower. "I stayed there as a kid." Derek gulped. "I came here once for two weeks in the summer. I remember my classmates were jealous that I was spending some of my summer vacation in Hawaii. It was the only time my parents ever visited here." Sweat lathered his brow. Derek swiped at it with the heel of his hand.

Leia linked her hands around the crook of his elbow. "What was your favorite part about the trip?" asked Leia.

"Um. Let me think for a minute." Derek glanced out at the lagoon, giving way to the ocean. His mind flooded with the trapped-up memories of the past. He stepped forward, walking again. Leia kept her grip on his elbow, slowly sliding it down his arm until their fingers touched.

"We went on a snorkeling cruise out of the marina back there. The fish were beautiful, and I loved every minute of it. My mom hated snorkeling. She lasted a mere five minutes, because she didn't like being out in the deep water. It scared her when she couldn't touch the bottom. So, my mom went back to the boat, but my dad and I swam for as long as they let us." Rubbing the back of his neck, Derek exhaled, making his shoulders droop. "Geez, I miss them."

Giving his hand a squeeze, Leia said, "I'm sorry. I can't even imagine how much."

"Sometimes, it's like I can't breathe. Knowing that I don't have one single person on this earth who's attached to me— it's incredibly lonely." Derek gripped his chest, waiting for the thunder of his pulse ringing in his ears to dissipate. Exhaling, the tightness in between his shoulder blades loosened a tad as his breathing evened out. "And being around you and your family has made me remember the feeling of security and love that comes when you have people in your life who care about you. You are lucky, Leia. So very lucky."

Gnawing on her bottom lip, Leia said, "I know how much I have and not everyone has that. I'm so thankful for my parents, Kai and Alana, and the magic we have together at Kama Farm." Flipping her hair over her shoulder, she paused then added, "You don't have to feel so alone anymore. You have me now. I care. I'll be only a text or phone call away. I'd love for you to stay a part of my life."

Derek wanted to scream it wouldn't be enough, not with an ocean in between them. But instead, he leaned over and kissed Leia on the temple. "I appreciate that. I'm sure I'll take you up on the offer. I'll probably call and text you so much you'll block my number."

Leia laughed, whittling away at the tension inside of him. "I highly doubt that, because once you get back to your real life you won't have time for me."

Opening his mouth to reply, Derek was interrupted by a large group passing by them on the tight sidewalk. They sidestepped out of the way, letting the group walk past. Once the group was gone, they continued toward the restaurant. Derek stared at the water as he walked, remembering the day from so long ago. It was like his parents were there again with him, if only for the briefest second. He waited for the dull ache to enter his being, but instead he felt grateful for the memories he shared with his parents. Giving Leia's hand a squeeze, Derek knew the difference was her, there with him.

After they arrived at the restaurant, they were led to a table overlooking the ocean. Settling into their chairs, they took their menus from the host. The host brought some bread and water, before leaving them to settle in.

As she scanned the menu, Leia asked, "So you've heard the shrimp is good here?" She took a sip of her water.

Laying his menu flat against the table in front of himself, Derek asked, "You haven't eaten here before?"

"Never," said Leia. Flipping her dark silky hair over her shoulder, the strands glistened from the last light of the sun. "I don't come to Ko Olina much. It's way on the other side of the island from the north shore and with the traffic it takes far too long."

"What about when you worked as a lifeguard at Waikiki Beach? Wasn't that a long drive?" asked Derek.

"Oh." Leia replied, "I used to stay with one of my many great aunts who has an apartment in Waikiki. She let me sleep over at her place on the days I worked. I usually would work two or three days in a row then I would have the next three or four days off, so I'd go home. But I only worked there in the summers during college to save money for my expenses."

"I know you're plenty strong." Derek glanced at the menu again. "You saved me after all, so don't take this the wrong way, but aren't most of the lifeguards on the island men?" asked Derek.

Leia whacked him on the arm. "Hey, you don't think a woman can be a lifeguard?" She raised an eyebrow, giving him a pointed look.

"No." Derek shook his head. "They absolutely can be lifeguards. Like I said, you were plenty strong to save me, but I'm only curious what made you want to do that when most of the other lifeguards were men."

"Do you want the truth?" asked Leia while she fiddled with her silverware.

Derek shifted closer to her and placed his hand over Leia's fidgeting hand. "I do." He weaved his fingers through hers.

"I wanted to prove I could do it, do something most women couldn't." With her free hand, Leia took another sip of her water. "Kai was always making fun of how weak I was. He liked to say I used it as an excuse to get out of doing chores around the farm. The weak thing got stuck in my head, and I had to prove him wrong. If I could be strong enough to be a lifeguard with a bunch of men, then I was strong. Does that make sense?" She stared back at him.

Derek sat in awe. Her determination he found incredibly attractive. "A thousand percent," he said.

Grinning, Leia said, "It also didn't hurt that I spent my college days around a bunch of ripped guys. It certainly made the job more enjoyable." Her lips twitched.

Derek laughed, "I'm sure it did."

The server finally came by and took their order. Both ordered garlic shrimp along with a slice of macadamia nut pie for dessert. After the server left, they sat staring out at the ocean. The sun disappeared, being replaced by a full moon with bright glowing stars. Derek dreaded tomorrow.

Leia broke the peaceful silence. "When do you leave tomorrow?" She turned toward him, pulling her gaze away from the ocean to him.

With a quick glance at her, Derek stared out at the ocean not wanting to look Leia in the eyes. "Early," said Derek. "I'll be gone before you get up."

Nodding her head, Leia paused then asked, "Do you think you'll ever come back?"

"Boy, I hope so," said Derek.

"Then I guess that's that. You'll go home. I'll stay here. And this …" Leia waved a finger between them, "this will just end."

Exhaling, Derek wondered how to reply. He wanted to say no, surely there was a way for them to be together. A way for the impossible to be possible, but he didn't have a solution. Maybe Leia had been only a distraction from Heather? But the argument didn't hold up. His mind was a muddled mess. Nothing made sense anymore. How could one woman make him question everything?

His throat suddenly dry, Derek gulped and replied, "I don't want it to end, but I don't know how to make it work either."

"See?" asked Leia. "We both knew it was foolish getting involved with one another. I wish I had listened to my gut on this one."

The air crackled with kinetic catastrophic energy. He knew what he needed to tell Leia was about to make everything a thousand times worse. But Derek couldn't slink away. It wasn't right, and if he did, she'd hate him even more than if he'd only fessed up.

Taking a deep breath, Derek said, "And, Leia, my investment firm is not investing in the farm."

Her jaw dropped, and every sound in the universe was instantly silenced.

CHAPTER 14

Derek left.

Leia stayed.

He called.

Leia didn't pick up.

Derek texted, and Leia didn't respond.

The funky dance of avoidance, Leia played it out for a few weeks, hoping she'd stop caring about Derek. Or better yet she dreamed of forgetting him all together. When her family asked about Derek, Leia quickly changed the subject. In the end, Derek ended up being nothing he claimed to be, and Leia was embarrassed she had thrown caution to the wind and acted so recklessly with her own heart.

One evening a few weeks later, Leia was working in the office trailer. Kai had hired an official accountant who was way better equipped to help the farm get back on track financially. Leia only inputted the receipts for the day to assist in a small way. When Leia inquired what Kai was going to do without the promised investment money, Kai told her he had figured something else out. His lips were sealed, but Leia was relieved.

The jingle of the trailer door made Leia pause in place, her fingers hovered over the keyboard. Kai popped his head in. "Hey, Leia. I saw the lights on when I was passing by, I wanted to double check I hadn't left them on. I didn't realize you were still working."

Stretching her arms above her head, Leia then folded them against herself. "I'm finishing up. I should be done in another fifteen minutes or so."

Lingering in front of the door, Kai asked, "Are you still hung up on Derek?"

Her back stiffened. "Whoa, that came out of nowhere." With a clenched jaw, Leia said, "Kai—" she gave him a pointed look, "I don't want to talk about him."

"Why? Because you might be in love with him?" asked Kai.

With an eye roll, Leia seized the end of the desk, scooting herself closer. "We spent a short amount of time together. You can't fall in love that fast. Besides, I could never be in love with someone who only gave empty promises."

"What promises?" asked Kai.

Pushing up her chin, Leia replied, "Derek shouldn't have promised to invest in the farm. I thought he was different." Shaking her head, Leia continued, "Apparently, he wasn't."

Taking a step closer, Kai said, "Derek is a decent guy. You need to get over this, and stop being angry at him for no reason."

"How can you of all people be saying this?" asked Leia. "I know you had to scramble to find another way to pay off the bank loan."

"You've got it wrong, Leia." Kai paused, shoving one hand into his pocket. "Derek made me promise not to tell you, but I think you deserve to know."

"Know what?" asked Leia.

"Derek is the one who paid off the bank loan. He didn't want you to know because he didn't want that to sway your feelings for him. But you've been moping around since he left, so I couldn't stand not telling."

Gnawing on the inside of her cheek, Leia let the revelation settle. "So, Derek paid with his own money, not the investment firm's money?" asked Leia.

"Yes, and I'm working to pay him off little by little. We get to keep the whole farm this way. Leia, Derek isn't a bad guy, he's one of the good ones," said Kai.

"I— I—" stammered Leia. "I don't even know how to unpack this whole thing. It doesn't change the fact that he lives in Los Angeles. There's no way for us to be together."

"Oh, come on, little sis," said Kai. "You and I both know you could figure something out."

"I'll think on it," said Leia. "Thanks, Kai."

Kai nodded then turned and left. Leia leaned forward and threw her face into her flat palmed hands and moaned.

The next morning, Leia woke to the blaring of her alarm clock. After slapping the buzzer off, Leia wiggled her way out of the covers and changed into her running clothes. With her shoes laced up, Leia hoped the morning run would give her time to clear her head before going to her teaching job. So, Leia ran and thought, ran, and thought. She wished Derek had told her the truth to begin with. Why didn't he trust her enough to know she was a good judge of character?

For miles, Leia pushed herself harder and faster than ever before. Finishing the final stretch, Leia's body was drenched in sweat and chest fully heaving. The feeling exhilarated her in a way it hadn't since Derek left. Slowing to a walk, Leia curved toward her parents' home. Noa and Teresa sat out on the front lanai enjoying the morning sunrise over the ocean.

With a wave, Leia walked up the gravel walkway. "Good morning," greeted Leia. She climbed up the front steps, stopping at the top step of the lanai.

"Good morning, Leia," said Teresa. Her gaze slid down her frame. "How many miles did you run today?"

Her breathing evened out. "Nine," replied Leia. Double checking her watch, Leia continued, "I don't have time to chat. I need to go shower before heading off to work."

Teresa patted the top of Noa's hand. "We understand."

"Do you know how things are going with Kai starting up the farm tours?" asked Leia. Shifting her weight, Leia put a hand on her hip. "I saw him yesterday, but I completely forgot to ask." Leia lifted the bottom of her tank top and used it to wipe sweat trickling down her temples.

"I believe they're going really well." Teresa looked toward Noa. "He told us they're going to start two tours next week."

Leia smiled and replied, "That's wonderful." Swiping some sweat off her brow, Leia readjusted her tank top. "I need to get going. I hope you both have a lovely day." Leia twisted around and took the stairs down.

"Leia—" said Teresa, stopping Leia on the second to bottom step of the stairs.

Once on the bottom, Leia turned around and faced Teresa. "Yeah, Mom?"

"Are you still talking to Derek?" asked Teresa.

Feeling defensive, Leia put a hand on her hip. "No, I am not. Why?" Leia didn't want to add, she had every intention of finally calling him tonight to clear the air between them.

Clasping and unclasping her hand, Teresa said, "I ran into Bane."

"Bane, like my old college boyfriend, Bane?" asked Leia.

"Yes, that Bane," said Teresa.

Leia hadn't thought about Bane in years. Their breakup had been a somewhat amicable one. Bane didn't want to stay in Oahu, and Leia did. After graduation, Bane moved to Idaho and got married shortly after his arrival there.

Dropping her hands down at her sides, Leia said with an edge, "Okay, and what?"

Teresa stood, walking to the edge of the lanai. Glancing down the stairs at Leia, Teresa said, "He's coming for dinner tonight with his mom."

"What?!" Leia stumbled a step forward, knocking the front of her foot on the bottom step of the stairs. "I don't want to see him," scoffed Leia.

"But Bane is back in Hawaii after a really long time," said Teresa.

"I still don't see why you think I'd care," replied Leia.

"He's divorced. Three years. His ex-wife cheated on him." Teresa wagged a finger. "I always thought you two had some unfinished business."

"Mom …" Leia pinched the bridge of her nose, forcing her voice to even out. "Why?"

"Because I need you to get over Derek. He isn't coming back. You had some fun, but Derek was a distraction, nothing more. It's time for you to wake up and realize you're going to end up alone if you don't move on. Bane jumped at the chance to come over. I could tell he *wanted* to come," said Teresa.

A loud groan escaped her. Leia knew she didn't have time to hash out this entire ridiculous thing. She had exactly thirty minutes to shower and get herself to work. "This is unbelievable. Why?" Leia wailed.

"Because I'm your mother. I know this thing with Derek could drag on for years, where you end up with nothing. You're not young anymore, Leia. I won't see you long for someone who isn't coming back." Teresa stamped her foot. "It's a huge mistake. Bane and his mom will be here at six." She straightened herself.

"I'm not coming," replied Leia.

Teresa walked down three of the steps. "Yes, you are. I know where you live and don't think for a second, I won't send Bane over to your place to fetch you come dinner time."

Pivoting to leave, Leia said over her shoulder, "I don't have time to argue with you."

"Great," said Teresa. With a sickly-sweet voice, Teresa continued, "I'll see you at six."

The entire way back to her apartment Leia grumbled to herself. Once home, she stripped off her soaking wet running clothes and jumped in the shower. Her hurried morning left her little time to stew about her looming dinner with a guy she hadn't seen in fifteen years. And with teaching, her day flew right on by.

So, as six o'clock neared, Leia dreaded the prospect of an awkward evening.

In the middle of changing into a pair of khaki shorts and floral blouse, her phone rang. Swiping it off her bed, Leia caught Derek's name flashing across the screen. The guy certainly was persistent, even with a month full of her ignoring him, he hadn't stopped trying. For a second, she hesitated, gnawing her bottom lip vigorously. Maybe it was time to talk? She sure did miss him.

Hitting accept, Leia placed the phone to her ear. "Hey, Derek. I don't have much time to talk." Putting the phone on speaker, she set her phone down on her bed. "If you're calling to apologize for leaving me high and dry, I'm listening."

"Umm," stammered Derek. "I can't believe you picked up. I thought for sure you were going to have it go to voice mail. You've ignored me for a month. I'm thrilled you picked up. What gives?"

"What can I say? I'm a woman of mystery," said Leia.

Derek paused then said, "It's good to hear your voice. I've missed you."

Warmth crept up her neck, Leia couldn't deny she missed Derek, too. Hearing his voice was making her feel all the feels, feelings she wondered if she had made up. "Ahh, I might have missed you a tad too." Leia paused for a moment. Clearing her throat, Leia continued, "I listened to all your voice messages and read your texts. And I've decided I can't stay mad at you. I wish I could, but it appears I can't."

"That's a relief. I'm sorry for how things ended," said Derek.

Gnawing on the inside of her cheek, Leia said, "I know. I'm sorry too for how I acted. I hope we can start over being friends."

"Friends?" asked Derek.

"Yes, friends, Derek," said Leia.

"I guess I have to take what I can get," said Derek. "Though, for the record, I like *like* you."

"What are we, like twelve?" asked Leia.

Derek laughed. "No, but I'll drop it." A long pause followed, Derek asked, "Are you headed somewhere? You said you couldn't talk long."

Opening her closet door, Leia said, "I've something tonight, and I'm not sure when it'll end." She bent down and dug out a pair of strappy sandals from her closet that were more comfortable than visually appealing.

"Oh, really. Where are you going?" pried Derek.

Sitting on the corner of her bed, Leia slipped her foot into her first sandal. "Only to my parents' house for dinner." She buckled the back of the sandal then moved onto the next sandal. "But my mom invited a guy for me."

Partly, Leia wondered how Derek would react. Would he be jealous of the prospect of another guy in her life? Or were they only friends, and he would react indifferently?

"Ahh. Anyone you know?" asked Derek. "Or is this a blind date set up thing?"

With her sandals strapped, Leia stood, snatching her phone off the bed. She continued to her bathroom. "Yeah, my old college boyfriend, *Bane*." Setting her phone on the top of her bathroom counter, Leia opened a drawer, taking out her makeup bag.

"It sounds like you're busy getting ready to meet *Bane*. I should let you go," said Derek.

Makeup bag out, she unzipped the top. Leia pulled out her

mascara first. "I've got a few minutes to talk." She unscrewed the top of her mascara, applying some to her top lashes.

"So, what's the story with you and Bane? Does Teresa think you two have unfinished business?" inquired Derek.

Leia's jaw dropped when he used almost exactly her mother's words, making her halt in place. "How did you know?" asked Leia.

"Why else would Teresa invite him over," muttered Derek. Clearing his throat, Derek asked, "And?"

"There's no story." Leia moved onto her other eye, sweeping the top with a coat of mascara. "We dated in college. We broke up when Bane moved away to Idaho. End of story. Why? Do I hear a hint of jealousy in your voice?" Mascara recapped, Leia threw it back into her makeup bag. Staring at her reflection in the mirror, Leia waited for Derek to answer. "Are you still there?"

"I'm here ..." Derek's voice faded away. Finally, Derek stated, "I might be a little bit jealous, though I have no right to be."

Picking up her phone, Leia took the phone off speaker, placing it to her ear. "I'm glad," said Leia matter-of-factly.

Laughing, Derek said, "You're happy, because I'm miserable here in Los Angeles alone, and I'll spend the entire night wondering if you made a love connection with some old flame."

"Precisely." Leia missed talking to Derek, more than she imagined. A knock at the door alerted Leia to the time. Eyeing her watch, Leia said, "I need to run. I'm late, and I know my mom sent Bane to my door to fetch me. I'll talk to you later."

"Bye," said Derek.

Leia said goodbye and hung up.

Double checking her appearance in the mirror, Leia slid her phone into her pocket and left her bathroom. Walking to her front door, Leia swung it open, and her gaze landed on Bane. He was fifteen years older, but boy, time had been good to him. His once chubby face and shabby hair were replaced by a chiseled jaw and slick dark hair cut close to his temples.

Leia gulped. "Hey," she managed. The single word came out shaky. Suddenly, her knees became wobbly. "It's nice to see you again, Bane."

Bane took a step closer to the opened door, casually leaning one shoulder against the door frame. "Hi, Leia." His dark eyes smoldered back at her. "You look exactly the same." He smirked.

Gathering her long strands of hair with her hands, Leia swooped it all over one of her shoulders. "I'd say the same about you, but I'd be lying." Her cheeks burned.

Straightening himself, Bane replied, "Oh— how so?"

Without thinking, Leia said, "You've managed to get better looking."

Bane laughed as his hand found Leia's. He tugged her closer to his body. "You are as beautiful as always." He hugged her.

Leia hugged him back then broke their embrace. Thoughts of Derek drifted away. Maybe tonight wasn't going to be so bad after all? Pulling the door closed behind her, Leia replied, "But not beautiful enough to keep you from fleeing to Idaho."

Wagging a finger at her, Bane replied, "I can see you're as sassy as always."

Her chin jutted. Leia said, "I'm not *sassy*."

"Yeah, you are." Bane shoved his hands into the pockets of his shorts. "But I always liked that part of you, and still do."

Rolling her eyes, Leia waved her hand. "Come on. Let's go get this dinner over with. From the way my mom phrased it, she had to arm wrestle you to attend."

They walked down the path weaving from her apartment to her parents' house. For a few moments, they walked in silence. Leia made sure to leave plenty of space between them to keep their arms from grazing each other. Her parents' house came into view.

"For the record—" Bane glanced from her parents' house to her. "I should've never moved to Idaho."

"It was like fifteen years ago," said Leia dismissively. "I'm completely over it. But why are you back? Did you not like living in Idaho?"

Bane pulled his hands out of his pockets, glancing down at his feet. "I didn't like it, and the snow was awful." He peeled his gaze from his feet to her, boldly meeting her eyes. "I should've never left Hawaii. I've missed this place every day since I've been gone. I've missed you, Leia."

The rhythmic crashing of the waves on the shore filled the silence. Fiddling with her hair, Leia stammered, "I— I—" as she tried to think of a good response.

"Leia! Bane!" Teresa yelled. Leaning over the railing of the lanai, Teresa craned her neck toward them. Spotting them, Teresa waved them over. "Come on. The food's getting cold."

Bane motioned for Leia to go first. Leia brushed past him, moving toward the stairs leading up to the front lanai. The outside world dimmed, and only the thundering of her temples let her know this wasn't a dream. This was happening, and she had no clue what any of it meant.

CHAPTER 15

The call ended. Derek shoved the phone into his pocket. Stomping into his bedroom, he swung open his closet and ripped three shirts off their hangers and tossed them onto his bed. If he was smart, he'd jump on a plane and head back to Oahu tonight instead of his scheduled flight to Boston. Boston, which would make the time difference with Leia an entire six hours. The gap between them was growing wider by the day.

His pocket buzzed. Without thinking, he clicked accept and answered, "What?" he half-yelled.

"Geez, Derek," answered Tyson. "You sound ready to bite my head off—which seems to have become the norm these days."

Running his free hand down the length of his face, Derek took a deep, settling breath. "I'm sorry." His shoulders dropped, loosening the pinch between his shoulder blades. "Any particular reason you're calling?" Derek reached back into his closet and pulled two button-up shirts off their hangers, throwing them on the bed too. "I'm packing."

"Is that what's causing you to be cranky? A little packing?" countered Tyson.

"I'm sick of traveling every week," muttered Derek.

"Since when? You're the one who has always volunteered to go, even when I've offered to go in your place," said Tyson.

On his knees, Derek peered under his bed and patted around until his fingers hooked onto his rolling carry-on suitcase. He placed it on his bed. "I've changed my mind. I have no life outside of work, making every one of my relationships doomed from the beginning. Heather and I are a perfect example of this." He unzipped his suitcase with his free hand.

"You told me you're over Heather," replied Tyson.

"I am." Derek placed his phone in the crook of his neck, picking up his shirt to fold it neatly. "This isn't specifically about Heather. It's the fact I have zero chance of being with anyone real if I don't slow down for a bit, stay off the road, and finally set down some roots."

"I thought you bought your house last year. Isn't that some roots?" asked Tyson.

Sighing, Derek picked up his button-down, folding it and placing it inside of his suitcase. "It's a start, but I know it's not enough." He picked up his next shirt and folded it. "After this trip to Boston, I want you to fly to the next place. We're going to have to start trading off the travel or I don't see this arrangement working for me anymore." His shoulders drooped, and Derek sat down on the edge of his bed, pinching the bridge of his nose.

"Umm, let's back up a second. We have no investment company without you. I've been working with you since we graduated from college. We'll figure something out. I'll travel more or we can hire another person. If we need to so you can take on more remote work." Tyson paused, "You're my best friend, and I want you to be happy."

"I wish I knew what would make me happy," replied Derek. "But it isn't this. I'm miserable."

Derek tried to remember the last time he felt happy.

It was back in Hawaii with Leia.

"Go to Boston. When you get back, we'll figure something out," stated Tyson.

Derek wadded up his T-shirt and threw it into his suitcase. "I'll call you after I meet with the potential clients." Then Derek said goodbye and ended the call.

After Derek finished packing up his suitcase, he tried not to think about Leia getting all cozy with her ex-flame. It proved to be incredibly difficult. With the tenth glance at his phone, Derek forced himself to turn his phone off to avoid the temptation to text Leia and find out how the evening was going. Leia deserved to be happy, even if it was with some other guy. He was relieved at least that she had finally picked up her phone after ignoring him for a month.

With nothing left to do, Derek shoved his phone into his pocket and left for the airport.

Before boarding, Derek turned back on his phone in hopes a string of unanswered text messages would pop up. Nothing. Right before taking off, Derek shot Leia a text message.

> Leia I'm headed to Boston. My phone will be off for the next several hours. I hope you had a nice evening with Bane.

After staring at his phone screen, Derek watched the message change from delivered to read. The three little cursor dots danced below his message. Shifting, Derek waited for Leia to text him back. As the dots danced, Derek buckled his seat belt and readjusted his messenger bag under the seat in front of him.

The dancing dots continued to dance. Derek wondered if he should send another message. But the dots stopped dancing, and Leia didn't respond. His chest pinched tight. Over the loudspeaker, the flight attendant announced electronic devices needed to be switched to airplane mode.

Quickly, Derek's fingers zipped across the screen.

I have to turn my phone off. I'll talk to you later.

He hit send then tapped the button to turn the wifi to airplane mode.

Then Derek spent the next six hours worrying about Leia kissing some guy, reigniting a flame that apparently had never died. By the time he landed in Boston, Derek was practically batty. With jetlag, sleep deprivation and full-on love sickness, Derek was a mess. Because a fifteen-minute conversation with Leia, confirmed what he already knew; he wanted Leia, but he had no clue how to make her his.

Once they landed and the flight attendant instructed them, they were allowed to unbuckle their seatbelts and take their phones off airplane mode, Derek immediately flipped his phone off the airplane mode. It took a few seconds for it to reconnect to his network. Sometimes there was a lag when it came with text messages coming through, but after a full five minutes, Derek knew his phone remaining silent wasn't a mistake. What had he expected? A simple phone conversation and then—bam— everything would be back to how it was?

Rubbing the back of his neck, Derek contemplated texting Leia again, but then he remembered though it was morning in Boston, it was the middle of the night in Hawaii. He cranked his neck both directions, loosening the tension building in his shoulder blades. The rows in front of him had almost completely exited the plane, so Derek shoved his phone into his pocket and fetched his messenger bag from between his feet and carry-on from the overhead bin.

As Derek exited the plane and walked through the airport, his mind was a muddled mess. His client had promised to send an employee to the airport to pick him up. Derek didn't have a checked bag, but he walked toward baggage claim to where drivers held up signs for airport pickups. Scanning the signs,

Derek spotted his name. He strode toward the middle-aged man with salt and pepper hair.

Once in front of him, Derek stopped and said, "I'm Derek."

Smiling, the man folded the paper, shoving it into his pocket. Holding out his hand, he said, "I'm Steven. I know I said I would send an employee, but I decided to pick you up myself."

Adjusting his slipping messenger bag on his shoulder, Derek shook Steven's hand. "It's nice to meet you."

Steven half turned, waving Derek on. "Follow me. I'm parked in the lot." They walked toward the exit. "We'll go straight to the office. We are located right off the red line, so you should have no trouble getting to your hotel on your own this evening."

"Excellent. I appreciate it," replied Derek.

They wandered around the groups of people filling up the area, trying to find the best way out of the airport.

Glancing over his shoulder, Steven said, "Are you ready to learn about a cranberry factory?"

"I sure am. My last client owned a farm in Hawaii—fruit. I was out there a month or so ago. So, cranberries will be right up my alley," replied Derek.

Steven scoffed, "You had to go from a tropical paradise to here?" Shaking his head, Steven continued, "Last night, with the wind chill, the temperature here dropped below freezing."

As if on cue, the sliding glass doors to the outside swung open. Though they were several yards from the exit, Derek shivered. Icy air nipped at his skin. Glancing down at his pants and long sleeve shirt, Derek said, "I think I need to pull out my coat from my carry-on. For some reason, I didn't think fall weather here would be this cold."

Laughing, Steven paused. "I told you. It's bone chilling. I'm sorry you aren't in Hawaii."

Unzipping his carry-on, Derek pulled out the jacket he had shoved on the top. "Me too." He pushed his arm into his less than adequate jacket. His body shook from the cold penetrating air.

His body competed against the impending doom of the outside. "I don't think this jacket is going to be enough."

"It won't be." Steven watched Derek zip his suitcase closed. "But luckily, I've an entire closet full of jackets. I'll let you borrow one while you're here."

"I'd appreciate it." Derek zipped his windbreaker up to his chin. He readjusted his messenger bag and tightened his grip around his suitcase. "I don't have much use for thick coats. I live in Los Angeles."

A knowing look crossed Steven's face and he added, "And you spend your free time in tropical climates like Hawaii. I see."

"Yes, in fact, I'm thinking about moving to Hawaii," said Derek.

The words slipped right out of his mouth with no ability to pull them back. They came as no surprise to him, because the idea had been brewing in his mind since he left Hawaii last month. There wasn't any reason he couldn't relocate to Hawaii and make that his home base. Sure, the flights to the states would be expensive and longer, but Derek didn't care. Leia was in Hawaii. And sometimes you rewrote your entire life for the chance to be with someone.

"Hawaii, huh," said Steven. They walked through the sliding doors, fighting their way against the cold. "Come on. Let's get to the office so we can talk about how to make these cranberry bogs better."

CHAPTER 16

Leia's phone vibrated in her pocket right as dinner was winding down. Bane leaned in close as her phone vibrated again, and Bane whispered, "Aren't you going to check that?" His gaze went to her pocket.

Tilting her head toward him, Leia met his gaze. "I know who it's from." She tugged her phone out of her pocket.

"I'm intrigued." Bane raised an eyebrow. His glance skidded across her face, studying her. "And who is this person you don't want to answer?"

Shaking her head, Leia peered down at her phone, tapping on the message from Derek. Two messages to be exact. Her finger lingered over the response box. The cursor line blinking back at her. "It's from—" She looked up at Bane. "A guy. We—" biting her bottom lip, she continued, "but he lives in Los Angeles." The reality of their nonexistent relationship made Leia close her screen, shoving her phone back into her pocket.

Derek lived in Los Angeles. And not here. Now a hot, good-looking Bane was beside her. It was time for her to lean into what the universe was throwing her way.

Running a single finger in a circle on the top of his glass, Bane asked, "But if he didn't, you'd be together?"

Shrugging, Leia reached for her glass, taking a sip. "Perhaps. Who knows?" She glanced out at the others at the table.

Teresa rose, "Dessert anyone?" she asked, ending their exchange.

"Here let me help you, Mom." Leia sprung from her seat.

"Can you find the dessert plates and forks for me?" Teresa pointed to the top cupboard. "I made chocolate kahlua pie."

"Please don't tell me you're joking." Bane shifted in his seat, leaning forward, he rested his forearms on the table. "Did you remember it was my favorite?" asked Bane.

Grinning, Teresa opened the fridge. "I sure did." Taking the pie out, Teresa popped her hip against the fridge door to close it. "I made it especially for you."

"Thanks." Bane waved a hand. "It was completely unnecessary but thank you."

"You don't say." Leia rolled her eyes. "Since when did you remember Bane's favorite dessert?" Walking to the table with a handful of forks and a stack of plates, Leia set them down on the table.

Moving back to the table with the pie in her hands, Teresa added, "Since, Mila told me when I texted her." Teresa set the pie down and walked back to the kitchen counter, selecting a knife from the wood block.

Mila laughed. "True story. Teresa texted me this afternoon asking what Bane would like to eat."

Slipping back into her chair, Leia didn't realize the extent of Teresa's scheming until now. While Bane and Leia dated, Teresa had been lukewarm toward him, but now Teresa was singing a different tune. What gives?

Derek.

"Maybe you really made it for Dad," said Leia. Leia reached

out, giving Noa's shoulder a squeeze. Then she turned toward Bane. "No offense, but I think she's lying. Chocolate kahlua pie happens to be my dad's favorite too. I think it was a happy coincidence."

Bane smirked. "Does it really matter?" He winked.

"It does to me," muttered Leia under her breath.

Teresa slapped the first slice of pie onto a plate and held it out to Bane. "Here you go." Teresa shot Leia a warning look. Squirming in her seat, Leia straightened her back. Putting the next slice of pie on a plate, Teresa held it out to Mila. "Bane why don't you tell us about how you came to your senses and moved back to Oahu, permanently."

With a shrug, Bane said, "What's to say? I made a mistake. I moved to Idaho. While I was there, I met my ex-wife. She was from there …" Teresa cut a slice of pie for Leia, Noa, and herself. Once everyone was served, Leia passed everyone a fork and they started to eat. "It didn't work out. I decided I hated the cold, and nothing was keeping me in Idaho, so I moved back." He shrugged, cutting into his piece of pie, taking a bite.

Shaking a fork at Leia, Teresa said, "I bet you regret leaving this one."

"*Mom*," hissed Leia. Shaking her head, Leia cast her gaze at her dessert. "You've got to be kidding me," she muttered under her breath.

Bane laughed. "I have a lot of regrets, unfortunately." Under the table, Bane tapped his knee against hers. "Leaving Leia for Idaho is at the top of my list."

Cheeks burning, Leia said, "You don't have to say that." Forcing herself to cut into her pie, Leia shoveled a bite into her mouth.

"I know," replied Bane. Leia stole a glance in his direction. Locking eyes with her, Bane said, "I wanted to." Without looking away, Bane took another bite of his pie.

Dang. Her nerve endings tingled. Was Bane always this smooth? This confident? But then Leia remembered he left her high and dry, and she cried for a month over his rejection.

Smugly, Teresa wiggled in her chair triumphantly.

They finished eating their pie in silence. Once done, Teresa insisted Bane and Leia go sit out on the lanai while Mila and she did the dishes to catch up.

After they settled into side-by-side wingback chairs, Leia and Bane stared out at the serenely perfect view of the ocean.

Itching to end the million questions whirling around in her mind, Leia leaned on her armrest, cradling her chin. "Bane, tell me what really happened with your ex-wife."

Shifting a bit, Bane brought his leg up, resting his ankle on his opposite knee. "I could always count on you to not beat around the bush." Turning his face from the view to Leia, Bane met her gaze.

"I know. You always told me how much you liked that about me." Leia gathered her hair and swept it over one shoulder. "But enough with the compliments, I must know, what happened."

"You mean after I skipped town and didn't even dignify you with a conversation before I left?" Bane raised an eyebrow. "I'm sorry about that. It was such a chicken way to leave. I completely regret it."

Waving him off, Leia said, "We agree, you were an idiot."

Bane burst out laughing. "Finally, we can agree on something."

"You're avoiding the question." Leia tapped the top of her armrest with her fingertips. "Why did you and your wife get a divorce?"

"Because I never got over you." Bane threw up both his hands. "Obviously."

Leia tsked, "Again, avoiding the question."

"I know," said Bane. He ran his finger around in a circle on top of his armrest. Exhaling, he continued, "She decided she didn't want kids even though when we married, she told me she did. I thought I could live with it, but it ended up tearing us apart. I tried for a lot of years to come to terms with what I wanted and she wanted would never line up. Finally, after years of fighting, we decided it was best to part ways with one another. We divorced. She stayed in Idaho, and I moved back here."

With no eloquent words to say, Leia simply said, "Wow. Okay then." Nodding, Leia turned back to peering out at the view. "I can't believe you ever left this place."

"I know," Bane exhaled, "again, being an idiot comes into play here."

The sun sank lower, hovering on the edge of the water. Taking a deep breath, Leia drank in the tangy saltwater air as memories of those years in college with Bane came roaring back. He had broken her heart when he left her for Idaho with zero explanation. Today with the softening lens of time, Leia no longer felt the same way. Everything happened for a reason, and the life experiences Bane had in Idaho were part of his story.

"It sure does." Pointing out to the ocean, Leia raised an eyebrow. "How could you ever leave a view like this?"

Bane shifted toward her, making his shoulder touch hers. "I won't ever leave it again." He made a cross motion over his heart. "Promise."

Honestly, it didn't matter to Leia either way. Their relationship ended for a reason.

"Okay, so you say you're staying in Hawaii," Leia scooted an inch away from him. "I think our relationship ran its course. You ditched me for *Idaho*." She raised an eyebrow and shot him a pointed look. "Idaho."

"I'm different now," replied Bane. "I'm not the rash decision maker I once was. And I wouldn't hurt you again."

"Ahh." Leia tsked. "People don't change … not that much."

"I disagree. You've changed. Teresa told me you run

marathons now. You always refused to go running with me when we dated," said Bane.

Blue turned to black, the sky painted a canopy of stars. Leia stared up at them. "That's completely different. Becoming interested in a certain type of exercise is vastly different than changing one's entire decision-making process," said Leia.

Crossing his arms, Bane replied, "Idaho taught me a lot of things. My failed marriage even more. I'm different now. Promise."

Leia pulled her gaze from the twinkling diamond stars to Bane. "I know you're looking for something Bane, but it's not me. You don't know how much I wish it was, but it's not."

Forming his hands into fists, Bane lightly tapped both his armrests with his fisted hands. "Because you've got your guy in Los Angeles?" asked Bane.

A big exhale made Leia slouch. "Unfortunately, he might be part of it, but even if he wasn't part of the equation," she wagged a finger between them, "we will never be."

"Teresa says he isn't coming back. The California guy," countered Bane.

Leia wanted to argue with him, but she had no snappy response. "I hope there is a way for us to be together." Speaking the words out loud, to another person, made them even more real. Tilting her head toward him, Leia said, "I'm holding out for it. Idiotic, probably, but I've got to at least try. Especially, now that I'm over being mad at him."

"Why were you mad at him? Was it because he left you?" asked Bane.

Waving him off, Leia replied, "That's part of it, but there was more to it than that."

Leia wasn't about to reveal the entire reason Derek came to Hawaii in the first place.

"Then I hope you figure it out. I hope you can have a happy life," said Bane.

"I do have a happy life," replied Leia.

Tipping his head closer, Bane replied, "I know, but one where you can share it with someone, because I hope to find that too."

Then they both shifted away from each other, staring out at the glistening moon reflecting a big circle on the ocean waves. Leia wished Derek was there sharing this moment with her, and not Bane.

CHAPTER 17

Derek pulled his borrowed coat tight against his body, crossing his arms. He tried not to shiver as Steven cranked up the heat in his luxury sedan. Yesterday, Derek had met with Steven and the rest of his employees in the office in downtown Boston. But today, he was headed with Steven out to the cranberry bog on Cape Cod.

Rubbing his hands together, Derek attempted to get some feeling back into his fingertips. "How often do you visit the cranberry bog to check in with the employees there?"

After their car pulled out of the parking garage, Steven turned onto the street. "I try to visit twice a month. During the harvest season, I stay up there in my cottage on the weekends."

"I see," replied Derek. After reviewing the business records, Derek believed they simply needed investment money to upgrade their equipment to maintain efficiency. Equipment was expensive, but Derek believed they could come up with a deal that would ensure the business received the equipment they needed while giving Derek and Tyson a nice return on their investment. "I'll hold my feedback until after I take a tour of the cranberry bog acreage."

"I'm sure you'll have plenty to say." Steven entered the interstate. "When I took over as CEO, I made a lot of changes too. But it wasn't enough. The family who owns the business has very particular opinions on how things are done." This wasn't news to Derek. He had done his research. From the articles he read online, Steven was named CEO three years ago, though he wasn't related to the people who owned the cranberry bog. Steven shrugged, gripping the steering wheel with both hands. "But maybe they'll listen to you."

Staring out the windshield, Derek remarked on how the Boston interstate could challenge any freeway in Los Angeles. "I think they won't have a choice. If they don't upgrade their equipment, they'll only continue to waste time and money on the inefficiency." Steven swerved across three lanes of traffic without pausing. Derek gripped the handle above his door. "Are you trying to get us killed?" Turning wide-eyed to face Steven, his heartbeat rapidly increased.

Steven chuckled and replied, "Is this the first time you've driven anywhere in Boston?"

"I've been here before, but I've always stuck to public transportation. This is something else," said Derek.

"I promise, this is how everyone drives." Steven honked loudly at a car who cut him off. "You're getting the real Boston experience, but I'll make sure we get there and back safely," said Steven.

Steven then changed lanes, holding down his horn again. Derek flinched from the sound and prayed he made it to the Cape in one piece. His phone vibrated in his pocket, temporarily distracting him from his fear of crashing on the interstate. Pulling it out of his pocket, a message from Leia flashed across his screen.

Any interest in running the Honolulu marathon with me? You still have time to train.

A smile slowly grew across his face. Derek shifted in his seat. Scratching his head, he wondered if he really had the ability to get himself in shape in the limited time he had before the marathon. Either way, he didn't care. He'd walk the thing if it meant Leia was inviting him to visit. Swiftly, his fingers moved across his phone.

> One hundred percent. I'll be there.

> I'll send you a running schedule. You only have eight weeks, which isn't ideal, but I still think you can do it.

> You underestimate my natural athleticism. I'm up to running ten miles. I know I can do it.

> Just like your surfing.

> I would smugly challenge you, but I know you're a way better runner than me.

> Say that again … for those in the back.

> LEIA IS A BETTER RUNNER THAN ME.

> See that wasn't so hard.

> Not hard at all. Oh … whoops I just remembered I said I'd run a marathon in eight weeks.

> That you did. Call me tonight. I want to talk.

> I will. Bye.

With a wistful sigh, Derek slid his phone back into his pocket.

Steven gave him a sideways glance. "Was that your significant other? I've been around too long to know that wasn't a business message."

"It's someone I'm hopeful about," replied Derek. Then as a second thought, he continued, "But she lives in Hawaii."

"And you live in Los Angeles," added Steven. Derek gave a quick nod but didn't say anything else. After a few seconds, Steven added, "and your job requires you to travel a lot."

The traffic eased as they drove further from Boston toward the Cape. Derek's shoulders loosened a tad. "I know. It's not exactly a big selling feature when it comes to trying to convince a woman to be in a relationship with me," replied Derek.

"I see ..." Steven changed lanes then put the car on cruise control. "I don't know much about love. I was married once. It didn't stick. But if I found someone who I clicked with again, I'd do things differently. I'd find a way to make it work."

Staring out the passenger window, Derek watched as they buzzed past beautiful foliage. Trees painted with the brightest colors of fall; orange, red and yellow, lined both sides of the interstate.

"Ok," said Derek.

Derek had zero interest in getting personal with a guy he barely met. So, Derek changed the subject back to business, asking additional questions about the processing part of the cranberries. The subject of him and his relationship troubles was dropped.

Later in the evening, after the tour of the cranberry bogs and farm, Derek returned to his hotel room exhausted and depleted. Loneliness enveloped him, as he set down his take-out meal on the small desk. With the time difference, Derek knew Leia was at her teaching job. He couldn't call her for at least a few more hours.

Instead, he decided to call Tyson to go over his assessment of the cranberry business.

Tyson picked up on the third ring. "Hey, Derek." He didn't pause but hurried forward. "I'm looking at the assessment you emailed over. This is looking good and pointing toward a sound investment for the company."

Putting his phone in the crook of his neck, Derek pulled out his to-go pasta from the bag. "I think this is a straightforward investment, and we should be able to see a quick return. I believe you'll find the same thing after going over the numbers I sent you." Derek sat down at the desk in his hotel room.

"I agree, and I'm glad we're on the same page. You shouldn't have to stay much longer. I bet you could finish up the loose ends tomorrow. I'll have the contract drafted up and sent over to you tonight," said Tyson.

"Excellent." Derek rubbed the back of his neck. "I don't want to stay in Boston any longer than I need to."

"So, about what we discussed earlier about your traveling—" said Tyson.

"I want to relocate to Hawaii," Derek sputtered out. "There's nothing holding me in Los Angeles anymore. I need a change."

"But you have a home in Los Angeles. You only bought it a few years ago," replied Tyson.

"I know, and I'm not going to sell it right now. I think I'll rent it out, and I'll find a furnished apartment to rent in Hawaii. Maybe something that is a short-term lease," said Derek.

As the words spilled out of him, Derek's back straightened. He had a plan. One which got him closer to Leia, without completely throwing away everything he'd built. If things didn't work out with Leia, he could always return to Los Angeles in a few months, and he'd still have his home waiting for him.

"That's a huge move. Are you sure you've thought this thing through? Last I knew, Leia wasn't even talking to you." asked Tyson.

"She just asked me today to run the Honolulu marathon with her. So, no I don't think this is one sided," said Derek.

"But a marathon where you go visit for the weekend is very different from you rewriting your entire life to move there," said Tyson.

"I know, but Tyson you have a family. You have a wife and kids. We live twenty minutes away from each other, and we used to work together in person all the time, now we never see each other. I'm grateful for the upgrades in technology that allow us to meet over video conferencing, and it's time I took more advantage of it. This is my chance to possibly be in a relationship, so I must try. If I don't, I believe it will be the biggest regret of my life," said Derek.

"If this is your chance, then you've got to take it. You've my support," said Tyson. He cleared his throat. "I mean don't get me wrong, I think you've completely lost it. But I understand why you want to take a risk. The heart wants what it wants. I know that was how it was with me and my wife."

"Thanks, Tyson," said Derek.

"Okay, we'll talk soon," said Tyson.

Derek ended the call. His shoulders instantly felt lighter than before. He had a plan, one which would allow Leia and him the needed time to see if this thing between them could work.

CHAPTER 18

Early in the morning, Leia exited her apartment, hiking up her purse on her shoulder. Leia calculated the time difference between her and Derek. If she texted him when she arrived at school, he should be available. Leia walked past her parents' house toward her car. Up on the lanai sat Noa in one of the wingback chairs, Leia waved, wondering if Teresa was outside or inside.

On the far side of the front yard, Leia saw Teresa pulling weeds. Leia approached her and asked, "Mom, why are you out here so early?" Leia peered from Teresa to the ocean. Slowly, the sun inched upward, warming her body.

Teresa stood with a bunch of weeds in her hands. "Noa couldn't sleep, and I was sick of trying to sleep myself. So, we watched the sunrise together. Then I decided to get to these weeds before I head inside to make some breakfast." Without glancing at her, Teresa took her handful over to a big pile, Teresa tossed the ones in her hands on top. Teresa brushed past Leia, returning to her original spot.

Her icy demeanor wasn't lost on Leia. She chose to ignore it. The sunlight blinded her, Leia dug around in her purse until she found her sunglasses and put them on. "I'm off. I need to get to work a little bit earlier to run off some copies before the bell rings."

The smell of manure tickled Leia's nose. Back on her knees, Teresa aggressively yanked out another weed. "Mila said she and Bane had a nice time the other night …" Teresa's voice drifted off. She tossed the weed she pulled into the pile. "But she said you told Bane there wasn't anything left between you both."

Leia pinched the bridge of her nose. "I can see you've been busy," replied Leia.

"No, Mila texted me on her own. I think she had as high hopes for you two rekindling your old flame, as I did," said Teresa.

"I'm sorry," Leia fidgeted with her purse, finally pulling out her keys. She continued, "to disappoint you."

Out popped another stalk, Teresa moved onto the next one. "I hope Derek's worth it." She didn't look back at Leia, but instead kept her gaze on her flower bed.

"He's worth it," said Leia.

With an edge, Teresa stated, "But he lives in Los Angeles, Leia. I think Derek is a nice guy, but …" aggressively Teresa used both her hands to tackle a deep-rooted weed, "you live here. How will you ever be together?"

Defensively, Leia squared her shoulders, Leia said, "He's going to run the Honolulu marathon with me."

The weed in Teresa's hands dropped back into the overturned dirt. Teresa leaned back on her heels. "Then what?" She used the back of her wrist to swipe at the sweat glistening on her brow. A pointed glance over Teresa's shoulder made Leia cower for a second. "So, he comes for a weekend. It doesn't change anything."

"It could change everything," said Leia.

Leia wanted to go on, laying out her carefully crafted reasoning, but she didn't have anything to back up her presumption that Derek returning could fix their insurmountable distance.

Clearly exasperated, Teresa wiped her dirty hands on her jogger pants and asked, "How?"

Leia tossed up a hand, making her keys jangle. "It just will. I need to go. I don't want to talk to you about Derek anymore, so please don't bring it up. If I have something to share, then I will."

"It's your life," muttered Teresa.

"It is," said Leia, forcing herself to keep her voice even and undeterred. "I'll see you later." Leia waved at Noa then turned and walked the remaining distance to her car.

Her stomach soured as she swung open her car door. Was Leia wasting time on Derek? She climbed inside, tossing her purse on the empty seat. Maybe. Did she care? Not currently. With a swirling mess of thoughts, Leia drove to work.

Luckily, with her teaching job, Leia's day sped by without much time to dwell on things out of her control. After locking up her classroom, Leia finally dug out her phone from her purse to call Derek. Readjusting her purse, Leia pulled up Derek's number and hit call, placing the phone to her ear.

Derek picked up on the second ring. "Leia," he said breathlessly.

Walking toward the school parking lot, Leia asked, "Are you okay? You sound like you're working out."

Laughing, Derek replied, "I am. I decided to start my marathon training. Right now, I'm running through Boston Common. With the time change, I couldn't drag myself out of bed this morning, so I decided to run at night instead. Luckily, I have my earbuds in so we can keep talking."

A co-worker passed. Leia waved but didn't stop talking. She continued, "Are you sure you can run and talk?" asked Leia.

"No," chuckled Derek. "But it's freezing here. If I stop running, I'll no longer be able to feel my fingers or toes. Plus, I have a long way to go with such a tight schedule I need to be running fourteen miles by next week. Then I'll add two miles a week till I reach twenty."

"And to think only a brief time ago you could barely run three to four miles. I'm impressed. Maybe you are more athletic than I thought," said Leia.

"Are you complimenting me?" asked Derek.

Smiling, Leia arrived at her car. "I believe I am." She opened her car door and climbed inside.

"I knew it," said Derek. Leia could hear him smiling on the other end. Clearing his throat, Derek continued, "I'll be back in Los Angeles in the next day or two. Then the time difference will be back to only three hours apart."

Exhaling, Leia gripped the steering wheel with her free hand. "Only three hours. It still feels too far for me." A long pause on the other side of the phone made Leia double check the connection. "Are you still there?"

"I'm here," said Derek. "I'm trying to get closer to you, Leia. Please just hold out a little longer until I sort everything out. I'll try to stay longer than a few days for the marathon."

"Could you stay until Christmas? The marathon is on December 10. I know that's two more weeks, but I'd love for you to be here. My whole big extended family gets together at Kama on Christmas Eve. My uncle and a few of my cousins play songs on their ukuleles, and we sing Christmas songs together after a big feast," said Leia.

"I can't remember the last time I celebrated Christmas with anyone," replied Derek. "I'll see what I can do. I'd love to spend Christmas with you and your family. Thank you for the invitation."

"Kai should have the farm tours working smoothly by then, too." Leia couldn't hide the pleasure from her voice. "I think you'll be pleased with what he's done."

"I'm sure," said Derek. "I'm glad he's found a way to keep the farm up and running."

Leia bit her tongue, she wanted to tell Derek she knew about his investment in the farm. But for whatever reason, Derek didn't want Leia to know so she chose to respect his decision instead of trying to over-analyze it.

Instead, Leia asked, "So, you'll do it? You'll stay for Christmas?"

"Let me check with Tyson, and I'll let you know as soon as I can," said Derek.

A tapping at her car window interrupted their conversation. Leia saw her co-worker on the other side of her car door. "I need to run. A co-worker needs to speak to me. I'll talk to you soon," said Leia.

With real hope, Leia ended the call with Derek, rolling down her window.

CHAPTER 19

Derek placed some old knick-knacks into a box. Glancing around his home, Derek reassessed what he was placing in storage and what would stay. He was able to find a nice couple who were in Los Angeles for six months on a work assignment to rent his home, furnished. This made things way easier for him because it only required him to sort through the junk in his closets to determine what he needed to throw away, take with him, or place in storage.

His back pocket buzzed. Derek pushed his hand into it and took out his phone. The screen flashed Leia's name. With a smile, Derek clicked accept and placed it at his ear. "Hey, Leia." Derek snatched the packing tape with one hand and placed the phone in the crook of his neck.

"Hi, Derek. I was calling to see if you were able to get your last long run in?" asked Leia.

After he tugged a piece of tape loose from the dispenser, Derek pulled it across the top of the box and taped it closed. "I sure did. I can't believe the marathon is in two weeks." He sat down on the edge of the bed. "I have no idea how I'll run 26.2 miles when the longest I've run is twenty."

Over the last six weeks, Derek's feelings for Leia had only deepened. He looked forward each night to ending his day talking with her over the phone. The separation only proved to reinforce his need to be closer to her, and Derek believed Leia felt the same way.

"That's where the adrenaline of the race kicks in and carries you those extra miles," replied Leia.

Scratching his chin, Derek said, "Is that how it works?" He flopped backwards onto his bed, relaxing.

Leia wasn't aware Derek was going to stay way longer than the extra two weeks they had planned after the marathon. He hoped the entire thing didn't blow up in his face. Derek wasn't known for taking many risks for love. Packing up his entire life to move to Hawaii was certainly a huge leap of faith. He'd know soon enough if it was the right choice or not.

"Yes, trust me. This isn't my first rodeo," said Leia.

"How many marathons will this be for you?" asked Derek.

"Umm …" Leia paused. "I'm not sure. I lost count after twenty. Remember?"

"That's right." Eyes glued to the ceiling, Derek his arm behind his neck. "I'll be thrilled to only complete this one. I'm sure I'll come in hours after you. How long do I have again to run it?"

"Honolulu Marathon doesn't have any cut off time. It's one of the only world-class marathons where every runner gets to finish, so no excuses," said Leia.

"I guess you're right." Derek sat up and swung his legs over the side of the bed. "I must finish." He paused for a second. "Are you sure you're still okay picking me up from the airport?"

"*Derek*," said Leia. "I'm counting down the minutes until we can be together. Of course I'm picking you up from the airport. Then we can eat lunch again at Aria and Kalon's food truck."

With a smile, Derek said, "I can't wait either."

"And I'm taking you surfing again, too," said Leia.

"So, you can prove you are better than me at that, as well?" asked Derek.

"No," said Leia. "Because that's when I knew I couldn't deny whatever was building between us. We can go back to the same beach."

"After the marathon, right?" asked Derek.

"Of course, I'll let you recover for a few days before I make you do anything too strenuous," replied Leia.

"Then it's a plan," said Derek.

After parking the car, Leia walked to the baggage claim area. Derek said since he was staying for over two weeks, plus Christmas gifts, he had checked some extra bags. Wringing her hands together, Leia's stomach churned on itself. It was only Derek, but so much time had passed since she last laid eyes on him, part of her wondered if they'd fall back in sync or be off from one another forever.

Sweaty palms were no good, Leia had no choice but to wipe them on the sides of her dress. Leia forced herself to walk to the arrival screens to find out if Derek's airplane had landed. Eventually, she spotted his flight number. It indicated Derek's flight was at the gate. Smoothing the front of her dress, Leia paced the small area in front of the exit. She wondered what the proper way was to greet Derek. Did she hug him? Kiss him? Had their time apart created awkwardness between them?

Her insides tossed and turned; the waiting was doing funky things to her. Finally, the sliding doors opened and out walked Derek. Leia ducked and dived around the others gathering to wait for their own family and friends.

Waving, Leia bellowed, "Derek!"

Their eyes locked.

BOOM.

And Leia knew she was in love.

The love that made you put everything on the line, the love that only made sense to the two of you and nobody else, that kind of love.

"Derek," repeated Leia, in a quieter voice with a lot more shake.

When only a few paces remained between them, Derek dropped his bag down by his feet. Leia leaped into his open arms.

"Leia!" exclaimed Derek. He spun her around, making Leia giggle. Finally, Derek stopped. Leia's toes touched the ground again. Her hands traced the length of his chest eventually wrapping around his waist. Derek mirrored her movements, embracing her in a tight hug. "You're so beautiful," Derek whispered into her hair.

His words tickled her neck, sending goosebumps down her spine.

Smiling, Leia tilted her chin up toward him, meeting his gaze. "It's *so* good to see you," said Leia.

Taking a single finger, Derek weaved it through her hair, pushing it over her shoulder. Clearing his throat, Derek said, "I feel precisely the same way."

For a moment, in the middle of the airport lobby, it was only them. The world around them grew dimmer, making everything silent except for the steady beating of Leia's heart. In the here and now, it was only them, and Leia knew Derek was everything she ever wanted but never thought she would have.

Giving his middle a squeeze, Leia said, "Just so you know, since you're only here for two weeks, I don't plan on letting you out of my sight."

With a chuckle, Derek said, "I'll gladly comply with your desire." Then his gaze smoldered.

The air sizzled, making a fire rage in her gut. So much was being said through his glance, that the hairs on her arms stood straight up. *Kiss me, kiss me, kiss me,* Leia wanted to scream. But

Derek seemed determined to drag out the heat building between them.

He moistened his lips and continued, "I've waited so long to hold you," He whispered, cupping her neck with one hand. Leia closed her eyes for a second as the heat from his touch warmed her entire body.

With a shaky voice, Leia whispered, "I know."

Opening her eyes, Leia tugged his body against hers. Their hips knocking against each other. Standing up on her tiptoes, she made her lips collide with his. Immediately, Derek tightened his hold around her waist. Leia rested one hand on Derek's chest while the other dove into his hair. His tongue swept her bottom lip, and Leia parted her lips to allow his tongue to plunge inside. Her pulse galloped, making her dizzy and weak at the knees. But Derek supported her weight as she leaned into him to hold her upright.

People parted around them, but neither were aware of the disruption they were creating. Though it was busy and chaotic, Leia didn't notice. The dull ache in her heart, her constant companion for so many years of longing for someone, disappeared in the blink of an eye. With Derek here with her, she knew she'd never be alone again.

Eventually, a scrappy security guard came up beside them and announced loudly, "You two are creating a traffic jam. It's time to move it along."

In a daze, Leia pulled her lips from Derek's. Turning to meet the narrowed gaze staring back at her, Leia said, "Sorry, we'll get going." She dropped her tight grip from Derek's waist. Readjusting her dress, Leia jutted up her chin. "We've just reunited after a very long time apart." She smiled over at Derek.

His hand ran down the length of Leia's arm, and Derek said, "Yes, I don't usually act so inconsiderately."

Eyeing them suspiciously, the security guard said, "Sure you don't." The security guard pointed in the direction of baggage claim. "Please don't forget your luggage."

Interlacing his fingers with Leia's, Derek gave them a squeeze. Straightening his back, Derek said, "We won't. Thank you." He kissed Leia on the temple and spoke into her hair, "let's get out of here."

Twisting, Leia turned in the direction of baggage claim. They walked hand in hand. When they arrived at the baggage claim, only a few lone suitcases remained. Circling around and around, the baggage waited for their owners to claim them. Reluctantly, he let go of her hand. Derek yanked one suitcase off the moving belt, then another, and another. And when Leia thought he couldn't have any more, Derek took a final piece of luggage.

Amused with his unexplainable amount of stuff, Leia pointed at the pile of suitcases next to him. "Are you sure you didn't pack enough to move here?" asked Leia.

Derek's gaze darted away from her. He rubbed the back of his neck. "I— I— guess I did bring a fair number of things," replied Derek. Shrugging, he continued, "What can I say? I couldn't decide on gifts."

Leaning in, Leia kissed Derek on the cheek. "I can't wait to see what you thought was worthy of bringing all the way from Los Angeles." Her hand found one of the roller suitcases, and she continued, "But first things first, you have a marathon you're running tomorrow. After lunch, we need to go pick up our race packets. It has your bib in it."

With a groan, Derek replied, "I can't believe you've convinced me to do this." He took two of the other suitcases, while Leia helped with one more, so they had one in each of their hands.

As they walked toward the sliding glass doors, Leia remarked, "If I remember correctly, you jumped at the chance to run this thing with me."

"I jumped at the opportunity to see you again," corrected Derek.

Leia's cheeks splashed with heat. She glanced away from Derek toward the glass doors. They swung open as they approached them. Sticky humid air trickled in. "I hope you can handle running in this type of humidity," said Leia.

Once through the glass doors, Derek replied, "I'll survive. But I might be the last one crossing the finish line."

She tilted her head in the direction of her car and said, "You won't be alone."

"Ahh." Derek smiled. "No, I guess I won't be alone, because you'll be right there with me."

CHAPTER 20

Running past the twenty-five-mile sign, Derek wondered how he'd manage to continue running for another step, let alone another mile plus. The last five miles had passed in an excruciatingly difficult haze. Without Leia by his side, Derek would have walked the last several miles. But Leia refused to run ahead of him and leave him by himself.

Sweat dripped down his temples as the sun baked his skin, making it practically sizzle under its violent rays. Using the end of his shirt, Derek swiped at the sweat to keep it from dripping into his eyes. "I don't know how much longer I can go on," said Derek.

"Pick a landmark up ahead and tell yourself you only need to run to that specific spot. You can't think about the entire mile that's left, every runner knows that is the kiss of death," replied Leia.

His feet throbbed, neck ached, and his back stung. "Fine." Derek forced himself to look forward and not at the ground. Pointing up ahead, he said, "I pick that lady in the bright pink shirt holding some sort of sign."

Without an ounce of heavy breathing, Leia replied, "I see her. Perfect."

Focused on the lady in pink, Derek somehow managed to run past her.

Once the lady in pink was several paces behind them, Leia said, "Okay, now pick something else."

"Umm." Derek swiped at his brow with the back of his wrist. "I'm running to that grouping of palm trees in the park overlooking the ocean."

They weaved around a few slower runners in front of them, Leia said, "I see it."

Time slowed. Each step seemed to take longer than the one before, but as promised, Derek made it to the bunch of trees.

Leia interrupted his dreary thoughts. "We'll pass by the Waikiki Aquarium soon then we're almost there," said Leia.

His calves seized. "I'm never doing this again," muttered Derek.

Giving a high five to a passerby, Leia said, "That's what I said, too, after my first marathon, but then I ran one more. It was a better experience than the one before. And then I was hooked."

"I'm not hooked, not even close." His throat was scratchy and dry. Derek forced himself to swallow. "I'm regretting every major life choice I've made up until this point."

"But nothing— and I mean nothing beats the feeling of crossing the finish line. You'll see," said Leia.

Passing by the aquarium, the finish line came into view. Derek wiped tears from the corner of his eyes with the heel of his hand. He couldn't remember the last time he cried, but he couldn't hold back the feeling of relief of knowing this pain was nearly over. Then Derek spotted Leia's family. All of them. Every. Single. One. Teresa, Noa in a wheelchair, Kai and Alana with their kids were several yards from the finish line, jumping up and down cheering.

A tug in his heart made Derek long for Leia's family to

become his own. He knew he was taking twelve steps forward with so much ground to cover in the middle, but for a split moment, Derek imagined a world where he was no longer alone. A world where he and Leia, together, could face any obstacle.

The last several yards passed in a somewhat catatonic state, but when his feet crossed the finish line, he was euphoric.

Leia hugged him. "I knew you could do it. Doesn't it feel amazing?" Pulling away, her fingertips dug into his biceps. She searched his face for confirmation.

"It does." With hands on his hips, Derek leaned forward attempting to catch his breath. Gazing up at Leia from his hunched over state, he repeated, "It really does."

Volunteers placed medals over their necks. Then they were pushed along, moving them from the finish line toward the area where runners were reuniting with their families and friends. Someone handed him a bottle of water and an ice cold dripping wet towel. Derek swiped his salty, sweat-streaked face with it, before wrapping it around his neck to cool himself down.

They walked toward the exit of the sectioned off area, or Leia walked, and Derek hobbled along. His legs were tight and sore, and every part of himself ached. Derek wanted to find a grassy area to lie down on and possibly never get up again.

"I think I need to sit down." Derek placed a hand on Leia's shoulder, leaning his weight on her. "I'm not feeling so great."

Glancing over her shoulder, Leia's gaze skidded across his face. "You do look really pale." She slowed her walking pace, Derek leaned on her for support.

Derek gripped his stomach with his other hand. "I think I might vomit."

"There is some space up there." Leia pointed to the exit of the sectioned off area. "You can sit down for a bit."

Bile bubbled up his throat. Derek fought against the urge to vomit. They made it out of the staging area. Leia found a shady grassy area to stop at. Collapsing on the grass, Derek rested flat on his back, closing his eyes for a minute.

Soon Leia's family found them. Their chatter sounded far away. Derek couldn't concentrate long enough to make out what they were saying. Instead, he kept his eyes closed and forced himself to slowly breathe in and out to fight against the wave of nausea that wasn't going away. Eventually, the knot in his stomach loosened a smidge.

Leia knelt beside him and held a water bottle to his lips. "Here sip this. I think it will help."

Forcing his eyes open, Derek took in the view of Leia's entire family towering over him. "Thanks for coming," he croaked. "I know you came mainly for Leia, but it's great to see you."

A water bottle touched his lips. Leia urged him, "Drink. Tiny sips only."

Alana dug into her purse, pulling out a gallon ziploc bag of snacks. "I've ritz crackers. Would that help?"

After taking the water bottle from Leia, Derek took a few sips. Swiping the back of his mouth with the back of his hand, Derek peered up at Alana. "Actually, a few crackers might help settle my stomach."

Derek almost added it was what his mom always fed him when he was sick, ritz crackers and ginger ale.

Alana opened the top of the bag, pulling out the little tube of ritz crackers. "Here." Alana held them out to him.

With a crooked smile, Derek replied, "Thanks." He took a cracker out of the tube and nibbled on one. The salty texture immediately made his nausea lift a tad. "I think it's helping."

A look of relief washed over Leia's face. Glancing up at her family that were still standing, Leia motioned downward. "Sit. My neck is getting sore looking at everyone."

Her family sat around them in a circle on the grass under the shade of the palm trees. Teresa sat down next to Noa's wheelchair. For a few minutes, they sat in silence with everyone's eyes on Derek. Teresa remarked that color had returned to his face as he sipped water and ate crackers.

"I'm feeling much better." Derek forced himself upward and into a standing position. "We can get going."

"Whoa," said Leia, jumping up and wrapping an arm around his waist. "We're in no hurry. Take your time."

"I'd rather collapse face down on my bed than here," said Derek.

Squeezing his waist, Leia said, "I understand. We can head home."

Kai chimed in. "We'll drive you to your car. We were able to snag a spot not far from here."

Everyone rose to their feet too.

Removing her arm from his waist, Leia found Derek's hand. "Thanks, Kai," replied Leia, interlocking her fingers with Derek's. They moved slowly toward Kai's van. Kai and Alana's children ran back and forth due to Derek and Leia's snail speed.

Teresa pushed Noa along in his wheelchair. "So," said Teresa. "Leia says you're staying for Christmas." Her gaze landed on them holding hands.

Derek's back stiffened, adding to his already aching body. "I hope you don't mind me joining everyone for Christmas. Leia told me the entire extended family gets together and one more wouldn't be any trouble," said Derek.

"You're more than welcome to join us for Christmas. The more the merrier," replied Teresa in a flat voice. "But what happens after Christmas? You'll go back to Los Angeles, right?"

Leia interrupted Teresa and hissed, "Mom, enough. I'll discuss this with you later."

Teresa waved her off and gestured toward Derek. "Derek doesn't mind talking about this. Do you?" She raised an eyebrow, throwing a pointed glance at Derek.

"Ahh," stalled Derek.

Derek wanted to lay out his entire plan of staying for more

than Christmas. But as he glanced at Leia's entire family eyeing him suspiciously and waiting for his reply, Derek froze, and his mind went blank. He cowered.

Luckily, Kai announced, "We're here." He clicked the unlocked button on his minivan, making the automatic doors roll open. "Climb in, kids. I want you to take the seats in the back, so Leia and Derek don't have to climb back there with their sore muscles." Kai winked at them.

Teresa kept walking without stopping. Over her shoulder, Teresa said, "We'll see you when we see you, Derek."

Derek didn't have time to think about Teresa's obvious disdain toward him.

Kai fiddled with his kids' seats as Alana walked around to the front seat.

"Bye," said Leia. "Thank you for coming."

Teresa drifted further and further away, clearly not listening, or caring. Kai leaned against the side of the van, waiting for his kids to get into their seats.

Kai addressed Derek and said, "I want to give you a tour of Kama Farm and show you the changes we've made. So much has improved since you were last here."

"I'd love to see what you've done," replied Derek.

With the kids settled in the back, Derek climbed into the van after Leia. Kai swung the door closed. Derek wondered how he could win Teresa over. Maybe once Teresa knew he'd put everything on the line for Leia, she wouldn't be as worried about his intentions. Though every part of Derek ached, he couldn't help but smile as Kai and Alana's kids fought in the back seat on the drive, Hawaiian music danced through the van, and Leia reached for his hand across the aisle giving it a squeeze. His muscles were sore, but his heart was full.

CHAPTER 21

The days after the marathon marched toward Christmas way too fast. Leia dreaded Derek returning to Los Angeles. Living in a fantasy world sure was fun. With each passing day, Leia fell harder and harder for Derek, so hard, she spent most nights in bed plotting out how she and Derek could be together. Leia knew she needed to consider moving from Hawaii, surely she could find another teaching job if she relocated. But Leia didn't know if she could do it, leaving everything behind, her family, culture, home, for the chance to be with Derek. Ahh … what a risk.

Torn in a thousand directions, Leia's hands shook as she pulled on her red dress. In a little bit, she'd head over her to her parents' house for the annual Christmas Eve gathering. Leia's mouth watered as she caught a whiff of the kalua pig roasting deep in the pit behind her parents' house.

Two days.

Derek left in two days.

And then Leia's world would shatter.

Again.

With no resolution, Leia left the safety of her apartment

walking toward her parents' house. Her aunt and uncles had come over earlier and helped her and Derek pull out the folding table and chairs from their garage. They set them up on the grassy area in her parents' front yard. Being outside allowed her entire family to gather, without feeling cramped inside. Luckily, Hawaii's weather made meeting outdoors possible any time of year.

As she rounded the corner, Leia saw many of her family members out on the lawn, mingling. Kale and Kai carried the pig over to the table. Derek sat at a table next to Teresa and Noa. They were deep in conversation. Slowing her pace, Leia's stomach twisted on itself. As she approached, Derek shifted in his chair, catching her gaze. Their eyes locked, smoothing out the skittish feeling in her gut. And she knew she was in love, and Derek belonged. There. With her.

Derek stood and strode a few paces to meet Leia. "Leia, Mele Kalikimaka."

Arriving in front of Derek, Leia smiled and replied, "Mele Kalikimaka." She reached out, giving Derek's hand a squeeze. "I'm glad you're here to spend it with me."

Wrapping an arm around her waist, Derek brought her closer to him. Heat radiated off his skin, and Leia warmed from his touch. "Do you want to come sit by your parents?" asked Derek.

Leia tilted her head close to his and whispered, "Has my mom been behaving?"

Touching his head to hers, Derek quickly kissed Leia on her temple and whispered into her hair, "She has. We had a nice chat, and I think we're now on the same page."

"And what page is that?" questioned Leia.

They were interrupted by Alana arriving with Malia, and Hilo in tow. "Kai said the food is almost already," said Alana. Her gaze slid across Leia and Derek. "Do you like kalua pork Derek?"

Giving Leia's waist a squeeze, Derek replied, "I do. It smells delicious. I can't wait."

More of Leia's family arrived, making the space electric with noisy reunions. Leia's heart warmed seeing her family gathered. She didn't know how she could ever leave, but Derek, he was worth whatever sacrifice she needed to make for them to be together.

After introductions to her various extended family, Leia led Derek back to the table where her parents sat. Leia settled into the seat next to Noa with Derek on the other side of her. Derek wrapped his arms around her shoulders. Alana sat down with Malia and Hilo, too.

Shifting toward Malia and Hilo, Derek asked, "What are you hoping Santa brings you this year?"

Malia lit up. "Top of my list is a new art kit. All my markers are dried out, and my colored pencils are broken."

Alana's eyes widened. "Since when?" asked Alana.

"Since yesterday, when my last light blue marker ran out," stated Malia. "But it's okay, Santa will know."

Alana fidgeted with the tablecloth, smoothing out the fabric in front of her. "He might not work that fast. You can't be upset if Santa ends up bringing you something else."

Bringing her hands into tight fists, Malia replied, "But he's Santa!"

"Oh dear," muttered Alana. She gave Leia and Derek an exasperated glance.

Derek winked at Alana. "Malia, I think you're right. He's Santa, and I believe you'll get exactly what you want this Christmas."

Malia's tight fists loosened. "See, Derek understands."

Alana pursed her lips together. "Apparently," mumbled Alana.

Derek leaned extra close to Leia and whispered, "I have just the thing for Malia in one of my bags. I can get it to Alana after dinner for her to give to Malia from Santa."

"Food's ready!" bellowed Kai.

Their conversation was cut off. Malia and Hilo bolted toward the food table.

Exasperated, Alana rose. "I guess I'd better go catch up with them before they take too much or knock something over." She shuffled around the table.

As she passed by, Derek said, "I have something for Malia. I'll drop it off tonight. I think it will solve your predicament."

The worry lines on Alana's face softened. "Thanks. I had no idea how I was going to make her last-minute wish come true." Alana then walked quickly to catch up with Malia and Hilo in line behind a few others, making their way through the buffet line.

They waited until the food line died down before going to get themselves food. Everyone ate as the cheerful, jubilant spirit dangled in the air for Christmas. Kale and Kalon started playing Christmas songs on their ukuleles. Her family sang in Hawaiian to the popular Christmas carols. Derek wrapped his arm around her shoulders, listening to the familiar songs in Hawaiian, Leia couldn't remember the last time she had felt this happy and whole.

Kai came over with a printed page. "Here, Derek." He handed Derek the sheet of paper. "I printed off the words in Hawaiian. I thought it would help you follow along and maybe you can join in if you feel comfortable."

Smiling, Derek took the paper from Kai. "Thank you. I appreciate it," said Derek.

After nodding his head to the melody of Silent Night, Derek finally attempted to sing along with the others. As Leia listened to the sweet harmony of her family's voices, Leia's heart was filled with gratitude. Tears misted the corners of her eyes.

The evening ended too soon. Her aunts and uncles packed up their food dishes before bidding them a good night. Derek and Leia helped fold up the table and chairs, taking them back to the crowded garage. When they returned to the front yard, everyone had left for the night. Leia's parents had gone inside to settle in, and Kai and Alana had walked back with their kids to prepare for bed.

Rubbing the back of his neck, Derek shoved his other hand into his pocket. "Can I walk you home?" asked Derek.

"Sure." Leia interlaced her fingers with Derek's free hand. "Though it's only a two-minute walk." She gave his hand a reassuring squeeze though sadness seeped into her being.

Only two more days with Derek.

And the thought devastated her.

In no time, they arrived at her apartment door. Lingering in front of her door, Leia's voice cracked when she said, "I can't believe you go home the day after tomorrow. It's making me dread Christmas day more than rejoicing in it, because I don't want you to leave. I want you to stay here forever with me." Shaking her head, Leia met Derek's glance. "I can't be separated indefinitely from you anymore, but I don't know how to resolve our predicament." She placed a hand over her heart.

Derek took a step closer to her. His hand grazed her arm, sliding down the length of it. "What if I moved here?" asked Derek.

Her eyes dilated. "I— I—" stammered Leia. "How?"

His gaze skidded across her face, and Derek's hand brushed her unruly hair over her shoulder. His touch made her senses awaken. "Would you want me to move here?" rephrased Derek. He earnestly stared back at her.

Her heart hammered, making it difficult for Leia to think straight. "I mean ... of course I do. But you'd do that ... for me?" asked Leia.

Derek wrapped both his arms around her waist, tugging her close against his body so their hips touched. Leia rested a hand on his chest. "I would, I mean I've planned it out. I plan on staying after Christmas. I don't plan on going back to Los Angeles."

Her mind tried to play catch up. "What about your house? Your things?"

Shrugging, Derek said, "I've already rented out my house, and my things are in storage. I can go get them at some point."

Wrinkling her brow, Leia asked, "And when did you plan on telling me all this?"

"Right now," Derek glanced away for a second. "I didn't want to scare you off by being too forward. But I told your parents tonight, before you arrived, about my plan. Teresa seemed pleased and only wants what's best for you. I know her saltiness toward me was only because she was worried, that I planned on stringing you along for who knows how long. I think your parents now have a better understanding of how serious I am about being with you. They'll come around to the idea of us."

Leia laughed. "I can't believe this." Placing her hands over her warmed cheeks, she continued, "I had decided I would move to Los Angeles if I needed to so we could be together. I had no clue how I was going to do it, but I was willing to."

Smiling, Derek said, "And now you don't have to, because, Leia, I couldn't ever take you away from Kama Farm. You belong here with your family. And I hope someday, when the time is right for both of us, I can become part of it too. Because I love you, Leia. I've loved you since that day you saved me in Shark's Cove."

Shaking her head, Leia drew a finger across his chest. "You can't be serious."

"Oh, I am." Derek touched his forehead to hers. "I've loved you every day since then, and I hope if you'll let me, I'll go on loving you."

Going up on her tiptoes, Leia brushed her lips against Derek's. "I love you, too," she said through parted lips. "So, stay. Be here with me. And I'll promise to make you as happy as you make me."

"Deal," replied Derek.

Then Derek collided his lips with hers, igniting her insides. His lips danced with hers, reminding her of where she belonged. Under the canopy of stars, on a brilliant warm Hawaiian Christmas Eve, Leia received her Christmas wish. Derek. Here. In Kama. With her. Forever.

EPILOGUE

The sand at Waimea Bay Beach wiggled in between Derek's toes. He held onto Leia's hand as a wave hit the shoreline. Derek sighed as the warm water tickled his ankles. On his lips, he tasted the salty sea breeze. The loud cheers of people rock jumping vibrated in the air. Nudging Leia with his shoulder, Derek asked, "Do you remember when I jumped off that for the first time, way back when we were engaged?"

Leaning into his arm, Leia linked her hands around the crook of his elbow. "Do I?" Leia laughed, making her glitter against the bluest blue sky. "I thought you were going to have a heart attack when we finally arrived at the top of the rock. For a second there, I didn't think you would jump."

"And that's when I discovered I was afraid of heights." Derek peered toward the famous jumping rock. The top was lined with people. Down below in the water, people cheered on those waiting to jump. "I will *never* do it again."

Her lips twitched mischievously. "Come on," she bumped her shoulder against his, "Not even if our kids want you to take them?" asked Leia.

"Um," said Derek, "I'll cross that bridge when the time comes. But I have plenty of time to warm up the idea of jumping again."

Leia pursed her lips, dropping her hands from his elbow. "Let's sit for a minute. I love the view here." They walked up the small sand hill, plopping themselves down onto the hot sand.

Cradling his knees with his hands, Derek asked, "Did you sign us up again for the Honolulu Marathon?" Since running it together two years ago, they had run it again. If they ran it for a third time, Derek believed it would become a bit of a tradition.

"Umm ..." Leia shot him a glance then stared out the water. Sailboats dotted the horizon, and children were playing in the gentle waves. "I've been meaning to talk to you about that—" Leia wiped her sandy hands on her shorts.

"I thought you wanted to run it together. The first time we ran it we were only dating, then we ran it engaged, and this time would be the first time we ran it married. It's perfect," said Derek.

"I'm going to skip it this year," said Leia.

Derek rubbed his sandy hands together then wrapped his arm around Leia's shoulders. "What? Why? Is everything okay?" asked Derek.

"I'm fine." Leia turned and met his eyes. She placed a hand over his knee. Inhaling, Leia said, "I'm not going to run the marathon this year, because I'm pregnant."

For a moment, Derek thought the air was knocked out of him. Placing a hand over his chest, Derek sputtered, "You're pregnant?!" His jaw dropped.

"I hope you're happy." Leia's gaze skidded across his face. The worry lines deepened on her forehead. Tilting her head to the side, Leia continued, "Tell me you're pleased. I can't tell."

"I'm just shocked." Derek scratched his chin. "I mean the doctors told you not to get your hopes up. It was like a one in a million chance." His mind tried to play catch up. Their first year of marriage had been filled with a long string of disappointments. Only recently had they both come to accept that they most likely would never have children of their own.

Smiling, Leia said, "Well, I guess you'd better go buy a lotto ticket, because we are the one in a million."

Derek removed his arm from Leia's shoulders, cupping her face with his hands. "I'm so happy." He kissed her gently on the lips. "I was happy before because I had you, but this is fantastic news."

Leia kissed him again. "Thanks, Derek. Thanks for giving me everything I've ever wanted. I love you."

"I love you, too," replied Derek.

Tipping her chin, Leia's lips grazed Derek's. Derek sighed as he reveled in the blissful feeling of the sun on his skin, the salty air in his lungs, the sound of the ocean waves, and Leia's lips on his. This place really was paradise.

MEET THE AUTHOR

Emi Hilton is a California native who was born at March Airforce Base, to an officer in the US Army Combat Engineer Battalion father and an English professor mother. Emi followed in her mother's footsteps and graduated from Brigham Young University in English. While in college, she took a year and a half break from her studies to serve as a full-time missionary for her church in the Canary Islands.

Emi writes sweet contemporary romance novels. Both her debut novel, Memories in Morro Bay, and second novel, Bluebird Sky, were nominated for Whitney Awards.

When Emi isn't writing, she enjoys training for marathons, fishing off local piers with her husband and three sons, or visiting her other love, Spain.

OTHER TITLES FROM

5 PRINCE PUBLISHING

www.ingramcontent.com/pod-product-compliance
Lightning Source LLC
Chambersburg PA
CBHW020836260626
47169CB00003B/1009